ALSO BY AMBER D. LEWIS

FIRE AND STARLIGHT SAGA

THE NIGHT THE STARS FELL

SCARS: ALAK'S STORY

THE STARLIGHT IN THE SHADOWS

STAR-CROSSED: CAL'S STORY

THE STARDUST IN THE ASHES

STRAY: KAI'S STORY

TO WISH UPON A STAR (SHORT STORY)

THE STARS AMID THE STORM

FATE OF ELODIA

BETWEEN FATE & FAILURE

FATE OF ELODIA | BOOK ONE

AMBER D. LEWIS

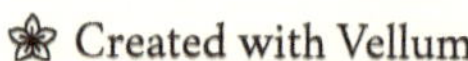 Created with Vellum

PRAISE FOR BETWEEN FATE & FAILURE

Captivating from the start, where friendship and love blossom amidst a tangle of royal drama.

—ARIEL RAE, AUTHOR OF *BLOOD HUNTED*

Once again, Amber D. Lewis delivers a rich fantasy complete with a whole new world for exploring, found family to adore, and a unique magic system, all wrapped up in a high-stakes tale that still makes you feel cozy.

— MANDY, INCOHERENT FANGIRL PODCAST

Lewis does it again, creating a masterpiece with lovable characters you won't be forgetting any time soon.

— MEGAN, BOOK INFLUENCER

To anyone named Mandy; I'm sorry I made you a bad guy.

Except that one Mandy. You know who you are and what you did.
Screw you.

Panbrio Isles
New Hingling
Elodia
Rosana
Shepherd's Shack
Langsworth Manor
Brookshire
Maximburg Estate
Temple of the Divine
Cabin
Netherfield
Brushwake
Hallowbridge
Bonesburrow
Greymaster
Lord Brackbill's Estate

AUTHOR NOTE

Please note that this book is meant for an adult audience and contains adult language, adult content, and adult situations.

This book also contains

- Anxiety & panic attacks
- A sick/dying parent
- Blood/injuries
- Battles/fight scenes resulting in death
- Vomiting
- Drunkenness/consumption of alcohol
- Very brief reference to a previous experience where a cat "accidentally" caught on fire but was not harmed (No animals are physically harmed or killed on-page.)
- Raised voices between characters in a domestic-like situation (Everything is resolved calmly and without physical violence.)

CHAPTER ONE

FREYA

I suppose most people think of clever things when they're plunging to their deaths after being pushed over the edge of a cliff. Or perhaps their life flashes before their eyes and they have a moment of reflection and whispered prayers. I, however, am thinking up sarcastic comments and replies to the twat who pushed me. A lot of good they'll do me now. As I twirl and twist through the air, I almost feel relief over fear. At least I won't have to marry the pompous pain in the ass that's Prince Tybalt. I know the kingdom technically needs me, but I can't help but wonder if he'll feel the same immense relief. I know his mother probably will.

My body jerks and breath whooshes from my lungs. I'm a bit surprised not to be dead. I should be scattered across sharp rocks with waves lapping at my corpse. But I'm not. At least I don't think I am. I stretch out a hand and discover I'm suspended a few feet above my would-be watery death by a firm surface of condensed air.

"There are better ways to fall for His Highness than off a cliff." A crisp, prim voice cuts through the darkness.

I groan. "How are you tonight, Bastion?"

He huffs and his air magic tugs me unceremoniously toward the shore. My hands flail about, trying to keep my dress from flying over my head and showing Bastion . . . well, everything. When I'm safely over land, he yanks his magic away, and I fall into a heap on the sandy shore. I glare up at him, not surprised in the least he's dressed in all black, completely swallowed up by the night so he's hardly visible, even as close as he is. I can easily understand why he's considered one of the top assassins in Elodia. I understand less why he's here, not that I'm completely ungrateful I'm not fish food.

"There," he mutters, brushing his hands together as if to wipe away any memory of his magic touching me. "My good deed for the day is done. Mind you, it's past midnight, so do try to keep yourself out of trouble for at least twenty-four hours."

He spins on his heel and marches toward the castle while I gape at him.

"I'll have you know," I cry, scrambling after him and nearly tripping over my own two feet, "that I didn't plan to leap of a cliff. I was *pushed* by another jilted or jealous lover of my husband-to-be."

"Don't care," Bastion replies, flicking his hand.

His long strides are nearly impossible for my much smaller ones to keep up with, but I huff and puff after him all the same.

"You should care!"

He glances over his shoulder at me and, since the full

moon was last night, there's still more than enough light to illuminate the half-smirk curling on his lips.

"But alas, I don't, Princess."

"I'm not a princess."

He laughs and stops short, spinning to face me. I'm still going full blast to catch up with him and plow directly into his chest. His hard, perfectly chiseled—I'm assuming as I've never actually seen it—chest. He scowls and places his hands on my shoulders, shoving me back.

"You might as well get used to the title, *Princess*, because come the Fae moon, that's what you'll be."

I cross my arms and raise my chin defiantly. "Not if people keep pushing me off cliffs."

His sharp, deep gray eyes hold my blue ones for a moment, some sort of challenge etched in the sharpness of his gaze. Like hell I'll be the first to look away. My eyes are starting to water when he finally blinks, shaking his head as he turns and resumes his march to the castle.

"Stay away from cliffs and it won't be an issue."

"That's fine and dandy," I shout, not bothering to continue my chase. To be honest I'm still catching my breath a bit. "I'll just find another castle that's not literally *surrounded by cliffs*"—I throw my arms out, gesturing dramatically—"to be held captive in while I await my imminent doom."

I half-expect Bastion to turn back around and scold me for my disrespect like he usually does, but he manages to resist. I'm pretty sure his shoulders stiffen, though, and his pace definitely increases. By the time I start walking again he's far enough away I'm alone, and I rather prefer it this way.

"I HEARD BASTION HAD TO FISH YOU OUT OF THE WATER LAST night."

I jerk up in bed, eyes falling on the lean figure perched in the easy chair a few feet away. Prince Tybalt Shadowmoss, Crown Prince of Elodia and my fiancé, leers at me, a crooked smile on his face. The room isn't well lit, but even in this lighting he's stupidly handsome. Centuries of perfect genes have crafted a masterpiece. He has light brown skin, soft, dark curls that hang loose across his forehead stopping above golden-brown eyes, and a physique that I'd only previously seen on statues.

Once his unwelcome presence fully registers, I grab my blankets and pull them up to my chin.

"What are you doing in my room?" I hiss.

Tybalt cocks an eyebrow. "Preeeeetty sure you're in *my* castle which makes all the rooms mine, including this one." He leans back in the chair, stretching out his legs and crossing his ankles. "Besides, we're to be married anyway. No one will question your virtue."

"One," I spit, clutching the blanket tighter, "it's not about my virtue—it's about privacy. And two, you want to marry me even less than I want to marry you, so why spend any more time with me than necessary?"

He sighs and stands in one fluid motion. "Yeah, well, don't have an option there, so might as well start getting used to each other."

He flashes me a wide, very fake smile before strolling to the nearest window and throwing open the blinds. Golden sunlight washes over the room and I blink as my eyes adjust.

His gaze remains fixed out the window, and I almost wonder if he's forgotten I'm here until he speaks.

"I love my kingdom. I really do. I'll do whatever it takes to make it run as it should. Even if it means marrying someone without a lick of nobility in their veins in order to keep the Fae magic alive."

I shoot a nasty look his way even though he can't see it.

"I'm sorry my heritage isn't as pure as you'd like. Perhaps if *your* ancestors hadn't slaughtered all the Fae, some might have been around to create other options for you."

Tybalt shrugs, clearly unfazed. "Perhaps." He twists his head a bit to shoot me a wicked grin. "At least you got the good end of the deal since you get to marry me."

I clench my teeth to hold in my retort.

"Anyway," he says, far too cheerfully. "You're wanted downstairs for brunch with my mother."

"What? The queen? The queen wants me?" I sputter. "Why? She hates me."

I can count on one hand the number of times over the past week I've been in the same room as the queen when she didn't look like she wanted to set me on fire with a mere look. The idea she wants to spend extra time with me is more than baffling.

"Oh, I know. There's no telling what devious plans Mother might have for you this morning, but she has to keep up appearances for the public and hide her open disdain just like we do." Tybalt grins, glancing toward the ornate clock sitting on my bedside table. "I'm pretty sure you're late."

"Shit," I mutter, scrambling from the bed. The sheet gets tangled around my ankles, and I plunge face-first onto the floor with a loud thud.

"Ah, what a creature of grace and beauty, my future wife."

"I. Hate. You."

"Such a pity, darling, because you're rather stuck with me and I with you. Don't worry, I'm sure you'll come to love me soon enough." Tybalt blows me a kiss. "Now, up and at it."

He claps his hands three times for emphasis and I lunge toward him with a growl. He steps from my grasp effortlessly, grinning. He strides toward the exit, pausing in the doorway.

"By the way, I told your maid you wouldn't need her this morning, so you'll have to dress on your own." He glances back at the clock and grimaces dramatically. "Better hurry."

He slams the door and I scream, standing and kicking at the sheet still trying to be my undoing. I can't stand Prince Tybalt Shadowmoss or his Guard and best friend Bastion Shamblefoot. I hate Castle Thornebridge and all it stands for. But the thing I hate the most is that I'm stuck here with no way out.

CHAPTER TWO

FREYA

Thankfully, my outfit for the day isn't overly complicated, so I handle dressing well enough without a maid. By pure luck, I manage to pull myself into a presentable version of a princess before flying through the corridors in a very unprincess-like manner. I'm entirely out of breath when I reach the brunch room, but I try to contain my gasping as I force a smile and walk inside. Much to my chagrin the queen isn't alone. Nope, I'm not lucky enough for that. Not only is she brunching with two absolutely gorgeous girls—much more suitable matches for the prince, if you ask me—but the golden-haired Cressida is the one who shoved me off a cliff last night.

"Ah, Freya, dear, I'm so glad you could see fit to join us, even if we are quite nearly done."

I dip into a curtsy, nearly toppling over, and incline my head. "I'm terribly sorry, Your Majesty."

I briefly wonder if blaming her son for my lateness would win me any sympathy, but I know she won't care. She wants me married to Tybalt even less than I do, and that's saying something.

"No matter," Queen Lyra says, waving her hand like it's nothing to be late to brunch with the queen, and she wouldn't have me thrown away if she could. "Please, take a seat and we will make do with what time we have remaining."

I bob my head in thanks and take the only available seat next to Cressida. I allow an attendant to pour me a cup of tea while I take a couple pieces of fruit and a pastry from the tiered tray in the center of the table.

"I'm pleased you were able to make it," Cressida says with a wry grin. "I thought you'd be *drowning* in activities today."

I take an aggressive bite of my pastry before replying. "Yes, well, I've always been one to keep my head above water."

Cressida's smile falters slightly but her friend, Lady Nadia —I think that's her name—is more than willing to try to knock me down a peg as well.

"I do so wish I could eat like you do," she says with a drawn-out sigh. "But if I did, I'd never fit into my dresses."

I make eye contact with her and shove the rest of the pastry into my mouth. I'm well aware that I don't have the slim bodies of most of the nobility, but I don't care. So what? I have curves. I didn't care before I came to the castle, and I certainly don't care now.

"Pity," I manage after I've swallowed the pastry and washed it down with some tea. "It might give you an excuse for new dresses so you wouldn't have to keep dressing like that."

Cressida and Nadia gasp and exchange a scandalized

look. I'm grinning into my teacup when the queen clears her throat. Oh, if looks could kill.

"Speaking of dresses, Gregorian Greengrass will be arriving later this evening to measure you for your wedding dress and the dresses you'll need for the other wedding activities, including your tour."

I blink. "My tour?"

The queen sighs like she's tired of having to lower herself speaking to me while Cressida and Nadia grin.

"Yes, my dear. Your wedding tour. You and Tyablt leave on your wedding tour in three short days. I do hope that you will be properly prepared?"

I barely contain my confused scowl, offering the queen a tight smile in its place. I have absolutely no idea what she's talking about, but there is no way I'm going to admit that to her face, especially not with Cressida and Nadia watching.

"Of course, Your Majesty."

The conversation shifts away from my impending wedding, thank the gods, and I might as well not even be present. My mind drifts to other things, so I'm not paying attention when everyone starts rising. I stumble to my feet and Cressida snickers.

"I will send someone to fetch you when Liege Greengrass arrives," the queen says, making her exit before I can respond.

I sigh, shaking my head, and step out into the hall, Cressida and Nadia on my heels. Nadia stretches her foot in front of me and I stumble, grabbing the door frame to keep from tumbling to the ground. I spin and glare at her.

"You're a pathetic excuse for a princess," Cressida mutters, shaking her head.

I grit my teeth so hard it hurts. "I didn't ask for this."

Cressida scoffs. "As if anyone asked for you." She takes a step closer and leans in to whisper in my ear, though her voice is nowhere near quiet enough. "You're a disgrace to this kingdom."

I rear back. I know I'm a disgrace. There are a million people better suited for this than I am, but there's no way I'll admit that to Cressida.

"And you're so much better?"

Cressida straightens, flipping her hair over her shoulder. "Of course I am." She smiles and levels me with a look I'm sure is meant to intimidate me. It fails. "If you hadn't come along Ty would be marrying *me.*"

Nadia's head bobs in agreement but I laugh. Cressida's grin falls into a sharp glare.

"I've been here for barely two weeks and I've been confronted by eight different women claiming to be Prince Ty's true love." I pause, tilting my head in feigned thought. "And three gentlemen."

"You're lying."

Now it's my turn to grin. "Oh, I'm really not. You're not special to the prince. You're merely the latest in a long line of lovers, meant to fill his time until I came along."

I should see the slap coming, but I don't. Cressida's hand finds its mark, and my cheek stings something fierce. Her face is red with fury and it's only the fact that I know I've made my point that keeps me from striking her back. I raise my chin and meet her eyes defiantly.

"Hate me all you want, Cressida, but you're not even close to first choice for Prince Tybalt. You never have been, and you never will be."

"You're wrong. I may not have as much Fae blood as the Crown thinks is necessary, but I can find a way to make it work. If I can get you out of the way, Ty will choose me." She spins, motioning for Nadia. "Come on, Nadia. We're done here."

I watch them stride away and shake my head. As much as Cressida might want to be in my position—and, believe me, I'd trade with her in a heartbeat—I know there's absolutely no way it could happen. Her blood simply doesn't contain the necessary signs of Fae heritage. If it did, I wouldn't be in this mess. If we want magic to be accessible in the kingdom, we need my blood.

Hundreds of years ago, possibly even thousands of years, there was no magic in Elodia. Then the king fell in love with a Fae woman. Like all Fae, she had magic and she wanted to share that magic with her lover's kingdom. When they were wed, they both placed their blood on a magical crystal, binding the human king's red blood with the Fae queen's golden blood. Together, they activated a magic that could be shared throughout the land.

Every time the crown passed to a new ruler, the magic of the land passed with it. Before receiving the crown, they would wed and be bound to their chosen spouse. They'd add their blood to the crystal underneath a Fae moon, which occurs roughly every three lunar cycles. Something about the magic woven into the marriage oaths activated the whole thing and made the magic strong enough to spread across the kingdom. As time went on, the Fae blood slowly left the royal line, and in order for the magic to remain intact, the bride—or in rare cases, the groom—had to prove their Fae heritage. They didn't necessarily have to be full-blooded Fae, but their veins needed to contain signs of the Fae's golden blood for the magic to work properly.

All was well and good until a war broke out between the

humans and Fae a couple centuries back, and the Fae were pretty much wiped out. The few that lived fled Elodia, leaving them without the strong Fae line to continue that magic.

As time passed, the magic weakened. The magic was no longer open and available to all and could only be channeled through magical crystals. Of course, since the crystals were relatively rare, not just anyone could have one; they were only meant for the richest and those with connections to the royals. But even that magic grew weaker so that each crystal only provided enough for basic magic, typically little more than tricks and brief flashes, unless, of course, the bearer had Fae heritage of their own to strengthen the magic. Without a strong mix of Fae and Human blood to keep the magic active, all magic would be lost. Thus, arranged marriages became the norm, forcing the heir to marry whoever could be found with the most Fae blood coursing through their veins.

Apparently the current king, Tybalt's father, married two others before Queen Lyra, but when they completed the marriage bond, their blood wasn't strong enough to hold up the magic. Magic almost faded away for nearly two years, only held up by the weak bond from his father. Queen Lyra's blood proved to be enough to restore the magic, enough that it held once the previous king died. With Prince Tybalt's blood even more diluted than his father's, he needs someone with a significant amount of golden Fae blood. With the pressure on, they scoured every corner of the kingdom. That's how they found me, a poor girl living on a farm, so far from being nobility the match was laughable.

That was a little over two years ago when I was seventeen. In order for the bond to work properly, however, I would need to be at least eighteen. The plan was for me to live my life until I turned twenty-one, when the magic bond would be strongest, but I know the delay was really so they could continue searching for someone better, since the queen insisted I should only marry the prince as a last resort. When the king's health took a dive and he found himself clinging to life, that plan got bumped up. The kingdom was out of options. If the king dies before Tybalt and I are bound and wed, magic may very well die as well.

So despite what Cressida thinks, only a miracle will stop the wedding at this point.

CHAPTER THREE

TY

"You're a dick, you know that, right?"

I push away from the wall where I've been leaning, waiting for Freya to get out of brunch with my mother, and turn to Bastion as he strides toward me with those long, wonderful legs. His black hair is getting a little long, hanging down a bit into his gray eyes, but honestly, he wears the look well.

"Oh, I'm quite aware, Bash, but what exactly happened that caused you to remind me?"

Bash stops a couple feet away and crosses his arms. "You insisted on waking Freya yourself and promised you'd make sure she made it to brunch—"

"I did!"

"—on time."

"Okay, so maybe I failed on that last part, but I went in there and she just looked so peaceful and I couldn't wake her."

"Stop with the bullshit, Ty."

I raise my hands defensively. "Fine. I had every intention of waking her on time, but I got distracted."

"Distracted by your own pettiness, which is why you also sent her maid away."

I grin. "I can't have life be too easy for my beloved. Ruling a kingdom is hard, and it would be cruel not to put her to the test occasionally."

"Did you know she wasn't the only one invited to brunch?"

My stomach drops in a momentary bit of guilt. Did I heap more trouble on Freya than she already had? That wasn't my intent. I only wanted to mess with her a little, not get her in serious trouble. Thankfully, the guilt doesn't stick around.

"No. Who else was invited?"

"Cressida and Nadia."

I wave Bash off with a scoff. "Who cares about Cress and Nadia? Freya certainly doesn't."

"Does your opinion on that change if I tell you I'm pretty sure Cressida shoved Freya off a cliff last night?"

My eyes snap to Bash's. He knows that changes things. To be honest, I didn't think Cress had it in her to be so . . . violent. She's not the kind of person to get her hands dirty. I'm impressed she took the initiative to do something of her own free will, or I would be if it hadn't involved nearly killing my fiancée.

"Are there witnesses?"

Bash nods once. "A couple. They're all hesitant to say anything truly condemning, so Cress could easily manipulate the facts if it came down to it."

"Fuck," I mutter, rubbing the back of my neck. "How many attempts is that on Freya's life since she arrived?"

"Cressida's attempt makes two that I know of, but given

it's only been a couple weeks, I consider that a significant amount."

"Doesn't she know we need Freya alive or we lose magic?"

"I doubt she can string two thoughts together, so no. She probably acted rashly without remotely thinking it through."

I groan and collapse back against the wall, squeezing my eyes shut in an attempt to block out the world. I mindlessly reach up and fiddle with the oblong citrine crystal hanging around my neck on a black leather cord. Normally, touching the source of my magic is comforting, but right now the struggling hum is just a reminder of how weak magic is and how much the kingdom is counting on my marriage to Freya.

"I hate this."

"I know, Ty," Bash says, placing a careful hand on my shoulder. "But like it or not, this is your life now. In less than a month, you'll be married and probably not much after that, you'll be the king."

I open an eye and peek at Bash. "I'm only twenty-one. What kind of king am I meant to be?" I sigh and close my eye again. "I was supposed to have two more years to undo the mess that I am. I'm not ready for this."

A gentle touch on my cheek has my eyes snapping open to find Bash's soft smile mere inches away.

"I know. I also know you're stronger than you give yourself credit for and that you can do this—marriage, ruling, everything."

I push away from the wall, opting to lean forward on Bash instead, pressing my forehead to the crook of his neck. "What would I do without you, Bash?"

Bash snorts. "I don't even want to imagine a world where I'm not here to corral you."

I straighten and offer Bash a grin. "Yeah, I'd truly be a lost cause without your guidance. I barely survived the last two years while you were gone. Lots of near misses. It's a good thing you came back when you did. You're a true lifesaver, Bastion Shamblefoot."

He breaks into a full grin, shaking his head before sobering, taking a wide step back to put more space between us. It takes every bit of willpower I possess to stay put instead of moving back into his space again.

"Do you want me to do anything about Cressida?"

I choke on a laugh. "I don't need her dead."

He rolls his eyes. "I don't *always* kill off the problem." A feral smile slips onto his lips. "Sometimes 'accidents' happen that make them reconsider things, though."

I bite back a grin. "Accidents, huh?"

"Yep. Need me to arrange one? Or will you take care of it?"

I gnaw on my lip and glance away for a moment as I think. Honestly, Cress could do with an "accident," but really, she's mostly harmless and I don't need any questions raised. Her father holds too much power and sway with the other dukes to do anything drastic.

"I guess I'll take care of it or she'll try again."

"And you're going to do it in a perfectly calm and rational way, right?"

I smirk, meeting Bash's eyes. "Now, what fun would that be? If I'm not dramatic and over-the-top, Cress won't get the point."

He shakes his head. "Just don't do anything that will

compromise things with her father, or I really might have to step in."

I scoff, waving him off. "She'd never tell her father—or anyone for that matter—anything she finds embarrassing or she thinks might harm her reputation."

"I can't say you're wrong about that. Since you don't want me to deal with her directly, is there anything else I should do?"

"I don't suppose you could keep a closer on eye on Freya?"

Bash cocks an eyebrow. "Closer than I've already been?"

"I know you don't like protecting her but—"

He waves me off. "You know I'll do whatever you ask of me. One problem, though."

"What's that?"

He grins, a mischievous twinkle in his eye. "Who will keep *you* out of trouble if I'm watching Freya?"

I laugh. "I've had some practice keeping myself out of trouble the past couple of years. It wouldn't hurt for me to learn some more."

He opens his mouth to say something but is silenced as a door opens nearby. I throw hand over his mouth, pulling him out of sight. I peek around the corner and watch my mother exit, her head held higher than ever. A moment later Freya marches out with Cress and Nadia close behind. I can't hear what they're saying, but I gather they aren't making plans to get together later for tea. Standing next to Cress and Nadia, it's clear how different Freya is. She doesn't fit in at court.

I watch as they interact, lost in Freya's movements. It's impossible not to compare her to the other girls. They're so prim and strait-laced. They hide their venom in carefully constructed conversations. Freya doesn't hide at all. She's all fire, emotions written on her face. She lacks the ethereal beauty and grace most noblewomen have, but she's not ugly. Not by far. She's gorgeous in a simpler way. Her ruddy-brown hair never seems quite contained, always flying about in loose curls that make her look free. She's plump with soft, alluring curves, especially in comparison the rail-thin noble-women. She's a bright star in a dark castle, and I hate the way I'm drawn to her.

The conversation ends with a slap and harsh words, and had Cress and Nadia not turned our way, I would likely have gone out and made a spectacle. I quickly duck back around the corner, shoving Bash in the direction Freya will go.

"Protect her."

Bash arches an eyebrow. "What are you going to do?"

Footsteps sound as Cress and Nadia approach.

"Only what needs to be done. Now go."

I give him another shove, and he leaves with a sigh. He nearly brushes shoulders with Cress as she rounds the corner. He offers her a quiet nod before disappearing. Cress ignores him, her eyes finding me.

"Ty! What a pleasant surprise!"

I grin and shoot her a wink. "A pleasure indeed." I turn my attention to Nadia. "Would you mind leaving us alone for a moment?"

Nadia's eyes brighten as she glances to Cress and back to me. She dips into a curtsy. "Of course, Your Highness."

"Thank you," I reply, inclining my head.

Once Nadia is well out of hearing range, Cress leans toward me, crowding my personal space. It takes every ounce of training I have not to shove her away in disgust.

"We're alone," she purrs, her lips nearly brushing my ear. "What did you have in mind?"

I take a wide step back and look around. "Not here," I whisper. "We need somewhere more . . . private. Follow me."

I take her hand and drag her through the hall. She trips along behind me, nearly falling twice. I bite back a grin. When we come to an empty room often used for meetings, I pull Cress inside and shut the door behind us.

"Now," I say, turning to Cress, "we can talk."

Cress pouts. "Talk? I thought we were going to do something far more entertaining."

She once again presses into my space and places her hand on my chest. This time I don't have to play a part. I grab her hand so hard she squeaks and tries to pull it away, but my grip is firm.

"Ty, what are you doing?"

"Did you push my wife-to-be off a cliff last night, Cressida?"

Her eyes widen and I can see her debating whether she's going to tell the truth or not. A lie is on the tip of her tongue, but I tighten my grasp on her wrist and she winces.

"Maybe, but, Ty, you can't marry her!"

I release her hand with a jerk and she clasps her wrist to her chest, taking several steps back.

"And you thought throwing her off a cliff would allow you to take her place?"

Cress starts to nod but quickly shifts to shaking her head. "No. I—It was an accident."

I laugh but it's without humor. "We both know that's a lie."

She blinks at me for a moment but finds some sort of fire inside and stomps back toward me.

"Fine. I tried to get her out of our way. She's a good for nothing little bitch who isn't even good enough to clean the shit from your shoes."

Anger rises and my hand is around my dagger before I register my movements. I lift the gleaming blade in the air, and Cress gasps, true fear flashing on her face as she stumbles back into the wall.

"Ty, what are you doing?" she whispers.

I smirk at her, turning the blade over so it catches the light. "Your turn to talk is over. Time to listen. Understand?"

She nods, eyes filling with tears. I almost roll my eyes. Like I'd actually cut her. Imagine the mess I'd have to clean up—literally and figuratively. She's not worth the energy. But clearly she doesn't know that. I take a step closer.

"Let me be perfectly clear—you mean *nothing* to me. You never did and you never will. Even if Freya wasn't in the picture, you would never be queen. Got that?"

"Y-yes," she whispers, visibly shaking.

I step closer, my face mere inches from hers, and raise the dagger to her throat, not touching her, but she winces anyway.

"Keep your hands off my fiancée. I will marry Freya in four weeks and there's nothing you or anyone else can do about it. You touch her or even breathe her way and I will end you. Am I clear?"

Cress nods, her tears spilling free.

I press the dagger a little closer to her throat. "I need verbal confirmation."

"Yes, Ty. I swear it. I swear!"

"And you can't have any of your minions touch her, either."

"I don't—"

I allow the cool metal of the dagger to kiss her skin. Her eyes widen and she swallows hard.

"I'll keep them in check."

"Good." I yank my dagger back and she gasps dramatically even though I wasn't even almost hurting her. "Get out of here."

Cress scurries away without another word, leaving the door open behind her. I take a deep breath and run a shaky hand over my hair, praying I didn't make a mistake threatening her. But what's done is done. Now I should probably track down my fiancée and see how her brunch went. Hopefully I'll get a word in before she tries to kill me.

CHAPTER FOUR

BASH

"You can stop following me, Bastion," Freya says with a sigh as she pauses in the door leading into one of the side courtyards. When I don't immediately move from the shadows she adds, "It's not like you're being all that stealthy."

"I wasn't trying to be stealthy," I say, stepping to her side, squinting against the sunlight. "If I wanted to be stealthy, I can guarantee you wouldn't know I was there."

"Why are you following me?"

"Who said I was following you?"

She crosses her arms and levels me with a glare.

"Fine. I thought it might be a good idea to tag along and make sure you arrive at your wedding alive."

"I don't need a babysitter."

"Last night's events prove otherwise."

"Leave me alone."

She huffs and spins away from me, walking quickly out into the empty courtyard, but it takes no effort for me to not only catch up but also pass her. I step directly into her path and come to a halt. She slams into my chest. She stumbles back and shoves me. It does absolutely nothing; I don't even waver. I smirk down at her.

"Come on, Princess. I'm sure you can do better than that."

Her jaw twitches in frustration and she crosses her arms, glaring up at me.

"Is it really going to be like this? You following me everywhere?" She scowls, glancing around. "Aren't you supposed to be watching over my beloved husband-to-be?"

I cock an eyebrow. "I go where I'm needed."

She brushes past me. "You're not needed here."

I cut her off a second time. I can't hold back the chuckle when she slams into me again.

"Leave. Me. Alone." She growls and pounds her fists into my chest with each word.

"No."

She steps back and drops her shoulders. "Please?"

Her voice is barely a whisper, verging on the edge of desperation. I study her for a moment. I know what it's like to have my every step dogged.

"Why do you want to be left alone? Especially considering there are people literally trying to kill you."

"Because!" She gestures wildly.

I stare at her. "Because . . . ?"

She sighs. "I'm not used to so many people being underfoot. I hate it in the castle. It's so stuffy. Plus, everyone hates me and wants me dead."

"I don't necessarily want you dead," I counter, knowing I can't really disagree with her other points.

A small laugh escapes her. "But you hate me."

I lift one shoulder in a shrug and hum in agreement. I have my reasons.

She glances away, her eyes trailing over the palace grounds. "I'm trapped here and having you follow me everywhere reminds me of the fact I'm no longer free."

I pause, considering her predicament. I know firsthand how much being trapped here sucks—it's one of the reasons I left—but even though she's far from my favorite person, I can't begrudge her the need for some semblance of control and privacy.

"Fine, I'll leave you alone." Her eyes light up and I hold up a finger, silencing any would-be rejoicing. "But—"

She groans. "Of course there's a but."

"—you have to prove to me you can handle any more assassination attempts on your own."

She licks her lips. "Okay. Yeah. I can do that."

"Excellent."

I lunge forward in one swift movement and hoist her over my shoulder. It's entirely too easy.

"Bastion!" she screeches, pounding her fists on my back as she struggles in my grasp. "Put me down!"

"Fine."

I dump her on the ground with a thud. She glares up at me through a mess of curls that have fallen loose.

"You know, Princess," I say, folding my arms across my chest as I grin down at her, "you seem to like being in a heap at my feet."

"Because you keep dumping me here!"

I smirk and glance off.

She scrambles to her feet, glaring at me with as much hate as she can. "Is it your goal to babysit me or torture me?"

I cock an amused eyebrow. "Why can't it be both?" She opens her mouth to retort, but I wave her off. "No matter. You want to prove to me that you can survive an assassination attempt, yet you can't even avoid getting thrown over my shoulder and subsequently thrown into a heap at my feet."

"You gave me no warning!"

I huff, shaking my head. "Right. And most assassins introduce themselves and give you a heads up before thrusting a knife in your gut."

Her eyes sparkle as she opens her mouth to retort, but I cut her off.

"Cressida doesn't count." Because of course Cress is the kind of person who would do exactly that.

"Fine. How many more attempts on my life can I expect?"

How many indeed? I honestly don't know how many dalliances Ty had over the past couple years while I've been away—I don't *want* to know—but I've heard enough rumors to know that if even a quarter of his ex-lovers come forward, she's in trouble.

"A dozen or so maybe." I shrug. "It doesn't matter."

She blinks at me like a flustered owl. "What? How can that not matter?"

"Because you're under my protection now."

"I—"

"*And* because I'm going to teach you some basic self-defense."

She crosses her arms, narrowing her eyes. "Why would you do that?"

"You think I *want* to babysit you, Princess? Because I don't. I have a million better things to do. If you can handle your own shit, that means free time for me." I pause, taking a step back. "Show me what you can do."

"What I can do?"

"Yes. I assume since you've made it this far in life you

have some basic self-preservation skills. You complained because I gave you no warning before my last attack, so this is your chance to act with a little warning. Prove to me you can protect yourself, I'll add on to those skills, and then you will be free to wander on your own without me dogging your every step."

She considers me for a moment and then nods. "Okay, I can do that."

I step back a little more to give her additional room. She rubs her palms on her thighs and stares me down, trying to figure out her attack. When this continues for a good minute, I raise an unimpressed brow and cross my arms.

"I'm waiting, Princess."

"I'm thinking!" she snaps.

"Maybe your method is to simply bore your attacker to death?" I taunt, wanting to get a rise out her.

"Shut up, Bastion!"

"Hmm. Slinging pathetic insults. Rather weak, but I guess for some it could work."

She growls and charges, throwing her full weight into me. I stumble back half a step before I regain my footing and sling her to the ground.

"That all you got?" I chuckle.

She huffs in frustration and throws her arms around my calves, pulling hard. Before I can fight her off, my knees buckle. Instead of falling back like she's probably hoping, I force my weight forward, falling on top of her. She scrambles to get out from under me, but I'm quicker, grabbing her ankles. She kicks back hard, her foot hitting my shoulder. I swear loudly, releasing her. She doesn't get long to bask in her success before I jerk her back, making her face plant in the grass as I drag her toward me. She struggles in my grasp, flipping over as she swings and kicks wildly. She manages to land another blow on my mouth, splitting my lip, and knees my stomach, winding me a bit.

"Enough," I grumble, grabbing her wrists and pinning them above her head.

"Let me go!" she huffs, wriggling and trying to kick me away.

I merely grin and straddle her in a way that keeps her completely pinned so no matter how much she wiggles there's no escaping. I brace my free hand to the left of her head and grin. She glares up at me.

"I must confess, Princess, you did better than I antici-pated. Still a pitiful display, but it proves you're not entirely helpless."

"See, I don't need you following me everywhere." She jerks beneath me. "Now let me up!"

I chuckle, shaking my head. "It took me ten, maybe fifteen, seconds to make you entirely immobile."

I lean down, my body pressing against her as I whisper in her ear. "Imagine all the things someone could do to you once they got you in this position."

Her face flushes and I grin against her ear. It takes her a second to find her fight again, but I am pleased she didn't give up.

"Let me up!"

I laugh again, pushing back.

"What is going on here?" Ty's cheerful voice cuts through the air. "I always seem to miss out on the fun."

I brace myself above Freya and give her a final wink before I effortlessly leap to my feet. I turn to Ty, who stands off to the side grinning like a cat.

"I was attempting to teach your fiancée some basic

fighting skills," I say, matching Ty's grin as he steps to my side. "She needs a lot of work."

She rolls over into a sitting position and stumbles to her feet, glaring at us. "I wasn't entirely helpless. Your bloody lip is proof enough of that."

"Your skills, if you can even call them that, might allow you to get away from someone equally pathetic like Cressida, but against a real threat, you wouldn't stand a chance. If I had wanted to kill you, you'd be dead."

Ty cocks his head and studies Freya for a moment. I try to figure out what he's seeing. Her dress is wrinkled and covered with dirt and grass stains, and she's practically dripping sweat, her hair a chaotic mess. Does he find her attractive like this? Would anyone? Appreciation stirs in me in a way I don't want to recognize. I merely admire that she's not a quitter. There is something attractive about that.

She twitches under our assessing gazes, smoothing her palms over her dress, though it doesn't help her state at all. She raises her chin defiantly.

"How much work will it take to get her to a point where she can hold her own against a basic attack?" Ty asks.

I shrug. "Depends on how quickly she learns."

Ty hums, tapping his chin as his eyes rake over her. "We leave in three days. Think you can work with that?"

I open my mouth, but Freya cuts in before I can reply.

"Stop talking about me as if I'm not standing right here! And what's this tour we're supposed to leave on? The queen mentioned it at brunch."

Ty's eyes twinkle as an amused smirk curls on his lips. "It's the wedding tour. You know, the tour of the kingdom that every royal couple goes on before they officially wed?"

"No, I don't know. I wasn't exactly alive when your

parents tied the knot, and, unlike you, I wasn't fed royal traditions from infancy. I have no damn idea what the tour is or why I have to go on it."

Ty lifts his shoulder in a half-shrug. "I suppose that's fair. Well, the tour serves two basic purposes. One, we make nice with all the significant people around the kingdom to gain their approval before we officially get married and take the throne. Normally it lasts months, stretching from one Fae moon to the next, but since we're on a tight schedule, ours has been condensed to about three weeks."

She nods. "And the second purpose?"

"You'll fetch the crystal needed to keep magic going, of course," I answer.

She frowns, looking from me to Ty. "Wait, the crystal isn't here at the palace?"

Ty shakes his head. "No, it's kept at the Temple of the Divine—bit on the nose name for a temple, if you ask me— on the opposite end of the kingdom. Something about it preserving the magic better."

"And we have to visit the nobles on the way there and back?"

"Correct. We'll be staying at a new location pretty much every night, charming our host and whatever other nobles traveled there for the occasion."

"What happens if they don't approve of us, of me?"

Ty frowns, all previous amusement vanishing, and looks at me. He knows what I think of the approval of nobles. He also knows I understand better than anyone what their disapproval can mean. My gut twists uncomfortably.

"Well, back when the line of magic was strong, the nobles could veto a marriage. They could also declare a king unfit for the throne and demand another heir be chosen from the line." He sighs, rubbing the back of his neck. "As it stands, you and I are the only truly viable options."

"So it doesn't really matter if they like us?"

"Unfortunately, it matters more," I answer for him.

She frowns. "How?"

"Because, while you and I may be king and queen after my father dies," Ty jumps in, "we still require the support of various nobles to pass laws and uphold our commands. We need them to uphold the laws we make, or we might as well not bother making them at all. There are examples throughout Elodia's history where the nobles worked together to override and undermine the Crown's wishes. It didn't end well for anybody. If the current nobility decide I'm too young and reckless"—he spits the words with a level of bitterness I feel to my core—"or if they find you completely unsuitable, they might coordinate against us and essentially run the kingdom, making me little more than a figurehead. At the very least, they'll make life hell for me—us."

"That means, Princess," I cut in, needing to make sure Freya understands exactly what's at stake, "that not only are there chances people will attack you and you'll need to defend yourself, but also you'll need to try to fit the role people are already assuming you can't. You need to prove to them you'll be the queen they want and need."

"Okay."

Ty's eyes widen with surprise. "Okay?"

"Yeah. Okay."

He narrows his eyes at her in suspicion and she sighs.

"Look, I don't exactly want to be your queen and I know I'm not your favorite person, but it obviously benefits us both if I play the part correctly. I'll train with Bastion and put some effort into my stupid princess lessons."

Ty manages a small smile that doesn't reach his eyes. "All right."

"And, in exchange, maybe you can at least pretend to like me?"

Ty laughs and nods. "Fine. When we're in front of people, I will tolerate your presence."

"Good."

She looks at me expectantly. I hold up my hands and smirk. "I make no such promises, Princess."

She rolls her eyes, but it looks like she's holding back a smile.

"Well, are you at least going to train me, or do you want to continue chatting like ladies of the court over tea?"

I don't bother keeping in my grin. She might be incompetent and a poor match for Ty, but at least she's got some fight. Even I can appreciate that.

CHAPTER FIVE

TY

Watching Bash train Freya is a treat I didn't expect, but all good things come to an end. After roughly thirty minutes of watching her flail and fall, one of her tutors finds her and drags her off to lessons.

"Want to go a few rounds?" Bash asks, rolling his neck.

I grin. Even if he won't admit it, I know Freya put up a decent fight and he could use a break.

"Nah, I'm good." I glance over my shoulder at the castle and my grin falls. "I, uh, I have something I need to do."

I look back to Bash and offer him a weak smile. He takes a step closer and places a hand on my shoulder.

"Want me to come with you?"

I meet his eyes and swallow. A piece of me wants to say yes, wants me to allow Bash to hold me and comfort me when I'm done. But I don't give in to that part, shaking my head instead.

"I think I need to go alone this time."

Bash nods knowingly and steps back, hand dropping to his side. "If you need me after, I'll be in the weapons room."

I manage a weak smile. "Thanks, Bash."

I head off, entering the palace through a side door so I'm less likely to run into anyone. I slink through the back halls and corridors, making my way up to the floor that houses the royal chambers. I stop outside a pair of heavy oak doors carved with the tree crest of our kingdom and take a deep breath. I'm reaching for the door handles when the right door opens. I jump back, startled.

"Ah, I'm sorry, Your Highness," Doctor Adbar says with a slight bow. "I wasn't expecting you."

"I came unannounced." I lean forward and peer over the doctor's shoulder into the dimly lit room. "Is now a bad time?"

"On the contrary, your timing is impeccable. The king is awake and alert. He's having a good day. I was merely checking him over before preparing and administering his next dose of medication. That is where I am off to now, to mix it up. You may go in and have a few minutes alone with him, if you'd like."

I offer the doctor a forced smile. "Thank you."

He gives me a parting nod and shuffles away, leaving the door ajar behind him. I take one last fortifying breath and push my way inside, shutting the door behind me. It takes my eyes a moment to adjust to the darkness in the room, but once they do I make out the slight figure of my father on his bed, propped into a sitting position on a pile of pillows. Even in this poor lighting I can tell how small his frame has become, such a contrast to the strong man I looked up to as a boy, his normally rich brown skin pallid and clammy.

"Tybalt?" my father calls out, his voice hoarse.

"Yes, Father," I say, approaching his bed with quick steps. "It's me." I reach the edge of his bed and place my hand over where his rests above the covers. "Doctor Adbar says you're doing well."

My father huffs. "I'm no worse, I suppose."

I give his hand a squeeze. "That's good. He'll have you up and back on your feet in no time."

My father's smile is sad as he says, "Perhaps, but I suspect you didn't come to discuss my health."

His words are slow and pained. Some days he's unable to speak at all, but the doctor was right. Today is a good day.

"As always, Father, you are correct. I was only wondering . . . Well, you and mother had an arranged marriage, I know, but you always seem happy together."

My father studies me for a moment but when I don't elaborate, he smiles softly. "I suspect there's a question there, but I'm not quite sure what you're seeking, Son."

I clear my throat. "Freya, the girl I'm marrying on the next Fae moon, she's so . . . different. We have to leave on our tour in three days. If I can't see her as my queen, my partner, how can I expect the nobles to see her that way?"

"Ah, I understand now. Perhaps you should—"

My father's words fall away as a cough overtakes him. He leans forward a touch, lifting a handkerchief to his mouth. My heart pounds in my ears, and I quickly look around, eyes falling on a glass of water nearby. By the time I'm handing it to him, his coughing has stopped, but I spot drops of blood on his handkerchief before he hides it and takes a sip of the water. I set the glass back on the side table and readjust the pillows as my father settles back down. He closes his eyes for a moment, and I'm considering leaving when he speaks again.

"What do you like about the girl?"

"What?" I ask, taken aback by the question.

His eyes open partway and he looks up at me. "You do not love the girl yet, but surely she has some redeemable qualities, things you admire about her?"

"I . . . Yes, I suppose there are some things."

"When I was first courting your mother, I found it helpful to focus on those things I liked about her. The more I got to know her, the more that fondness grew until it became love. Tell me what things you find enjoyable about your fiancée."

I pause, thinking. The question shouldn't be so difficult, but I've spent so long focusing on the negative, it takes a moment to remember the positive.

"She's brave, I suppose." I recall her not backing down from Cress this morning and a smile twitches on my lips. "She definitely doesn't back down from a challenge. She's fiery and determined."

My father hums and nods for me to go on.

"She's pretty, beautiful even, though it may not be obvious at first. She's confident when she needs to be. She'll make a regal queen, I think."

"Good. Good. And what do you have in common?"

A small scoff escapes before I can stop it. My father raises his eyebrows.

"Nothing? Not one thing you share?"

"She likes horses."

"Horses?"

"Yeah, when she first arrived she spent so much time in the stables I thought she was hiding from me. To be fair, she probably was to an extent, but the other day I walked in on her talking to the horses. She was so bright and happy and . . . warm." I realize with a start I'm smiling at the memory.

"If I recall, you always preferred horses to most people," my father says, a smile on his own lips.

I laugh despite myself. "Well, you've met the noblemen's sons."

"Hmm. Indeed. What else?"

I take a deep breath, scrambling for something else. "She . . . likes books. She didn't have many when she came—I guess they don't have many book merchants come through her farming village—but she enjoys reading." I pause, looking away from my father. "And she's as stuck as I am when it comes to this marriage."

"Tybalt," my father says a bit sharply, drawing my attention back to him. "You will make a good king. Why the gods ensured the Fae line passed through this girl, I do not know, but you can still have a happy marriage. Focus on these good things and let fate take its course."

I nod, but I'm fighting back tears. "I feel like I'm caught between fate and failure, destined to lose either a piece of myself or my kingdom."

"I know she isn't the partner you wanted," my father continues with a heavy sigh. "I wish you could have kept him, but you can still find a way to be content."

"I know, Father."

"I want the best for you, Son. I hope you can—"

He breaks off into another coughing fit, this one much worse than the first. I'm thrusting the water toward him, but he's too lost in coughing to even manage a sip. Panic overwhelms me as I watch blood splatter on the blankets. I barely register the strong hands of Doctor Adbar pulling me out of the way as he steps to my father's side. He mutters to my father as he presses a vial of medicine to my father's lips. I watch helplessly as he settles my father back onto his pillows, numbness prickling over my skin as my chest tightens.

"Breathe, Tybalt," Doctor Adbar says, turning his attention to me.

I struggle to understand why he's talking to me when my dying father is lying right there, mere feet away. Dizziness washes over me and I realize I'm not breathing. I gasp, letting in a rush of air, and nearly choke.

"In. Out. In. Out," the doctor instructs, placing his hands on my shoulders and meeting my eyes.

I follow his instructions and slowly the thrumming in my head lessons and I can feel my fingers again.

"Better?" he asks and I nod, releasing another shuddering breath. "Good."

He drops his hands and glances over his shoulder at my father whose eyes are closed. When he looks back to me, he forces a weak smile.

"The medicine will make your father sleep for a while, I'm afraid."

I nod, shoving my shaking hands into my pockets. "We were done."

The doctor gives me one more nod and I slip away. Sometimes talking with my father helps to lighten my troubles; other times it only adds to them. I'm not sure where our conversation landed today.

I debate going off to see if Bastion still wants to spar a bit, but I'm not sure I want to be around anyone else right now. Instead I head up to my room. I kneel next to my bed and reach underneath. My hands fumble blindly until I manage to grasp a wooden box, pulling it out. At first glance the box doesn't look like it belongs in the room of a prince, but it's far more precious to me than almost anything you could find here. For one, it was crafted by someone I will always hold dear. For another, it holds one of my greatest secrets.

I carefully open the lid and peer down at the chaotic mess of papers. I reach to pick one up, but pause, hand hovering just above the opening. I swallow and squeeze my eyes shut.

"Come on, Ty," I whisper. "Find the good things."

I take a deep, shaky breath and open my eyes. I pluck up one of the papers and adjust my position so I'm leaning against my bed. My heart flutters in my chest as I unfold the paper and read.

"Find the good things."

CHAPTER SIX

FREYA

Between training with Bastion, my inane princess lessons, and more fittings for dresses I have zero desire to wear, I have practically no time to myself. I suppose it's better that way, because every time I do find myself alone, I tend to overthink everything all over again. Loneliness rushes over me and I ache to return home. Having things to focus on makes for a decent distraction.

When the morning of our departure arrives, I'm shoved into a dress that makes no sense for traveling. It may not be as nice as the dozens of dresses packed into my trunks, but it's still levels above what any normal person would travel in. The corset I've been forced into pinches and constricts, and no matter how much I try to adjust my position, I'm uncomfortable.

"Stop that," Tybalt hisses from his seat across from me in our royal carriage.

"Stop what?" I hiss back, shifting to lean against the curtained window.

"That!" he says, motioning to me. When I scowl in return, he scoffs, shaking his head. "All that twitching and moving. It's annoying."

"Yeah, well you try finding a comfortable position in this dress," I mutter, opting to sit up straighter. "This has to be the most miserable way to travel."

"This isn't exactly my choice of apparel, either, but you don't see me fidgeting," he replies, rolling his eyes.

I pause and take in his outfit. He is buttoned up a bit more than usual, his more casual clothes replaced by tight gray britches and blue silk shirt with a high collar that compliments his soft brown skin flawlessly. A stiff, pristine jacket with golden buttons, each bearing a delicately carved emblem of an oak tree, completes the regal look.

"Why are we dressed so formally? Aren't we just stopping in a regular village today?"

Tybalt makes a sound between a sigh and a scoff. "That's our first stop, but once we've kissed their babies, we go directly to Lord Longfellow's estate. Since he's the Duke of Newmeadow, gods forbid we arrive in anything less than our finest silks."

"But once we arrive, won't we have to change into formal dinner wear?"

Tybalt cocks a smile. "Of course."

I groan and lean against the opposite window so I'm practically lying down across the plush, yet somehow uncomfortable, bench seat.

"I don't think I'll ever get used to the ridiculous rules you nobles make up."

Tybalt chuckles. "I've grown up my entire life with these regulations, and I don't see the point either." He pauses, tilting his head. "Maybe once I become king, that can be the first thing I get rid of."

I sit up, grinning. "Yes, we can throw a formal dinner and have the pure audacity to show up in the exact same outfits we've been wearing since breakfast."

"Or, better yet," Tybalt counters, leaning forward conspiratorially, "we show up in training clothes."

He feigns a scandalized look before breaking off into a laugh. I laugh along with him. Something flutters in my chest as I meet his shining golden-brown eyes. As quickly as the amusement came, he sobers, a shadow crossing his face as he sits straighter and glances away.

"If only it were that easy to make changes."

His voice sounds so sad. I study him for a moment, wanting to say something to bring the joy back to his eyes, but before I can find the words, the carriage lurches to a stop. A moment later, there's a knock on the door giving us only a brief warning before it's thrown open. Bastion stands outside dressed in the finest solider uniform possible, though his version is black and silver, differing from the standard navy and gold.

"We have arrived," he says with a bow.

"Thank you," Tybalt replies with a nod.

Bastion's head remains inclined as he steps back, holding the door open. I'm thrown seeing Bastion so formal. I logically know he's a soldier and a servant to Tybalt, but the relationship between them has never once hinted that their positions were different. It's unsettling to witness the awkward shift.

"Freya," Tybalt says, turning to me with a forced smile and extending his hand. "Shall we go?"

I swallow and manage a nod, placing my hand in his.

Tybalt helps me to my feet, releasing my hand once I'm standing. He meets my eyes and in that moment I sense he wants to do this even less than I do. He quickly breaks the eye contact and steps out of the carriage. When I go to step out, Bastion reaches his hand to help me. I hesitate a moment before I place my hand in his, descending from the carriage as delicately as possible. Tybalt steps forward and offers his arm. I accept as Bastion steps back and closes the carriage door with a click. Tybalt starts to take a step forward, but he pauses and looks back at Bastion, who's standing at attention.

"Bash," he whispers, his voice so low I barely hear him, "if it gets to be too much—"

"I'll be fine, Your Highness," Bastion says quickly with an unconvincing smile.

I frown, noticing the tension in Bastion's shoulders and the tightness in his jaw. I glance to Tybalt.

"What's—"

"Let's go," Tybalt cuts me off, his fake smile popping into place. "We shouldn't keep everyone waiting."

I try my best to force away my scowl, but I'm not entirely sure I'm successful as Tybalt escorts me around the carriage. Bastion falls into place a few steps behind us, along with at least a half dozen soldiers. The path ahead is also lined with soldiers, holding back what appears to be the entirety of the village. Nerves twist in my gut and I'm suddenly grateful Tybalt is there to hold me up.

"What exactly do we do?" I whisper to Tybalt.

Tybalt waves at some of the villagers as we step between their neat lines on either side of the road, leaning toward me slightly. "Mingle and make them feel seen and important."

I wonder exactly how I'm supposed to do that with

guards blocking most of the crowd, but I force a smile onto my face and try to at least meet the eyes of our onlookers. As we move toward the center of the village, I catch snippets of conversations. Some people are keeping their voices low, but others seem to have no issue speaking at regular volume. Most of it is frivolous, talking about our appearances and general, meaningless gossip. But some of it is less so.

"Just because she's dressed up so nicely doesn't mean we'll forget who she really is."

"Surely the prince could've found someone better. Someone from our village at the very least who knows *something* about the workings of the kingdom."

"I think she's pretty, if nothing else."

"She looks like she doesn't even have half a brain. How can she lead?"

"Are they sure her blood is good enough?"

I swallow, determined not to let their words bother me, but something must give me away. Tybalt shifts next to me, slipping his arm from mine and sliding it around my waist. He tugs me closer and I nearly stumble.

He leans in, his warm breath brushing my ear as he whispers, "Don't let them get to you. They're little more than prattling fools with wagging tongues."

I barely have time to register his words before he presses a quick kiss to my cheek and releases me to step toward the crowd. I blink at him as he smiles and waves at everyone gathered. The people press closer and call out to him and he replies with natural charisma. A small smile sneaks onto my lips. He's good at this. My smile slips. I'm not.

I'm wondering if I should take a step closer to him or if I should find a different part of the crowd to interact with when movement in the corner of my eye catches my attention. I turn just in time to see a little girl half-stumble, half-shoved past the soldiers standing guard. The little girl seems startled and looks up at the nearest soldier in wide-eyed terror.

"What are you doing?" he growls, drawing his sword.

The girl gasps and staggers back a step. "I didn't mean—It was an accident!"

The guard takes a step toward the girl and before I'm even fully conscious of my movements, I'm moving between them.

"I'm sure she's fine," I say quickly.

The soldier stares me down, but I know he won't strike or speak against me. Not publicly anyway. I turn my back to him and kneel down in front of the girl.

"Hello, what's your name?"

Her eyes dart around nervously before settling on my face. "A-Arabella."

I smile. "Arabella. I like that name."

"Th-thank you."

"Did you want to ask me something, Arabella? Or did you have something you wanted to say?"

She nods, looking up at the soldier towering behind me.

"Go on. He won't bother you," I assure her.

She doesn't look quite convinced, still eyeing the man, but she straightens her shoulders with determination. "I wanted to know if the rumors were true."

My stomach sinks but I hold my smile. "I guess that depends which rumors you mean."

"The ones where they say that you're a nobody." Her eyes widen as she realizes how her words could be taken and she hurries to add, "Not a nobody. I didn't mean that! Just, you know, not royal."

"Ah, well, yes, that is true."

Her mouth drops open. "Really?"

I nod. "Is that a problem?"

"No! It's amazing!"

A surprised laugh escapes me. "Amazing?"

Her head bobs vigorously. "Because that means even *I* could be a princess one day!"

"Hmm," Tybalt says, startling me as he takes a knee next to me. "A princess?"

The girl's eyes widen and she takes a step back. "C-can I be?"

"Well, in order to become a princess you'd have to marry a prince, and I'm afraid princes are in short supply right now. However, you could most certainly be a noble one day." Tybalt smiles and I notice it's one of his rare, genuine smiles I've only seen a handful of times since my arrival. "Yes, I think Lady Arabella has a nice ring to it, don't you, Freya?"

I smile. "It does."

Arabella's eyes are brighter than the sun as she stares up at us, but before she can find a reply, Tybalt turns to me, extending his hand. "Shall we continue?"

Tybalt helps me up, but I turn back to the girl. "It was lovely to meet you, Arabella."

"Yeah. Yep. Uh, you too. It was nice to meet you, too!" Her face is bright crimson as she attempts a curtsey and darts back into the safety of the crowd.

I allow Tybalt to guide me down the road until we come to the center of the village where a circular space has been cleared. People flood the road behind us, essentially trapping us in. The soldiers and guards line the entire circle, but I suddenly feel like a caged animal. I stand dutifully by Tybalt's side as his voice rings out crisp and clear, delivering what I'm sure is a well-rehearsed speech. He's clearly at ease with all the attention, but I feel like the world is closing in around me. I struggle to keep my breathing steady with a smile plastered on my face, but my heart rate is increasing with every moment.

When his speech finally ends and the crowd breaks up, I'm relieved. We don't seem to be heading back to the carriage, however, and I turn to Tybalt with a barely concealed frown.

"What now?"

He shrugs. "More mingling, I suppose."

I look around, realizing that while many people are going off to their own corners, just as many are milling about, likely hoping to get more of a one-on-one with us. I already feel exhausted and I haven't even had a conversation with anyone yet.

"Don't worry, we have guards," Tybalt says, misreading my concern. His eyes focus past me and he frowns. "Bastion?"

"Yes, Your Highness?" he says, stepping to Tybalt's side.

Tybalt clenches his jaw, the light in his eyes dimmed by the formality in Bastion's voice. "Are you all right here?"

Bastion nods sharply. "I cannot imagine why I wouldn't be."

Tybalt turns his full attention to Bastion. "Bash—"

"I am fine, Your Highness," Bastion bites out.

Tybalt sighs, shaking his head. "So be it. Why don't you take Freya over there to meet with those lovely ladies, and I'll go this way? Divide and conquer and all that."

Bastion bows. "Of course." He turns to me, not bothering to mask his displeasure. "Shall we?"

I frown but nod. Bastion follows a few steps behind as I

make my way toward a group of women. I answer tedious questions about court fashion and court customs before being pulled to another group asking much the same things. Despite being the center of attention, I've never felt so dull. If I can't get away, I'm going to scream.

CHAPTER SEVEN

BASH

Freya is clearly getting frustrated by the cycles of the same conversation, but I don't expect her to take off marching toward a tree off to the side of the safe area.

"Pr— Your Highness!" I call, racing after her.

How is she even moving so fast in that dress and shoes?

I still manage to catch up pretty quickly. I go to dart in front of her, cutting off her path, but realize that it's not proper protocol. I glance over my shoulder toward the other guards. They want me gone, and they'll take any reason to get rid of me. I fall a step behind her, staying close enough I could reach out and grab her if needed.

"Princess, stop," I whisper, my voice falling somewhere between a beg and a command.

We step under the shade of the tree and she slows, turning to face me. Something seems off. Maybe this whole thing has taken its toll on her. I'm not exactly a fan of crowds myself.

"Are you okay?"

She manages a smile that's not convincing in the least. "I couldn't talk about tea cakes and court and silks anymore. I needed air."

I nod knowingly. "I suppose that could be rather tedious." I glance over my shoulder again. A couple of the other soldiers are looking our way. "We shouldn't stay over here long, though."

She sighs and leans against the trunk of the tree. "I suppose not." She looks over my shoulder and I follow her gaze to where Ty is entertaining a group of villagers, the majority of other guards by his side. "How long do you think we can get away with?"

A smile twitches the corner of my mouth against my will. Something about me appreciates her penchant for going against the rules. "I can't say for sure. I should probably make you go back right now."

She arches an eyebrow. "Are you going to?"

"Five minutes."

She grins. "Thank you, Bastion."

I shake my head at her. "You know, Ty has put a lot of work into—"

"Well, well, well. It looks like the little mutt has returned home!"

I go stiff, looking to my right toward the approaching figure with the taunting voice. Rupert, my asshole half-brother. Out of the corner my eye, Freya leans away from the tree, assessing him. His clothes aren't quite as finely made as ours, but he's clearly in a station above a common villager. He saunters toward us, flanked by two more young men with perfectly coiffed hair and turned up silk collars. Of course he wouldn't leave home without Charlie and Wilhelm, his favorite cronies.

"Rupert," I say through gritted teeth, offering him a nod as he comes to a stop a couple yards away.

"Now, Bastion, you know that's not how you're to address me. It's 'Lord Bryant' to you."

I inhale sharply. My fingers twitch, eager to draw my sword, but I reel in my temper and bow my head instead.

"My apologies, Lord Bryant."

"Who are you, exactly?" Freya cuts in, her voice sharp as she glares at the newcomers.

Rupert turns to her with a wide, cocky grin I want to smack off his face.

"Ah, Your Highness—or soon to be Highness, anyway—I am Lord Rupert Bryant. My father is a Baron over these lands, over Netherfield." He offers her an overdramatic, low bow.

"Right. And why are you disparaging upon my guard?"

Rupert straightens, raising an eyebrow in mock shock. "Why because dear Bastion grew up in this village under my benevolent father's care until your prince took pity on him and whisked him away to the castle."

I grit my teeth. Freya doesn't need to know my history. I can't even look at her directly as Rupert's smile turns murky. He steps closer, leaning in like he has a secret to tell.

"You know," he whispers loudly enough he knows damn well I can still hear him, "given his heritage, or lack thereof, and the things he's done, I'm surprised he's allowed anywhere near you."

"Explain," she says, crossing her arms.

"You mean you don't know?" Rupert gasps. His companions snicker.

"I didn't ask you to blather on with more needless questions. I asked you—no, commanded you—to explain."

His eyes dance with far too much delight as he takes another step closer. I'm on the verge of drawing my sword and ordering him back, but I really don't need another mark on my record.

"I'm sure you know of all the blood on his hands as an assassin for the king? He got that job because he was a ruthless child, always preying on others and beating them down. He was a horrible boy, and I can't imagine he's good for much else than slitting throats."

Lies. I flare my nostrils but bite my tongue.

"It's one of the reasons my father cast him out of our house. Well, that and the fact that Bastion's a bastard, born of infidelity by our whore of a mother. She couldn't keep her knees together, and everyone knew it. Bastion's only proof. Thank the gods at least my father is legitimate or I'd be a worthless bastard, too."

That's it. My hand flies to my sword and I have it half drawn before I catch myself. Rupert catches the movement out of the corner of his eye, and turns to me, grinning wickedly.

"See? What a temper." He clicks his tongue. "Surely not safe for a timid and innocent young lady like yourself to be around. He's a poor mutt of a dog and should be taken out and put down, not assigned to such a high position and left to look after someone as important as yourself."

"Well, I must say that you have brought some very important information to light."

My heart sinks. Surely Freya doesn't believe this? Then again, maybe she's like everyone else, ready to be rid of me.

And she doesn't even know the real reason she should want me gone.

Rupert's grin widens. "I'm glad to be of service, Your Highness."

"Yes," she says, taking a step closer to Rupert. "I didn't know much about Lord Bryant, Baron of Netherfield, but I must say, it has been enlightening to discover his son is willing to badmouth a guard appointed directly by the king and therein also cast distasteful judgment upon my soon-to-be husband and future king."

Rupert pales. I quickly push back my own surprise, working to keep my expression as neutral as possible.

"I did no such thing," he protests.

She takes another step closer. "Oh, but you did. You stated quite clearly you think Bastion's appointment was a mistake, that he is not worthy of his position. You went on to insinuate he's not fit to serve me. So either you can admit that what you spoke was a fallacy, likely born out of your own pathetic jealously, or you can admit to treason."

What little blood is left in Rupert's face drains away completely as Charlie and Wilhelm exchange panicked looks. I bite the inside of my cheek to hold back my smile.

"Treason? I spoke no treason!"

"No?" she tilts her head. "I distinctly heard you doubt the king and prince's appointment. You openly spoke against them. Last I checked, that is treason."

Rupert shakes his head. "I meant no disrespect to the prince or the king."

"Only to my guard?"

"Yes! No! I—"

"I think you should apologize to Bastion."

Rupert's eyes widen to a comical level, and it takes every ounce of self-control and training I have not to burst out laughing.

"Pardon me?"

"I will not pardon you. Apologize to Bastion."

Rupert's eyes dart between me and Freya. "I—"

"Bastion, do you know much about the workings of nobility?"

I clear my throat. "I know some, my lady."

"Good, then I suppose you can tell me if a Baron's title can be easily removed?"

A smile threatens to break free for brief moment before I push it away. Rupert doesn't look as if he's breathing.

"I believe so, my lady," I reply evenly. "If you had good reason to present before the king, he could remove the title from the current Baron for his wrongdoing."

"My father hasn't done anything wrong," Rupert protests, relaxing a bit as he adds, "the king wouldn't touch his title."

Freya hums, placing a finger to her chin in thought. "Perhaps not." She looks back at me. "Is it possible to change the line of who should inherit the title?"

I nod. "I would imagine that would be even easier, my lady."

Rupert begins sputtering nonsense before he finally manages to pull together a string of coherent words. "You wouldn't. Not over someone like him!" He thrusts his thumb toward me. "He's not worth it!"

She takes one final step toward Rupert so she's barely an inch from his face. I really should step in and pull her back, but I love watching him squirm. Besides, it seems like she can handle herself quite well in this particular situation.

"You don't get to decide someone's worth."

Rupert swallows and stumbles back, casting a desperate glance toward his friends.

"I want you to listen carefully to what I'm about to say, because your inheritance may very well depend on it. Are you listening?"

Rupert nods once.

"Good." She straightens, lifting her chin. "Bastion Shamblefoot is one of the best men serving the prince. How he got his position and how he maintains it is none of your concern."

My hearts stutters at her words. No one has ever defended me besides Ty. Now Freya, the future queen, is defending me. I can tell by the ferocity in her voice these aren't empty words, either. She truly believes what she's saying, which is baffling to me. And she's not done.

"If you continue sticking your nose and your opinion where they are neither needed nor wanted, I will have the former removed. I know you've heard that I'm a nobody from a nothing village, and I'm sure you will use what I say today to fuel rumors about how unfit I am to be queen. So let me be abundantly clear. The kingdom needs me to wed Prince Tybalt or everything as you know it will fall. If anything happens to me or to Bastion and we can trace it back to your loose and wild tongue, I will give Bastion full permission to remove that as well."

Rupert has the decency to look terrified as he glances quickly to me then back to Freya. "Y-you wouldn't."

"You clearly don't know me." She tilts her head, studying Rupert. "But you do know Bastion. Do you really think that given even the slightest bit of permission from the Crown he wouldn't be ready to wash his hands in your blood?"

I step to her side and meet Rupert's eyes without fear. "Yes, Rupert, what do you think?"

Rupert looks between us, blinking rapidly before he straightens. Despite his display of faux confidence, I can tell he is truly terrified.

"Fine. If you feel you must reduce yourself to petty threats, then so be it. Associate yourself with whomever you wish, but when trouble finds you, don't come to me."

"You can trust me when I say I cannot think of a single situation where I would even consider coming to you," she replies.

Rupert huffs and storms off, his friends tripping along behind him. Once he's gone, I turn to Freya.

"I'm not sure if I should thank you or scold you."

She shrugs. "It doesn't matter. What's done is done." She looks to where Tybalt is still in the center of the village. When I glance that way as well, his attention is undoubtedly on us.

I straighten to attention. "I do believe your five minutes is up."

She sighs and takes a step toward the village, but pauses, turning back to me.

"I really don't care about what he said, you know."

My heart leaps into my throat. "What?"

"Everything he said, I don't care if it's true or not—well, I know the assassin bit is true—but the other bits. It doesn't matter. It doesn't change who you are, and I truly believe if you were dangerous Tybalt wouldn't trust you the way he does. If it doesn't matter to him, it doesn't matter to me."

"I—Thank you."

She offers me what is probably the most sincere smile I've

seen from her since her arrival at the palace. "No one deserves to be judged for things beyond their control."

"Still," I mutter with a shake of my head. "You didn't have to do that, didn't have to come to my defense, and yet you did."

"Honestly, it was no big deal," she replies as we walk up next to Ty, who's stepping back from his previous conversation.

Ty furrows his brow, shooting me a quick look of concern. "Did something happen?"

I open my mouth to reply, but pause, glancing to a couple of soldiers nearby. They don't need the worst bits about me confirmed.

"Everything is fine, Your Highness."

Ty looks less than convinced, turning to Freya. I shoot her a quick look that I hope conveys my desire for her to drop it.

"I got an up-close glimpse at some of the locals, and they were . . . less than pleasant." She says and I relax a bit. Ty's jaw clenches and she hurries to add, "But it's all been taken care of."

Tybalt looks back to me. "Truly?"

A hint of a smile twitches at the corner of my mouth as I glance to Freya then back to Ty. "Truly."

Tybalt looks more puzzled than anything, and I have to work to hide my smile. Tybalt shrugs and turns back to the crowd, but I know this won't be the last we speak of this.

"All right then."

He takes Freya's hand and brings it to his lips for a gentle kiss. My heart clenches and I remind myself that's what we're here for. He has to show off his bride. Or maybe, it's his way of thanking her for what she did without drawing more attention to the situation. He lowers her hand but doesn't release his hold, drawing her toward a waiting group of villagers. As he chats, he pulls her into the conversations while I take up my position several feet behind them. There's a new energy buzzing around them that somehow seems to extend to me. I think something may be shifting, but I'm not sure what exactly it is. Not yet.

CHAPTER EIGHT

TY

It takes several minutes of prying once we're alone to get Bash to confess what happened in Netherfield, but once he does I'm infuriated. I knew there was a chance Bash would run into trouble from his past, but I had hoped we could avoid it. It's probably a good thing Freya was the one there and not me, because there's a strong possibility Rupert wouldn't have walked away with all his body parts. I must admit, I am quite impressed with her response, and I feel like I owe her a debt. A debt I will happily pay back if she would only arrive in the damn drawing room.

The pre-dinner chatter is draining. The duke is a something cousin something-something removed on my mother's side, and he seems to think he has charm. He does not. His pompous sons aren't much better, but at least only one is in attendance tonight and he's taken up residence in the opposite corner of the drawing room. I glance at the clock in the corner. Freya isn't late yet, but if she doesn't arrive soon and save me from this boredom, I'm rescinding my gratitude.

Thanks to the arrangements made ahead of time, Bastion is allowed to act as my valet as well as my guard while on the road, but he's not permitted to escort me to dinner. Unfortunately, most people seem to think along the same lines as Rupert. Given Bash's lowly upbringing, questionable parentage, and "choice" of career, he's not considered significant enough to be allowed anywhere near a formal occasion, even though I doubt the dozen or so lords and ladies in attendance for this dinner are really all that more respectable when it comes down to it. The only difference is that instead of doing their own dirty work, they use their fortunes to pay others to commit their crimes. Meanwhile, Bash will be forced to slink in the shadows while they parade around like peacocks. I know he's probably twitching in the servants' hall, not being able to lay eyes on me at all times. Chances are he's in the hall right outside this room, hidden in the shadows.

I sigh and adjust one of my cufflinks, glancing at the clock again. How has only a minute passed? I blink and try to focus on what the duke is saying.

"So, of course you can understand our ongoing concern."

I manage a nod. "Naturally."

The man straightens and smiles. "I knew you would see my way of thinking."

Shit. What exactly did I just agree to?

"Perhaps we could—"

The duke is interrupted by the door opening, and I practically sag with relief. That relief is quickly replaced by awe. Freya is stunning, to put it simply. She was lovely enough in the dress she traveled in, but this dress is something else entirely. It's meant to show off her every curve while displaying wealth and power. For a brief moment, I believe we may actually be able to pull off this whole wedding tour thing.

"My dear," I say, crossing to her quickly and offering her my arm. She accepts with a small nod, allowing me to lead her further into the room.

"I hope I didn't keep you waiting long."

I force a smile. "Every moment we are apart feels like an eternity, but I managed well enough."

A quick twitch of her jaw is the only indication she knows I'm playing a part, but her lips fall into a smile of their own as she feigns delight.

"How precious," a voice sneers. I turn to find the duke's second born child and eldest son watching us, lips curled in disgust. Since he's only three years older, we've been forced into the same social circle more times than I care for, and I can say with all certainty the distaste between us is mutual.

"Now, now, Anthony," his wife admonishes, stepping to his side as she eyes us. "We cannot begrudge them for their . . . public affections."

Anthony scoffs. "Please, Annalissa. As if any of us believe this charade."

I open my mouth to retort but don't get the chance as a bell rings, announcing the start of dinner. As the guests of honor, Freya and I enter the dining room first, taking our places of honor near the head of the table. The duke and duchess take their seats next and everyone else settles in. I glance around, taking in the elegance of the room. The duke has spared no expense making this evening as formal and fancy as possible. I glance at Freya to try to gauge her reaction and find her blinking down at the plate arrangement. I look at my own and my stomach sinks. Practically every piece of silverware known to man has been laid out. I have no doubt that during this five-course meal, the duke and his family are hoping to trip Freya up with ridiculous formalities.

When the first course arrives, Freya hesitates only a minute before she's plucking up the correct utensil. I sigh with relief and dive into my own food. The conversation is boring as Hell but flowing smoothly enough. Lady Longfellow engages Freya in a conversation on artists and seems pleasantly surprised that Freya recognized the expensive portrait in the main hall painted by an artist named Brickhollow. Honestly, things are going beautifully until we approach the main course.

It starts when Lord Longfellow mentions the upcoming property taxes and Anthony casually mentions raising them to make more profit. Freya frowns, opening her mouth to voice her opinion and I shoot her a sharp glance to keep quiet. But Annalissa doesn't miss Freya's reaction, swooping in like a vindictive hawk.

"Did you have an opinion?" she asks, eyes glinting dangerously as she looks at Freya.

"I . . ." Freya hesitates a moment, looking to me. I shake my head almost imperceptibly and she wilts a little, looking down at her lap as a servant removes her plate to prepare for the main course. "No, I don't think I do."

"Oh, come now, dear," Lady Longfellow says with a wave of her hand. "We're all very interested in what our future queen thinks." She smiles at Freya, but it's more venomous than comforting. "Please, share your thoughts."

"Well, it seems as if you're well off without needing to

raise the taxes you're taking up, so I don't understand why you would need to take more." She glances to me. "You haven't changed what you're asking them to pay, right?"

"That's not the point, Freya," I say through gritted teeth. "There are other expenses to consider."

"Precisely," Lord Longfellow says, tipping his wine glass to me. "We are wanting to refurbish our sitting room and library. That costs money."

"But they looked fine," Freya protests, her frown growing.

"Freya," I warn, but she doesn't stop, shaking her head.

"No, I could understand wanting to bring in more money to fix things that need actual repairs, but to take more money from their tenants and workers just so they can upgrade frivolous things doesn't make sense." She turns her attention to the duke, who looks less than pleased. "Have you even asked your tenants what they need? Maybe there are needs that should be considered before your wants."

"Freya," I say, a bit sharper this time.

She shrinks back in her chair. "I . . ." She pauses, focusing on the plate of food a nervous servant is placing in front of her. "Perhaps I have a bit more to learn."

"Indeed," Lord Longfellow snaps as Anthony looks on in glee.

Freya looks on the verge of tears as she plucks up the wrong fork. I clear my throat discreetly and nod to the correct fork in my hand. She catches herself quickly, switching out her utensil for the correct one, but Lady Longfellow doesn't miss the mistake, exchanging a look of chagrin with her husband. Things get worse when Freya takes a bite of her lamb. It's been heavily seasoned with red sauce peppers from the south. Most people would recognize that the dish has significant spice and would take a small bite, but Freya apparently didn't get that message. She takes a large bite, her eyes widening as the heat floods her mouth. She chokes, cursing under her breath but loudly enough anyone sitting near her can hear, and barely manages to get her food down, her eyes watering.

"Something wrong, dear?" Lady Longfellow asks, smirking as she lifts her wine to her mouth.

"I-I'm fine," Freya sputters, trying to cover a cough.

She reaches a shaking hand toward her water, but in doing so, she knocks her wine glass, spilling wine across the table and into her lap. Freya screeches, jumping to her feet and sending her entire plate flying in the process. I manage to scoot away just in time to avoid being hit by the airborne food, but Freya isn't so lucky—wine, red sauce, and bits of vegetables splatter down her dress.

"I'm sorry," she says, tears brimming in her eyes as she looks down at the mess.

"You should probably leave and have the servants set that dress or it will be rather lost," Annalissa says, grinning like a cat.

Freya manages a nod as she steps back out of the way of the servants hurrying forward to clean up the mess. She turns to the duke and inclines her head.

"Thank you for the dinner," she says, her voice wavering. "It was lovely."

Lord Longfellow offers her a nod and she scurries from the room. Once she's gone and the servants have cleared her place, the duchess lets out a long sigh.

"I suppose it was only a matter of time."

"I'm surprised she lasted that long," Lady Pristina, the

duke's daughter who's a year older than me, says with a shake of her head.

I clench my jaw. "You expected her to spill her wine and topple her plate?"

Lady Longfellow chuckles. "Of course not, but I cannot claim I did not expect something to go wrong. She is from low farm stock after all."

My blood boils. "Farm stock? Freya's not an animal."

She waves her hand. "Not quite what I meant."

"But she might as well be," Anthony mumbles.

"Pardon?" I challenge, shooting him a sharp look.

Anthony seems entirely unbothered, shrugging as he cuts his meat. "She was raised on a farm and sold off to you for nothing more than what she can offer the kingdom. It's not like she has actual worth beyond her blood."

"Anthony, enough," the duke says before I can retort. His voice is sharp and I'm on the verge of thanking him when he adds, "She is disappointing, but a human nonetheless."

"Disappointing?" I say, managing with great effort to keep my voice level.

The duke meets my eyes. "This whole arrangement is disappointing, to say the least." He turns his attention back to his food. "I was trying to remain hopeful that the kingdom could be salvaged, but surely you cannot believe you can be a proper king with her at your side as queen."

"What exactly are you saying?" I say through gritted teeth as the duke lifts a forkful of lamb to his mouth.

He takes his time, chewing his food slowly before washing it down with a swig of his wine.

"I am saying, boy"—I bristle at his casual tone and address —"that the young woman whom you are set to wed is not fit for the title of queen any more than you are ready to be king."

I stare him down as he raises another bite of food to his mouth like what he just said isn't on the verge of treason. I take a gulp of my own wine in an attempt to steady myself before replying.

"I have been training since before I can remember to take my father's place."

He waves me off and I bite the inside of my cheek to keep my temper in check.

"There is a difference between learning how the kingdom is run and actually running it." He pauses, leaning forward and meeting my eyes. "After all, when did you find this farm girl? Two, three years ago?"

"It was two."

He nods knowingly. "Exactly."

"I'm afraid I don't see your point."

He sighs, shaking his head like he can't believe he has to explain something so simple, but it's his wife who answers in his stead.

"That girl may be lovely enough, but she is not prepared to be a queen, though she has had two years to learn. Did you hear her language? Shameful."

"Freya is—"

"Not good enough to sit on the throne as she is," the duke cuts me off. "She is that way because instead of bringing her to the palace two years ago to learn how to serve the kingdom and fit into her place, *you* chose to leave her behind in squalor."

My mouth goes suddenly dry and I wet it by downing the rest of my wine.

"You made a horrible decision," the duke continues. "You

put off what needed to be done. You cannot be trusted to run this kingdom."

"Thankfully, my father is still alive."

Anthony huffs and I turn my attention to him.

"Did you have something to add?"

He raises his palms in false surrender, a smirk playing on the corner of his lips. "I meant no offense, but what was the last thing your father did as part of his kingly duties?"

"Now, now, Anthony," Lord Longfellow says, his voice far too cheerful given the conversation. "The king is ill and likely on his deathbed, but we will not disparage his name."

At least the old windbag realizes that is straight treason. A servant steps forward and refills my wine glass as I return my attention to the duke.

"My father had no issues with the decision to leave Freya in her village. He did not want to uproot her entire life, and there were certain adjustments I had to make as well before she could be moved into the castle."

"Oh, we know about your adjustments." I bristle but the duke keeps talking, not giving me a chance to speak. "Your father indulged you and your boyish whims. He had faith in you and your bride that I do not. I cannot fault him for not seeing the future regarding his health, but I do believe his faith in you was . . . not wrong, exactly, but rather misplaced. If you continue this way, thinking of your own desires over the good of the kingdom, there is no way that you will be able to handle the demands of leadership."

He pauses to dab his mouth with a napkin while I indulge in more wine to keep myself from stabbing him with my fork.

"Thankfully, you will have my help," he says slowly, placing the napkin to the side. "As your cousin, I have royal ties myself, and I understand the ways of running a kingdom. I also have the ear of several other dukes and many of the counts and earls as well. We can guide you and direct your hand so that Elodia can prosper."

I catch a small snicker and glance across the table to Anthony. His eyes gleam and he isn't bothering to hide his smirk. I gulp more wine, emptying my glass a second time.

"What if I decline your help?"

The duke's eyes harden as they meet mine. "I do not believe you will have much choice in the matter. You cannot even competently present yourself and your bride at something as simple as a dinner. Then, when she's gone off and made a mess and embarrassment of things, you go to defend her. How can I expect you to run the kingdom when you can't control your queen and only make excuses?"

He shakes his head, looking down to cut another piece of meat. "No, for the sake of Elodia, I will support you by standing by your side and guiding your hand, unless by some miracle there is evidence of vast improvements before you are crowned."

Support? Hardly. It's a poorly veiled threat to take the throne. I have no doubt I will still be allowed to remain the figurehead, king only in name, while he and his crew of thieves call the shots.

"Now, enough of this dreary talk," the duchess cuts in cheerfully. "Surely there are lighter things to discuss?"

Everyone seems to agree, and the conversation shifts to gardens and horses and other mundane things as we finish our meal. My mind, however, is still on the fact my throne is being stolen from me, partially because Freya couldn't even play a part for one single evening. Everything had been going all right and she had to blow it. She may have been pretty in her dress and she may have momentarily enchanted the duchess with talk of painters, but when it came down to it, she failed their stupid test. And, while I know it's ridiculous to take it personally, it feels like she failed me. I needed her, and when the vultures swept in to pick at the carnage she left behind, she wasn't anywhere nearby to help me fight them off. But I feel like I failed her, too, and somehow, that almost hurts more.

CHAPTER NINE

FREYA

To put it simply, dinner was a disaster. My nerves were all heightened so I could barely hold it together. Maybe I should have been more careful about the things I said, but as their future queen, I thought it was only fair I shared my perspective as someone who has been on the other side of things. They obviously didn't appreciate it. I was already rattled when I made the mistake of reaching for the wrong fork—who even needs that many different forks, anyway?—and things went downhill so fast. My maid for the evening helps me change, but I can tell by the look she gives me when I ask if she can save my dress that it's a lost cause.

I suppose I could return to dinner after taking off my dress, but I really don't want to go back down there. I doubt they want me to return anyway. Instead I change into a ridiculous nightgown with a floor-length sheer robe. Honestly, even the sleepwear provided for this trip is over the top.

I sigh and sink into a chair, finding comfort in the pages

of a book I managed to sneak along. I'm debating going to sleep when I hear a voice in the hall. I pause, setting my book to the side as I listen.

"No, I need to talk to her."

I frown and rise from the chair. I'm reaching for the door handle when a loud knock echoes through my room accompanied by Tybalt yelling my name. I open the door and come face-to-face with an obviously drunk prince.

"You," he slurs, thrusting a finger in my face, "have ruined everything."

He stumbles inside my room without invitation, Bastion following with a nod of greeting to me.

"What—?" I start, closing the door with a click.

"You were doing so well, but you had to screw it up, didn't you?"

"It was an accident!"

"Sure. Sure." He waves his hand through the air. "Accidents happen, but it was more than that, you know. I tried to warn you, but you just kept talking."

I clench my teeth as Tybalt collapses into the recently abandoned chair.

"Every time I think you're done ruining my life, you fuck it up again. You already took—" He breaks off, frowning in something close to confusion as he looks toward Bash who tenses. Tybalt shakes his head like he's clearing his thoughts before he barrels on. "You already took someone—something—important from me, and if you keep this up you're going to take my kingdom from me as well."

Tears burn my eyes as his words bite into my chest.

"It's not like I'm having the time of my life," I snap. "I had a life outside of you and all your problems, you know. I don't want to be here. I don't want to be fucking up your life because I don't want to be part of your life."

"Good," Tybalt snaps, staggering to his feet. "I don't want you in my life." He stumbles toward me, stopping less than a foot away. "You're only here because I *have* to marry you." He leans closer so his face is barely an inch from mine. "We'll do the ceremony and save magic, and then you go do your thing and I'll do mine. You're not ruining anything for me ever again. I'm not letting myself hope again."

He droops a little, like the life has seeped from him. Sadness replaces the previous anger and, for a moment, he looks small and lost.

"It wasn't supposed to be like this," he says, his voice so quiet I wonder if he even realizes he's spoken out loud. "You were . . . The things she said . . ." He shakes his head, running a hand down his face. When he looks back at me, his expression is so stricken it startles me. "You and I were supposed to work. We should've worked. I looked for the good things, and they're there. They're there, Freya. They've always been there, as much as I pretend not to notice. I did notice and then I looked and found them again. I hate that these assholes get in my head and make me doubt all the things I know and feel."

He sounds so desperate as he rambles, and I take a step closer to him, my brow furrowing in equal parts confusion and concern. "What are you talking about? You're not making sense."

I glance to Bastion, but if he has any idea what Tybalt is rambling on about, he's masking it well, his expression tight.

"You're just so frustrating and I . . ." Tybalt's breathing is erratic as his frantic eyes meet mine. "I need . . . I want . . ."

He lifts his hand toward my face, but he freezes, fingers

inches from my cheek, and stumbles back a step, going a little green. I think for a moment he might puke, but he closes his eyes for a moment and steadies himself. I reach for him on some sort of instinct, but he jerks away from my grasp like a frightened animal. He watches me for a moment, eyes wide, breathing hard, before he shakes his head, turning his back to me.

"Let's go, Bash," he slurs, moving toward the door.

Bastion goes to follow him, but pauses, turning to me. "He's very drunk."

"I can tell," I mumble, hoping that Bastion can't detect the tremor in my voice.

"Dinner didn't go well," Bastion explains. "After you left, Lord Longfellow—"

"Bash!" Tybalt yells from the doorway.

Bastion sighs. "I should follow him and make sure he makes it to bed safely and doesn't fall down a staircase and break his neck."

"It wouldn't be the worst part of the night. It'd at least put both of us out of our misery."

Bastion's eyes flash as his expression goes cold. He straightens and all sympathy for me vanishes entirely.

"Right. Good night, Princess."

When the door closes behind Bastion and Tybalt, I collapse onto the plush yet uncomfortable bed and let my tears break free.

I DRESS IN THE MOST COMFORTABLE OPTION AMONG THOSE packed and head down to breakfast. I've never been so thankful to be able to leave a place before, and I'm ready to get breakfast done. When I'm escorted into the breakfast room, I find only the duchess and her youngest daughter in the room. The girl can't be more than fifteen or sixteen and had been absent during dinner last night but, judging by the delight in her eyes as I take my seat, she heard a full account of what happened.

We manage to avoid all small talk as I fill my plate. A very clearly hungover Tybalt stumbles in a few minutes later. He puts on a good face, but I can see the clear distaste in his eyes as he glares down at the breakfast offerings. I hope he pukes.

"Lord Longfellow had business to attend to first thing this morning, so I do hope you'll forgive his absence," the duchess says with a small nod to Tybalt.

He swallows, a muscle in his jaw twitching. "I understand."

We fall back into uncomfortable silence as we finish our breakfast. When we've eaten enough to be polite, the duchess escorts us outside where Bastion and our small fleet of guards wait with our carriage.

"Thank you, my lady, for your hospitality," Tybalt says with a nod to the duchess. "Please pass my regards on to your husband as well."

The duchess inclines her head. "I will, and I do hope, Your Highness, that will you will take my husband's words of wisdom into consideration."

Tybalt clenches his jaw for a moment but forces the corner of his mouth up into a small smile. "Of course."

He turns to me and offers me a hand up into the carriage. I accept and settle into my seat as a soldier locks and secures the door. Once we've gotten on our way, I take a moment to really study Tybalt. He's slunk low in his seat, leaning against the window, eyes closed. I'm not sure if it's just the hangover or if there's something else, something deeper upsetting him.

"What did she mean?"

He cracks an eye open and looks up at me. "What?"

"The duchess, what did she mean when she said you should take her husband's advice?"

He scoffs and closes his eye. "Nothing. Don't worry about it."

For a moment I consider dropping it, but I need to know what has him in this state.

"I'm going to worry about it, so you might as well tell me."

Tybalt sighs and sits up a bit, but he keeps his eyes closed and his head leaning back against the wall.

"They find me unfit to be king," he mutters. "The duke ever so graciously 'offered' to help me rule." He exhales through his nose and opens his eyes, allowing them to meet mine. "He basically told me that he's going to rule the kingdom for me because I'm clearly incompetent."

I frown. "How did he get to that conclusion?"

Tybalt snorts. "Because I couldn't keep you in check so clearly I can't control a kingdom."

I sit up straighter, my face heating with anger. "Control me? Like I'm a dog?"

"I believe you were compared to farm stock, if I recall correctly."

"Turn this carriage around and I'll teach that pompous old man a thing or two about how exactly I can be controlled."

The corner of Tybalt's mouth tips up. "I'm tempted to let you do it." He chuckles and then flinches. "Gods, my head is pounding."

I settle back against my seat. "How much did you drink last night?"

He shrugs. "I know I had at least four glasses of wine, but I'm not really sure." He pauses, glancing away. "I know I came to your room last night, and while I don't remember exactly what I said, Bastion assured me I was an ass."

A huff of a laugh escapes me. "To put it lightly."

He winces. "I'm sorry, Freya. I'm sure I didn't mean at least half of what I said." He offers me a half-cocked smile that borders on charming. "Forgive me?"

I consider him for a moment. On one hand, his words from last night still sting. Putting them in context now that I know how things went down with the duke after I made my exit definitely makes things clearer. And yet, I can't make myself believe that he didn't mean at least a little of what he said.

"Freya?" Tybalt says, leaning toward me a little, his brow scrunched in concern.

I look down at my hands clasped in my lap. "Do you really not remember what you said?"

"I—Not really. I remember yelling and . . . I'm sorry, Freya."

He scoots to the edge of his seat and places his hand over mine. I startle at the contact and look up into his eyes, which are filled with genuine concern.

"We both messed up last night," he says, his voice so quiet I barely hear him over the rumble of carriage wheels. "One of us more than the other, I think." He offers me a weak smile. "Regardless, we have to be able to move forward together. I can't do this without you. I screwed up last night and I'm sure I'll screw up again. Can you forgive me?"

"I don't know. I mean, I want to, but we need to be a

team. Right now I feel like I've been shoved aside like I'm worthless, and if you treat me like I'm worthless, why should anyone else treat me differently? I'll be on your side against the dukes and duchesses trying to take your throne, but I need you to be on my side, too. I can't take the whiplash."

Something I can't quite define flickers on his face for a moment, but he pushes it away.

"That's fair," he says quietly after a moment. "I promise to treat you like my partner next time."

I take a deep breath and release it slowly. "Okay, then I forgive you."

His eyes light up and a real smile curls on his lips. "Yeah?"

I can't hold back a small smile of my own. "Yeah."

"You know, if we're really in this together, you should call me Ty. At least in casual company."

I arch an eyebrow. "Ty?"

His eyes shine. "Yeah, it's what people who actually like me tend to call me."

"I never said anything about liking you."

A laugh startles out of him and it stirs something in me. Something warm. I shove the feeling aside and glance to the window.

"So, where are we headed next?"

Tybalt—Ty—shifts in his seat, making himself comfortable. "I believe the home of an earl. It will be less pressure and to-do than our most recent visit. In fact, that was probably one of the worst we'll have to deal with. If you don't take into consideration the ball."

I groan. "There's going to be a ball?"

Ty grins. "Yeah, held by Count and Countess Hallowbridge. They live near the temple where the crystal is stored so it will kind of be celebration of the halfway point of our tour. Most of the nobility we won't be visiting will be in attendance. As a plus, though, since a lot of people will be at the ball, we'll actually have fewer obligations on our return journey."

"Well, at least that's something."

Ty cocks his head, studying me. I frown.

"What?"

He shakes his head, shooting me an unconvincing smile. "Nothing, I just . . . nothing." He closes his eyes, tucking his hands behind his head as he leans back in his seat. "If you don't mind, I still have a bit of wine to sleep off."

I shake my head. "Fine. Sweet dreams."

A smile twitches on his lips, but he doesn't open his eyes as he says, "As you wish."

Something stirs in me again, and for a moment I really want to believe everything can work out.

CHAPTER TEN

FREYA

After the disaster that was our dinner with Lord and Lady Longfellow, the dinner with the Earl of Greymaster is a breeze. The man is on the younger side at only thirty-two and his wife is truly delightful. She's the first conversation I've had that was interesting and ventured outside the usual dress codes, feasts, court customs, and other things of higher society. When it comes time to turn in for the night, I'm a little disappointed our conversation has to end.

It doesn't take long before I'm ready for bed, but despite the plush comforts I've been given and the long day of travel, I can't quite fall asleep. After nearly an hour of tossing and turning, I push back my covers with a sigh and head to the balcony in the corner of the bedroom. Maybe some fresh air will help me sleep. I'm immediately greeted by a bracing wind the moment I step outside, and I wrap my arms around myself in a somewhat vain attempt to block out the cold.

"If you'd thought ahead, you could be wrapped in a blanket right now."

I startle and spin to my left. Ty stands on an identical balcony several feet away, grinning with a blanket draped over his shoulders.

"What are you doing?"

"Looking at the stars," he replies, glancing up to the clear sky above us. "They calm me." He looks back to me, offering a weak smile. "Sometimes when I have trouble sleeping, looking up at them helps settle my restlessness."

A smile twitches at my lips as a warmth settles in my chest. "Same here." I look up at the vast expanse above us. "Looking at the night sky makes me feel a part of something, makes me feel like I have true purpose beyond just my stupid blood." I shake my head. "I know that probably sounds ridiculous, but—"

"No, not at all," Ty cuts me off. "It kind of makes me feel the same way."

Another cold breeze whistles past and I shiver, wrapping my arms tighter. I should probably go back inside, but something in me wants to stay outside with Ty under the stars.

"I can share my blanket with you, if you'd like."

I huff a laugh. "That offer would be a lot easier to accept if you were actually near enough to share."

"I can hop over there. That's the whole point of lovers' balconies, you know."

"Of what?"

"Lovers' balconies," Ty repeats. "That's what these are. They're meant to be a way for two people to sneak into each other's rooms to be together at night without passing through the hallways under the eyes of nosy servants. Like conjoined rooms but less convenient given you have to jump across. Adds a little thrill to the rendezvous."

He waggles his eyebrows and I roll my eyes, swallowing a laugh. "You're making that up."

"I am not!" Ty cries indignantly. "I swear! It's a real thing! As evidenced by the fact that we're currently standing on the aforementioned balconies. Why else would they design the rooms with two balconies so close together if lovers weren't supposed to jump back and forth?"

A smile tempts my lips, but I manage to contain it. Ty doesn't need the encouragement.

"Right, and you expect me to believe people just leap across?" I step closer to the edge of my balcony, studying the space between us. "That's a good four or five feet at least. No way someone could jump that."

Something flashes in Ty's eyes as his mouth tips up into a smile. He pulls his blanket tighter around his shoulders. "Is that a challenge?"

"Is that a—" Ty's meaning lands and I take a step closer to him, shaking my head. "No, it's not a challenge!" Ty's grin grows as he clambers up onto the waist-high balustrade. "Tybalt whatever-your-middle-name-is Shadowmoss, don't you dare try to jump over here!"

But my words are pointless. Before I even finish getting them out, Ty is airborne, his blanket flapping behind him as he leaps from his balcony to mine. His foot just catches my balustrade and he falters, balance off, and he starts to tip backward. I lunge forward and grab the front of his night-shirt, tugging him toward me. He falls forward and down, landing on top of me.

"Oh my gods!" Ty gasps, pushing up on his palms to hover over me, his panic palpable. "Are you okay?"

I groan and glare up at him. "I'll survive, but what the Hell were you thinking?" I shove his chest to punctuate my point and some of the alarm leaves his face. "You could have fallen to your death."

Ty smiles. "But I didn't. And now I can share my blanket, though"—the previous mischievous glint returns to his eyes—"*this* is also a rather nice way to keep you warm."

My face heats and I push on his chest. "Get off."

"Fine, but you have to admit, it is a cozy way to warm up."

He pushes up and settles into a sitting position beside me as I also right myself. He adjusts the blanket around him so it's settled over his shoulders with the majority of it spread behind him like a cape. He lifts the edge of the blanket closest to me.

"My offer still stands—you're welcome to share my blanket. It's why I hopped over, after all. I risked death to bring you warmth."

"I can't decide if that was very chivalrous of you or just stupidity."

He cocks his head, grinning at me in a way that makes my heart flutter. "I prefer to think of it as chivalrous, but can it be both? I like to think I'm a master at combining the two."

I cross my arms and attempt to glare at him, but when another chilly breeze brushes past, I sigh and shuffle closer. Ty brightens as he tucks the blanket over my shoulder, but even as I pull my corner of the blanket around myself, I leave enough space between us that we're not quite touching, even if I am very aware of his warmth. For a few moments we sit in awkward silence, and I debate if I want to just call it a night and go back inside to stare up at the bed canopy until I finally drift off.

"Should we talk about the fact you don't know my middle name?" Ty asks, a hint of teasing to his voice.

"I'm sure I've heard it at some point, I just forgot in the moment."

"It's Adrian, for future reference. It takes less time to yell. I'm sure you'll need to middle-name me again before too long."

A small laugh escapes me. "I'll try to remember it next time." I pause. "Mine's Astrid, after my grandmother. Not that you asked but . . ." I trail off with a shrug.

"Astrid," Ty muses. "Freya Astrid Brambleberry. It's a pretty name. It fits you."

I've never heard my name sound so alluring before, but the way it rolls off Ty's tongue makes it sound decadent and rich. My stomach flips pleasantly and I adjust the blanket around me to give me something to focus on besides the prince beside me. We fall back into silence and I'm not sure if I'm grateful or not.

"Do you see that constellation?" Ty asks after a few moments, his voice soft against the quiet of the night. "The one with the cluster of seven stars all close together in a kind of squished circle?"

I look over at him to find his face tipped upward, his eyes fixed on a specific point in the sky. For a moment I'm rendered speechless, my breath catching almost painfully in my chest as I take in his beauty in the softness of starlight. When I don't say anything, he turns to me, and I try very hard not to focus on how close his face is to mine.

"So, do you see them?"

I swallow hard and force my eyes to the sky, looking to where he was moment ago.

"I think so."

I feel more than see his attention return to the stars, my heart lurching with equal parts disappointment and relief.

"That's the constellation of Caralea, the goddess of friends and lovers. She rules the night sky at this time of year. Some people say all seven stars represent her, with the topmost star being her head, the middle four being her arms reaching out to spread her love and friendship to the world, and the bottom two her feet. I prefer the idea that one star is her presence while the other stars are her lovers and closest friends, all huddling close and craving her presence and comfort." He turns his attention back to me, but I keep my eyes on the flickering stars. "Either way, I kind of like the idea of getting married under her sign. I feel like it bodes well for our union."

I slowly pull my gaze from the night sky and am greeted by even brighter stars shining in Ty's brown eyes. I take a shaky breath, trying to steady my suddenly racing heart.

"But we're not lovers or really even friends, are we?"

Something I can't quite define flickers across Ty's features before his lips tip into a tentative smile. His hand finds mine under the blanket where it rests between us and the warmth and gentleness of his touch does nothing to calm my heart.

"I'd like to be," he confesses. "Friends that is. Of course, I also wouldn't object to being lovers." He attempts a seductive grin, but it's weak, too soft around the edges. He shakes his head with a sigh. "Sorry. Habit. Honestly though, if we never become anything more than partners who share a bond to keep magic alive, I'd like for us to be friends. Do you think that's possible?"

I hesitate, not because I don't have an answer ready, but because I'm not sure I can voice the words I want. I'm afraid to admit that I want a friendship with him. A partnership is easier to commit to, but a friendship evokes emotions I don't want to name. I take too long to answer, and Ty's face falls as he turns away, his hand leaving mine.

"I'm sorry. I was foolish—"

"No, you're not," I rush to say. "Foolish that is."

He turns back to me and I can't miss the bright hope shining in his eyes. "Yeah?"

I lick my lips, pulling my gaze from him to look straight ahead. "Yeah. I think I would like to be friends. Good friends, even."

Honestly, sitting here so close to him, sharing our heat beneath the blanket under a clear sky of shining stars, I almost want to confess I'd like to be more. I'm not sure lovers is the right word, but it feels more correct than friends. I slowly bring my gaze back to Ty's and my breath catches in my throat. He's close and so beautiful. My eyes fall to his full lips and my heart somersaults in my chest. His lips part and everything in me screams for me to close the distance, to press my mouth to his, to taste him, to truly share his heat. Without even making the conscious decision, I shift closer to Ty, our arms brushing.

"Freya," he says, his uneven voice barely even a whisper. "I . . ."

"Yes?"

He hesitates, shaking his head. He adjusts his position so that our arms still have the slightest contact but he's facing away. "I was wondering if you had a favorite constellation."

My heart plummets in my chest as he turns his attention back to the stars. Tears of disappointment burn my eyes, and I remind myself it wasn't so long ago he was yelling at me about how much he hates me and how unsuitable a match I am for him. Even if we've made up, he's likely in no way ready for the sort of intimacy a kiss might bring. So instead, I push my feelings down and look up at the sky.

"Um, I don't think I have one. I honestly don't know that much about the stars. There's one about a dragon, right? If I had to pick, maybe that one."

He hums in reply. "That's two constellations in one—Barik the dragon hunter and the dragon he actually ended up saving. Or maybe the dragon saved him. Once again, stories vary."

He shifts his position once again so his arm slips behind me, a comforting and calming presence. I lean into him a little and I'm pleased when he doesn't move away.

"I can teach you a little about some more constellations. The stars have always fascinated me, and their stories never fail to entertain and enlighten." He turns to me with a gentle smile. "Would you like to hear my favorite ones?"

The smile that slips onto my lips is sincere. "Yes, I really would."

Ty's smile grows, shining in his eyes. He tips his face upward and dives into tale after tale, and I hang on every word. Little by little our bodies shift closer together, and at some point in the night, exhaustion takes us both. We end up curled together under our blanket, millions of stars watching over us as we sleep soundly, our hearts beating as one.

CHAPTER ELEVEN

TY

I wake with a start, wondering why my bed is so hard and why my pillow feels so warm. When I discover my pillow is actually a sleeping Freya, memories from last night crash in around me. Oh gods. I almost kissed her. I *wanted* to kiss her. I can't remember the last time I wanted to kiss someone as badly as I did last night without it being a prelude to luring them to do other things. Actually, I can, and that memory hits like the stab of a knife. I don't want to go through that again—I *can't* go through that again—but as much as I want the feelings from last night to dissipate, all I can think is how right it feels to be waking up with her in my arms. Something akin to guilt mixed with fear and longing swishes in my gut, and I pull away from her. Freya stirs and blinks up at me.

"What . . . ?" She registers our location and jerks into a sitting position. "Did we really fall asleep out here?"

I nod. "It would appear so."

She groans, rubbing her eyes with the palm of her hand.

"Great." She looks over toward my balcony. "Are you going to jump back across?"

A snort escapes me before I can stop it. "No. Nearly falling to my death last night was good enough for me."

She narrows her eyes at me. "Well, it's good to see you have more common sense this morning, but how exactly do you propose getting back to your room?"

I shrug. "Tha hallway?"

Her eyes widen in horror. "You can't just leave my room first thing in the morning! What will people think?"

"That we made sweet, sweet love?" Her horrified expression intensifies and I barely contain my laughter. "I'll be careful. I swear it."

"If you get caught . . ."

"I won't." I push up from the ground, pulling the blanket up with me. "I have plenty of experience sneaking from lovers' rooms."

I waggle my eyebrows at Freya as she stands with a heavy sigh. "Exactly what every bride wants to hear from her groom weeks before their wedding."

I grin. "At least you know I have experience when it comes to—"

"Okay," she cuts me off, holding up her hand to stop me. "I get it. As if I didn't already know you have . . . experience."

A fresh swarm of guilt washes over me and I mask it with a grin and a faux bow. "All the better to serve you, my darling."

She groans, but I don't miss the smile tugging on the corner of her lips as she gives me a playful shove. "Just get back to your room before we get caught and people assume you somehow made me fall for you."

I choke on a laugh. "Yeah, we definitely wouldn't want that."

I stroll into her room and she trails behind me. I carefully open her door and peer out into the hall to make sure the coast is clear, Freya looking over my shoulder. Once I'm satisfied that there's no one nearby, I slip into the hall. I'm closing her door when she leans forward and whispers, "Oh, and Ty, just so you know, I have a little experience of my own."

I barely have to time to register her words before she shuts the door with a wink and smirk. I stand, mouth gaping, staring at her door for a moment before I shake myself back the present, rushing to my room, thoughts swirling. This whole marriage arrangement may turn out to be a bit fun after all.

Not much later, I'm hurriedly dressing so I can join the earl and his wife for breakfast. I arrive first, but Freya makes her appearance shortly after. She acts like absolutely nothing happened, but she does shoot me the occasional smirk which I happily return. When we get on the road, her lack of proper sleep the night before catches up with her, and less than an hour into our journey she ends up curled up on the bench seat across from me, fast asleep. It's nice to know that she's comfortable enough to be vulnerable around me. I think last night went a long way to healing things between us from the harsh words I spoke a couple nights ago, but even I'm not foolish enough to think that everything will be smooth sailing from now on. Things just don't work for me like that. I tend to screw things up.

The carriage hits a bump and Freya's eyes flutter open. She takes a moment to take in her surroundings and sits up with a groan. I bite back a smile at her rumpled appearance.

"How long have I been out?"

"Not too long. Maybe half an hour?"

She makes a noncommittal noise and glances toward the window, even though she can't see out because the curtain is closed.

"Where are we going tonight again? A count's house?"

"A count's *estate*, but yes."

She rolls her eyes. "Estate. House. It's all the same."

"It's really not."

"It's a building where people live. I don't see much of a—"

She's cut short as the carriage jerks to a stop, muffled raised voices drawing our attention. Feet shuffle by with hurried action.

"What's going on?" Freya asks, scrunching her brow. "Surely we haven't arrived yet?"

I shake my head. "No, it's way too soon for that."

We don't have to wait much longer before the door cracks open and Bash peers inside, his eyes darting between me and Freya.

"Stay put," he orders, his voice firm.

I scoot to the edge of my seat. "Bash, what's happening?"

"There's a tree in the road. It could be nothing, but we're checking the area to make sure it fell on its own and not—"

Soldiers yell outside and Bash swears, drawing his sword as he steps back, slamming the door shut. Freya inhales sharply as the yells turn to screams. She looks terrified. I want to comfort her, but my own heart is racing so fast, I'm not sure I can find any words of comfort right now. Something—or someone—slams against the side of the carriage and we rock violently. Freya clutches the edge of the bench seat, her face paling.

"Bash will take care of them," I whisper, my voice a little hoarse. "He's the best."

She manages a nod, but I can tell she's not entirely convinced. The horses whinny and something scrapes against the carriage near the door. A moment later, the door flings open and a masked face peers inside. Freya gasps and scrambles away as the invader grins. A moment later, they're jerked backwards as Bash appears in their place. Blood is smeared across his face and uniform, but he seems mostly unhurt. The blood is too red to be his.

"You need to run," he says, out of breath.

"What?"

His eyes flash. "Run, Ty! Run! Get into the woods. I'll find you."

I stumble forward, Freya following. Bash stands guard, blocking an attack as we fall from the carriage. I take a second to gather my bearings. We're on a path in the middle of a forest, tall trees on either side of the road, chaos surrounding us. There are at least a dozen attackers. The soldiers should be able to handle them, but we have to get out of here.

I grab Freya's hand and dash toward the trees, pulling her along behind me, but she cries out and her hand slips from my grasp. I spin around and see her in the arms of another masked intruder. My hand is on my own sword a moment later.

"Let her go."

"*Bás ad faecræft*," the man says, lifting a sword to Freya's throat.

I still as his words register and translate. *Death to magic.* I'm still processing when the man hisses and Freya pulls from his grasp. I look down and discover a small dagger sticking in the man's leg. Freya yanks it out and stumbles forward. The man lunges at her, snatching the edge of her dress, sending her spiraling to the ground, her dagger falling away. She twists away from him enough that I stab my sword in his gut. The man staggers backward as I yank my sword out, turning to Freya. I sheathe my sword, making a note to clean it later, and grab her hand, pulling her up, but she hisses, stumbling back.

"My ankle," she whimpers, lifting her left foot. "I hurt my ankle."

Without hesitation, I loop my arm around her waist, giving her support. Together we stagger away from the chaos and stumble down the embankment on the side of the road. Someone tries to chase after us, but I call on my magic. I rarely use my magic, especially since it's become weak lately, but now I need it. I close my eyes and the crystal warms and glows against my chest. I reach out my free hand and release my flames. Our attacker staggers back, screaming as their clothes catch fire. With our escape no longer hindered, we disappear into the forest.

Running through the unfamiliar trees while supporting Freya isn't the easiest task, but fear and desperation drive us forward. As the sounds of the attack fade behind us, I slow and take in our surroundings. I spot an area not far ahead with a lot of underbrush surrounding a large tree and head that way. I ease Freya down to the ground first, and she leans against the trunk of the tree. I unsheathe my sword and lay it on the ground next to me as I settle at Freya's side.

"Are you okay?" I ask, scanning her over.

She manages a small nod. "Beyond my ankle and being shaken, yes, I think so."

I nod and scoot forward. I reach toward her foot but

pause, my hand hovering in the air above her ankle as I glance over my shoulder at her.

"Is it okay if I . . . ?"

She bites her lip and nods. I carefully lift the tattered edge of her dress and examine the injured area. Her ankle is definitely swollen, but it doesn't look too bad. I tenderly press my fingers to her skin and she inhales sharply, but she doesn't say or do anything to stop me.

"Well," I say, easing back beside her. "I don't think it's broken. Looks like a simple sprain."

"Is that your professional opinion?" she says, her mouth tipping into a smile.

A smile tempts my own lips as I meet her eyes. "In my professional opinion as someone who has broken my ankle before, yes."

"What then, in your professional opinion, should I do?"

"Hmm," I muse. "In my professional opinion?" She nods. "Stay off your ankle, prop it up on a pillow, and rest."

She snorts. "Easy enough to do in our circumstances."

I grin over at her. "It is if we think outside the box."

I shrug off my jacket—it was too cumbersome anyway—and roll it up. I carefully lift her ankle and tuck my bundled jacket underneath.

"There. That's basically a pillow."

"What about the rest and staying off it bit?"

I shrug and settle next to her, leaning on the tree, our shoulders brushing. "We have to wait for Bash, so you're pretty much required to rest for at least a little bit."

"Do you really think Bastion will be okay?"

I glance at her out of the corner of my eye. She's sincerely worried. I'm worried, too, but I don't want her to know that.

"Of course. It takes a lot to take Bash down."

She opens her mouth to speak, but a distant explosion from the direction of the road cuts her short. My stomach sinks. That doesn't seem good.

"He'll be fine," I repeat, more to assure myself than Freya. "He'll find us. He always finds me when I need him." I say the last part in a whisper, and if Freya hears it, she doesn't react.

I stare off toward the carriage and say a quick prayer just in case the gods are listening for once. I finger the crystal at my neck and pull on the magic, not enough that my flames flicker to life, but enough that I feel the warmth of the magic. It's been said when magic was at its height, those with strong connections could tether their magic to send feelings, thoughts, and the like. They could pull people to them and away from danger. I don't know if those rumors are true and even if they are, I doubt magic is strong enough to do that today. It doesn't keep me from trying, however. I close my eyes and push a thrum of magic into the air, sending it after Bash.

Find me, Bash, like you always do. Find me.

CHAPTER TWELVE

BASH

Relief washes over me as Ty and Freya disappear safely into the trees, but it's short-lived. Our attackers are still going strong, which doesn't make sense. Their constant movement makes getting their exact number a little hard, but I've counted at most fifteen of them. We have twenty-four soldiers plus myself. They shouldn't have been able to take us down so quickly. It did help their cause that their attack was a surprise, taking down several soldiers before we even registered the attack was happening.

I suspected the tree in the road was a trap, but of course, the captain in charge of the soldiers didn't want to believe me. In fact, he laughed at me. I glance to the ground where he lies with an arrow through his eye. He's not laughing now.

I catch movement out of the corner of my eye and spin, blasting a quick shield of air to block my attacker. They slam into it and stagger back. With a quick swipe of my sword, they're dead.

Most people don't understand how to effectively use magic to make it last, but I have a couple tricks. One, make it quick. A concentrated, brief flash of magic is an effective weapon. It's taken me a bit of practice, but I have it down to an art. Using those small bits of magic means it lasts longer before I start to feel the draining effects. Two, have Fae blood so your magic is naturally stronger. Obviously, the second isn't really something you can change, but I was born with more than an average amount of Fae blood. I practically bleed gold. It's how the baron knew I couldn't be his child.

I use another rush of magic to knock back a pair of attackers. Another solider takes one out while the other charges toward me. They have admirable sword skills, and I find myself latched on their every move. Their sword clashes against mine and manages to catch it at just the right angle to make me lose my grip. I shove them back with a harsh wind and gather my magic around them, sucking away their air. The eyes above their mask widen as they realize what I'm doing. Taking away their ability to breathe doesn't seem to hinder them as much as it should, however.

"*Bás ad faecræft,*" they spit.

The words sink over me like ice water, startling me enough I don't notice their hand pulling something from their pocket until it's too late.

"Get down!" I yell to anyone who will listen, diving to the side myself as they toss a small black object toward the carriage.

A moment later, the carriage explodes in a ball of orange flames, taking out everyone within several feet, both assailants and soldiers alike. I cover my head, protecting myself from the spray of shrapnel. When I lift my head, my previous attacker is staggering my way, their mask gone and blood dripping from the corner of their mouth.

"Your prince and his bride are next," they say, wiping the blood with the back of their hand. "They can't run forever."

I lunge forward and drag them to the ground. They struggle against me, but a moment later, I'm slicing a diamond blade across their throat. I stumble to my feet and look around. All the other attackers are either dead or have fled. Of the soldiers, only one is up. He meets my eyes, arching an eyebrow to ask if I'm okay. I offer him a nod, and he leans down, checking the pulse of a soldier. He shakes his head and goes to check another.

The carriage lets out a loud crack as it sinks in on itself, orange flames licking the sky. I take a deep breath and concentrate my magic around the carriage. The last thing we need is the entire forest catching fire. Sweat beads on my forehead as I suck the air away from the flames. It takes a fair amount of concentration and effort, but little by little the flames snuff out, leaving thick black smoke in their wake. When I release my magic, exhaustion overwhelms me. I pushed myself too much. I sink to the ground and allow myself a moment.

"Are you okay?"

I startle and look up at the soldier. Cooper, I think his name is. I manage a nod. I look past him to the smoking carriage and bodies.

"Anyone else alive?"

Cooper shakes his head. "Jack was, but he got hit by too much shrapnel from the carriage so I—"

He chokes off, but he doesn't need to finish. One of the first things you learn about wounds during a battle is that not everyone can be saved, and sometimes you have to make tough decisions. He offers me his hand and helps me up. A whinny catches my attention, and I look further down the road to a horse with her reigns caught in the trees. All the other horses have run off, long gone. I make my way over the bodies and approach her slowly. She jerks away from me at first, but I extend my hand and whisper calmly until she allows me to approach. I untangle her and lead her back toward where Cooper stands watching us.

"Back up the road a bit there was a fork. If you go to the left, there should be a little village a short way up," I say, passing the reigns to him.

Cooper frowns. "Shouldn't we go after the prince?"

I shake my head, already making my way over to the side of the road where I tossed my emergency bag. "No, *we* aren't going to do anything." I kick rubble out of the way. "*You* are going to the village to use whatever resources they have to get a message back to the palace. They need to know about the attack. Ah, there it is."

I lean down and pluck up my bag, shouldering it. It doesn't have much in it, but it will help our situation. I turn to face Cooper.

"*I* am going to go hunt down Ty—the prince. I'll make sure they're okay, tend to any wounds, and make sure they make it somewhere safe."

Cooper's frown deepens. "Are you sure that's the best idea? Shouldn't we find them first and then all head to the village? We can refresh our horses and supplies and—"

"No," I say, cutting him off with a wave.

His eyes flash, and he sets his jaw. Cooper is one of the few soldiers who didn't seem to mind me joining them, but he clearly doesn't like me giving orders and making decisions.

"We need to get the prince to his next location."

I shake my head, sighing. "That's not safe."

Cooper takes a step closer. "Those are our orders."

"Those were *your* orders," I counter. "My orders were what they always are—protect the prince at all cost. Did you hear what those people were saying?"

"They said something about getting the prince."

"But did you recognize the phrase they were shouting?" Cooper shakes his head. *"Bás ad faecræft* means 'Death to Magic.'"

Cooper's eyes widen as he registers what I'm saying. "The cult rebels?"

I nod. "They're here to stop the marriage, to kill magic. They want to take out the prince and princess and make sure that the nobles' access to magic is snuffed. This was a targeted attack, which means they likely know our path. I'm going to go against their expectations and take the prince a different route. It means he might miss a few stops on his tour, but I'll get him back on track as soon as it's safe."

Cooper studies for me for a moment before nodding somewhat reluctantly. "Fine. I'll make sure the palace knows."

"Good." I roll my neck, willing away the exhaustion tickling across my limbs. "Now, you head off your way, and I'll find the prince."

Cooper offers me one last nod before mounting the horse. I don't spare him another glance as I climb down the embankment and head off into the trees. It's a good thing none of the attackers made it far enough to go after Ty and Freya, given the very obvious trail they left behind. I'm a few steps into my trek when I feel a whisper of magic pulling me forward. Or maybe it's less magic and more intuition. Either way, I move quickly through the trees.

The feeling grows stronger and I feel like like I must be right on top of him when I hear whispered voices. My eyes dart around, looking for signs of Ty. I hear a soft laugh from Freya and something about it both soothes and grinds raw against my soul. I move toward the sound and finally spot the two of them huddled together behind some brush, leaning against the trunk of a tree. Ty's jacket is gone, but he seems unbothered. He's smiling at Freya and she's looking up at him with shining eyes. I clench my jaw and force down emotions I have no right to.

I take a deliberate step forward, a branch cracking beneath my boot. Both of them look up at me, fear flashing across their faces. Ty relaxes first, jumping to his feet.

"Bash!" He lunges forward, throwing his arms around me and tugging me into a hug. My heart leaps into my throat and I'm tempted to lean into the embrace. Thankfully, he's pulling away a second later, his eyes scanning me over. "Are you hurt?"

I wave him off. "Minor injuries."

He doesn't seem entirely convinced, so I remove my jacket to show him I'm fine. His attention drops to my left arm which bears a thin cut and his eyes widen. I look down at my sleeve which is stained with—

"Shit," I mumble, tugging on the gold soaked fabric. The skin beneath the sleeve is already scabbing over, the golden blood sealed away and hidden well enough, but my sleeve will be harder to hide. I know from personal experience that if the wrong person were to see my blood, it could cause problems. People don't like it when people like me have something that usually deserves honor.

"Everything okay?" Freya calls out.

I swallow and look past Ty to where Freya lies on the ground. It's only then I notice Ty's jacket tucked beneath Freya's foot to elevate it.

"Don't worry about me. Are you two okay?"

"I'm good, but Freya twisted her ankle," Ty replies, stepping back from me toward Freya. "Should we wrap it?"

Ty looks at me pointedly, raising his eyebrows as he says the last part. I furrow my brow. He focusses his attention on my sleeve and nods almost imperceptibly to Freya's ankle. What is he—Oh.

"Yes," I say, clearing my throat as I step forward. "We should probably wrap it. I'll just . . ." I rip the fabric of my sleeve with ease and kneel down by her side. I meet her eyes. "I'm going to touch your ankle now. Is that okay?"

Her teeth catch her bottom lip as she nods. I reach forward and carefully lift her foot, removing Ty's jacket and passing it to him. She inhales sharply but allows me to wrap my torn sleeve around her ankle. Once it's secured in place, the gold-tinted blood is hidden, but if anyone notices, they'll assume it's hers.

"There," I say, rocking back on my heels and pushing up to stand. I offer Freya my hand. "Let's see if you can stand on it."

She places her much smaller hand in mine and I pull her to her feet. She stumbles forward a little, catching herself by placing her other hand to my chest. She looks up and meets my eyes, her cheeks flushing as her mouth drops open. Something I don't want to understand flutters in my chest, but it's gone the next second as she takes a step back. She glances down and I realize I still have her hand in mine. I drop it like her flesh burns and take a wide step back, glancing around.

"We need to get going. I don't think any of our attackers came this way, but they undoubtedly have reinforcements nearby that will definitely be looking for you."

Ty nods, running his tongue across his lips. "So you heard what they said?"

I nod, but Freya frowns.

"What did they say?" she asks. "I heard them, but it sounded like another language."

"*Bás ad faecræft,*" Ty answers. "It means—"

"It means there are people nearby who want you dead, Princess," I cut in, forcing a mocking grin. "It means we need to get moving. We can discuss more later."

Freya scowls, clearly not happy with my lack of a real answer, but she doesn't argue, taking a step forward. She stumbles and Ty catches her, slipping an arm around her waist.

"I'll help you," he says, his voice warm. "You need to keep off your foot as much as possible."

A smile twitches on her lips as she meets Ty's eyes. "In your professional opinion?"

Ty's answering smile is soft and makes something lurch in my gut. "Exactly."

"Actually," I say, my body moving toward them without my permission. "I can help her."

Ty's eyebrows pinch together as he shoots me a puzzled look. "You're hurt, Bash, and I know you've probably drained your magic. Plus you've got your emergency bag to carry. I've got her."

He adjusts his hold on Freya, his hand finding its place on her waist like it belongs there. Which it does.

I clench my teeth but manage a nod. "If you get tired, let me know and we can switch."

Ty shoots me a sloppy grin. "Aye, aye, Captain."

I roll my eyes, biting back a smile, and fall into step next to him.

CHAPTER THIRTEEN

TY

We make it a decent way into the forest despite Bash's obvious exhaustion and Freya's foot before we stop for the night in a small clearing that still offers plenty of cover. Bash digs dried meat out of his bag to serve as our makeshift dinner along with some sort of medication for Freya that knocks her out. She's curled in a little ball on the ground, shivering occasionally. Even though the day was warm, the temperature is dropping quickly as the light fades.

"Are you sure we can't start a fire?"

Bash shakes his head. "We shouldn't risk it. Maybe if we had put a little more distance between us and the carriage, but we're still too close for comfort."

I nod reluctantly as Freya shivers again. I shrug out of my jacket and lay it across her. It's not as warm as a blanket would be, but she sighs and snuggles under it. She looks so peaceful. Movement behind me has me turning back to Bash. He's sitting on the ground, emptying out his pack. I sink down to the ground next to him, our legs brushing.

"What are you doing?" I ask.

Bash doesn't look up at me as he takes out the last few items, laying them in straight lines. "Inventory."

"Inventory?"

He nods. "I'm making sure everything that should be in here is where it's supposed to be."

I let my eyes trail over everything. He has a several knives and daggers, a few vials and packets that could be poison or medicine, a jar of salve, a little more dried meat, a map, a black strip of cloth, black gloves, a skein of water, and a bag of coins. I sit quietly as he takes note of everything and places it back in his pack one at a time.

"You should get some sleep," he says, avoiding my eyes as he ties the bag shut.

A huff of a laugh escapes me. "Me? I'm pretty sure you need sleep more than I do."

He finally looks at me. There's something in his eyes I can't quite decipher, but it's gone a moment later.

"Someone needs to keep watch," he says.

"I agree. That someone will be me."

Bash shakes his head and opens his mouth to protest, but I cut him off, placing my hand on his thigh. He inhales sharply, swallowing audibly, and looks down at my hand on his leg then slowly back up to me.

"I'm trained to protect myself, and you need sleep. Let me help you for once."

"Ty," he whispers, his voice warm but so quiet it's almost lost to the rustling of the trees in the wind. My heart picks up its pace and I'm suddenly aware of all the places we're touching.

"You know, that's one bonus to sleeping in the woods tonight," I mutter with a chuckle, pulling my hand back.

Bash scowls. "What?"

"You're using my name again. You realize it's been all 'Your Highness' this and 'Your Highness' that for the last couple days. Even when we've been alone, everything has been so formal."

Bash sighs and looks straight ahead. "You know that's how it has to be."

I nod and look down at my hands in my lap. "Doesn't mean I have to like it."

I look up at Bash, taking in his profile in the moonlight. He's so handsome. His gray eyes slide to mine and suddenly it's very hard to breathe. He must register something in the way I'm looking at him, because his lips part as his eyes drop to my mouth. My heart pounds against my ribcage, and I scoot closer, placing my hand back on his thigh.

"Bash," I whisper leaning closer. "I—"

Bash stands abruptly, nearly causing me to topple over. I blink up at him as he looks away.

"I'm going to check the perimeter one last time, and then one of us should take first shift."

I stumble to my feet. "Bash," I say, reaching for him.

He jerks away from my grasp and my heart plummets.

"No. I can't, Ty." He looks at me and everything about his expression is so broken my heart breaks right along with it. He takes another step back and it takes every ounce of willpower I possess not to close that distance.

"We haven't really talked since you came back," I say, not willing to give up yet. "You disappeared for almost two years. I woke up every day expecting to get news that you were dead." Tears burn my eyes, but I refuse to let them free. "I get that you needed space after . . . everything, but going off on suicide missions without saying a proper goodbye wasn't the way to get that space."

"They weren't suicide missions. Not entirely."

I take a step toward him, hands clenched into fists at my sides. "Then what were they?"

His shoulders drop slightly. "Do you really want to know?" He looks down and to the side, still refusing to meet my eyes. "You didn't seem to want to know before."

I take a deep breath, releasing it slowly. "I didn't want to know before because I wanted things to go back to normal as quickly as possible. Or at least as normal as they could." I take another step closer. "I could tell you didn't want to talk about the things you did, that the rumors bothered you. I didn't want to add to your discomfort, so I buried my questions. I was just happy to have you back. But now that we've found a bit of our old selves, I'd like to know, if you'd like to tell me."

He takes a shaky breath and slowly raises his eyes to meet mine. "I was struggling, as you know, so when General Harrow approached me with a mission, I took it. I knew there was a chance I wouldn't come back, and at that time, it seemed like the best option."

I inhale sharply but Bash continues talking.

"A group that had been thought to be dead, or at least latent, was reassembling. They had several people in their ranks who, if put into action, would easily take out their targets. I have always been toward the top of my class when it came to both one-on-one combat and group fights, and since I am one of few soldiers with access to magic, it made sense to send me."

His fingers absentmindedly reach for the crystal hanging around his throat. That stone is rare and he more than deserves it, but he's right. Very few soldiers are allowed the privilege of magic.

"What group?" I ask. "Can you say?"

"The *draíochta*." When I frown he adds, "The group that attacked you today."

My eyes widen. "What?"

"Once it was announced your match had been found, they seemed determined to kill you before you and Freya could create your bond. Since my . . . attachment to you was known to certain groups, I was the perfect candidate. I had the skill and motivation needed to go in and destroy their cult before they could get close enough to lay a hand on you. Had Freya's location been better known, they probably would've targeted her, but thankfully, I made sure that information never got out. I managed to take out a lot of their higher ups and the deadliest among them, but their reach was already larger than expected. We couldn't disassemble the entire operation. Obviously."

I shake my head, allowing his words to sink in. "How much of a threat are they?"

"Well, they attacked with roughly fifteen people today and almost succeeded, taking out twenty-three trained soldiers in a matter of minutes. They're trained from birth to fight and they have no problems sacrificing themselves for their cause, which makes them incredibly dangerous."

I pause, afraid to ask the next question that comes to mind. I open my mouth, but close it again quickly, shaking my head and looking away.

"Because I missed you," Bash answers softly, not even needing me to voice the words.

I take a deep breath and look at him. A small, sad smile twists his lips.

"Being away from you was more than difficult. I had no problem risking my life to keep you safe, but when your father's health began to fail, I knew my place was by your side."

"Bash," I whisper, taking his hand in mine. He tenses but doesn't pull away, his eyes locked on mine.

"I knew you would need a friend." He swallows and shifts closer so he's barely a breath away. "And I, selfishly, wanted to be the friend you leaned on. Plus, I know how reckless you can be, and I figured you would need a trained assassin watching over you."

His mouth cocks up into a teasing smile. I offer him a grin of my own, but it quickly falls away.

"It's a good thing you did come back, otherwise I might not have made it out alive today." I glance over my shoulder at Freya. "*We* might not have made it."

When I look back at Bash, he's not looking at me anymore, his smile gone. He slowly withdraws his hand from mine and takes a wide step back.

"Your marriage to Freya is important. The *draíochta* might want to stop you, but most of the kingdom supports magic and the Crown." He raises his eyes to mine. "*I* support you. I always have and I always will. And I"—he draws a shaky breath—"support this marriage."

My heart aches as it pounds against my ribcage.

"I want you to be happy, Ty," he continues, his voice tight. "I think you can be happy with Freya. You need to give her a fair chance."

I want to grab and shake him and make him take it back. I want to scream at him. I want to . . . I want . . . My shoulders drop. I want to do what's best for my kingdom.

He offers me a sad smile. "It's okay to love her. I'm told lots of people love their spouses."

I swallow and take a step closer to Bash. "Bash, I don't love her."

The muscle in his jaw twitches. "But you want to."

"I . . ." I trail off and glance over my shoulder at her, my heart flipping as warm memories from last night rush over me. I loved sharing the stars with her almost as much as I liked waking with my arms wrapped around her. Even though I struggle to admit it to myself, I know I want more of that. I look back to Bash.

"Yeah, I think I do." My chest constricts as my confession tumbles out in a timid whisper, as if speaking it aloud puts it all at risk. "I really do."

"Good." He clears his throat and looks back out into the trees. "I need to check the perimeter. Alone." The last word hits like ice. "If you insist on staying up for first watch, I'll sleep as long as you promise to wake me when you get tired."

I nod and realize he's not looking at me so I manage a weak, "Yeah, sure."

A moment later Bash disappears into the trees without another word. I take a seat on the ground. The wind whips around the trees and I shiver, drawing my knees to my chest. I rest my chin on my knees and stare off into the darkness, zoning out entirely. Something drops on my shoulders and I start.

"You'll have to be more aware than that if you expect me to trust you to keep watch."

I look up at Bash behind and cock a weak smile, tugging at his jacket that he draped over my shoulders. "Won't you need this?"

He shakes his head, settling down on the ground next me.

"Nah," he mumbles, stretching out and tucking hand behind his head. "I'm made of stronger stuff than you."

A small laugh escapes me. "Of that I have no doubt, but you know my magic keeps me warm."

He closes his eyes. "I'll take it back when you wake me up in a couple hours."

"If you insist."

He doesn't respond, but a smile twitches on his lips. A couple minutes later he's fast asleep. Despite having both Bash and Freya within reach, I feel more alone than I have in a long time.

CHAPTER FOURTEEN

FREYA

My back aches, which is weird because even in my vague, half-asleep state I know it should be my ankle that's hurting. I slowly crack open my eyes and an assortment of sticks and leaves come into focus. Oh, that's right. I'm in a forest, sleeping on the ground. No wonder my back hurts. I groan and roll over, coming practically nose to nose with Ty, who's still asleep. I take in his long, dark eyelashes and a smattering of barely-there freckles sprinkled across his cheeks and nose. I smile softly. I hadn't noticed his freckles before.

"It's creepy to watch people sleep."

I jerk away from Ty into a sitting position. Bastion leans against a tree trunk a couple yards away, arms crossed in a way that highlights his upper arm muscles.

"Gods, Bastion," I grumble, rubbing the sleep from my eyes. "You're the one watching people sleep."

"Uh-huh. So you staring at Ty was, what? Where your eyes naturally fell?"

I ignore him, shaking my head as I push up from the ground. I tentatively test my ankle, but find it more or less better. Putting my full weight on it, I brush dirt and leaves from my shambles of a dress and look around, realizing I really have to pee. I start to make my way to a bunch of trees to my left, but freeze when I hear footsteps crunching behind me.

"What are you doing?" I ask, turning to scowl at Bastion.

He arches an eyebrow "I can't let you wander off alone and unguarded in the woods with people about wanting you dead."

"Well, I don't need your assistance with . . . this."

He grins. "And what exactly are you planning to do?"

Heat colors my cheeks. "Bastion."

"Princess."

"I—Leave me alone!"

Bastion cocks his head, pretending to consider my demand for a moment before he shakes his head. "No."

I growl in frustration. "I just need to pee really quickly," I admit, face burning.

"Excellent timing because I too have to urinate." My eyes widen in horror as his eyes glint mischievously. He gestures ahead of us. "Ladies first."

"You can't be serious."

His grin tightens into a line but his eyes still smile. "Oh, I'm very serious."

I gape at him for a moment, but since I really, really have to go, I relent with a huff, spinning and marching into the trees. Bastion follows but goes off to one side while I go to the other. He turns his back to me, undoing his belt. I don't know if my cheeks can possibly burn any brighter, but my entire face feels on fire as I whip away. I pull up my dress and try to get comfortable as I hear Bastion doing his own business behind me.

"Are you done yet?" Bastion calls out. "I haven't heard anything."

"I can't do this with you watching."

"I'm not watching, but you have about five seconds before I turn around."

"Bastion!"

"One."

I close my eyes and will myself to pee.

"Two."

I am going to strangle him at my earliest convenience.

"Three."

Finally, my body snaps into motion and I finally feel relief alongside my embarrassment. Thankfully, Bastion stops counting. Once I'm done and have cleaned myself as best possible, I turn to find Bastion still facing away from me, his arms crossed.

"I'm done."

He turns to me and grins. "Excellent." He strides to me and offers me his arm. "Shall I escort you back to camp?"

I glare and push past him as his rich laughter fills the air. When I step back through the trees to our makeshift camp site, Ty is sitting up, blinking blearily at us.

"Where did you two go off to?"

"Freya needed me to guard her while she peed."

"I did not!"

Bastion leans toward me, waggling his eyebrows. "You know you wanted me there."

Ty's brow scrunches in confusion as he glances between us.

"Whatever," he mumbles, shaking his head as he pushes up from the ground. "I need to go as well."

I expect him to go off like we did, but he only turns his back and begins to undo his pants. The blood that was finally leaving my face rushes back as I spin away to look anywhere but at Ty. Bastion laughs so hard he has to lean against a tree to stay upright.

"You boys are horrible!"

Ty's steady stream silences and he shuffles behind me. I give him a moment to adjust everything before turning back around.

"Do we have any breakfast?" he asks, glancing to Bastion.

Bastion gestures to the forest around us. "Trees are edible." Ty scowls and Bastion chuckles before sobering. "All I have is what meat we didn't eat last night, and we really should save that. Keep an eye out. Caspian berries are in season, and I bet we can find a bush or two."

Bastion plucks up his bag and turns to me. "I assume your ankle is better?"

"Um, yeah," I reply, lifting my foot and giving it a wiggle.

Bastion nods. "Good." He looks up at the light peeking through the leaves. "We should get going, but if it starts to bother you, let me know. I can wrap it again or we can take a break and I'll give you more healing powder."

A moment later we're tramping through the forest with Bastion at the lead. About an hour later we stumble across a bush of berries that Bastion confirms are edible Caspian berries. Despite the fact they're extremely bitter, we each eat a couple handfuls before continuing. When the sun settles high in the sky, we stop and split the rest of the dried meat. My ankle is starting to ache a little, but it's not enough for me to make everyone stop.

It's nearly nightfall when we spot a pillar of smoke rising above the trees. Bastion and Ty both draw their swords and we approach carefully. When a small cottage comes into view, they sheathe their swords, but Bastion's hand rests on the hilt of his as we knock on the door. A middle-aged woman answers, her eyes knit together in confusion as she glances between us.

"Good evening, ma'am," Bastion says, inclining his head. "My sister, cousin, and I were traveling and our wagon wheel broke. Our horse ran off in the confusion as well, and we were wondering if you could spare us a bite to eat and place to sleep? Even better if you have some clothes we could borrow."

The woman looks very skeptical as she glances between us.

"We can pay," Ty hurries to add, and Bastion shoots him a sharp look.

The woman still doesn't seem entirely convinced so I step forward.

"Please, ma'am." I hold out my foot that's still wrapped in Bastion's sleeve. "I hurt my foot in the chaos and could really use the rest without worrying about wolves."

Her expression softens and she steps back, opening the door wider. "I suppose I can help a bit."

I step through the door first, Bastion and Ty right behind me. The cottage is cozy, a warm, flickering fire filling the small main room with light. A large knit rug takes up a good portion of the space near the fireplace. Off to one side is a kitchen area with a small, wooden table complete with four matching chairs. On the other side of the room are two closed doors.

"I can offer you dinner and a floor to sleep on," she says, closing the door. "And I suppose I can dig up some of my husband's clothes for you boys and a spare dress for you."

I incline my head. "Thank you, ma'am."

Bastion glances around, taking in the room. "Husband?"

The woman nods. "My Henry isn't here right now. He's taken some spare pelts and meat into the village and likely won't be back until morning."

"Which village would that be?" Bastion asks, his voice casual, but the woman eyes him warily before answering.

"Portersville."

Bastion nods, storing the information away. The woman stares him down a moment before heading toward one of the doors.

"Let me get you those clothes."

She returns a moment later with a stack of folded garments. She passes me a soft blue dress and directs me to the bedroom she just came from while pointing the boys to what is apparently a storage closet. She also provides us with a couple washbowls. The dress fits me fairly well, though it falls a little short. When I step back out into the main room, laughter bubbles out of me before I can stop it. Ty stands in the middle of the room drowning in an oversized off-white shirt as he does his best to adjust the belt on a pair of saggy brown pants.

"Stop laughing," he snaps, glaring at me.

"I'm sorry," I say through my laughter, not feeling sorry at all.

The door to the storage closet creaks open and Bastion steps out. The clothes he's wearing must be the same size as Ty's, but he's managed to make them fit. The sleeves of his shirt are rolled up to his elbows, showing off strong fore-arms, and he has the shirt tucked in so that it fits nicely across his broad chest. Even the pants are adjusted in such a way they almost seem made for him.

"That is so not fair," Ty grumbles, crossing his arms like a petulant child.

Bastion frowns, bending down to put his old clothes in his spare bag. "What?"

"That! You!" Ty cries, gesturing wildly at Bastion.

Bastion stands straight, arching an eyebrow as a smile twitches on his lips. "Me?"

"Ty's just jealous you look better than him," I reply.

Bastion's attention pivots to me, and he smirks. "You think I look good?"

My mouth drops open with a sharp inhale as I stumble back a step, my face heating. "No! I . . . Ty just . . . Oh, shut up!" I snap as he starts laughing, eyes dancing. Even Ty looks amused. Thankfully, I'm saved by the woman returning from outside, a basket of freshly picked vegetables in her arms. She looks between us curiously but doesn't say anything as she heads to the kitchen.

We chat with her a bit as she preps dinner. Bastion turns on a level of charm I didn't know he possessed. We find out our hostess's name is Mandy and her husband is a trapper. He also gets more information on how far away the closest villages and towns are. Portersville, the village where her husband went, is only a few hours on foot, but Bonesburrow is roughly half a day with a horse and cart but close to a full day on foot. It also turns out that Bonesburrow is the direc-tion we should head to get back on track.

Dinner is a simple root vegetable soup, but after not having had a proper meal in well over a day, it's delicious and satisfying. After we're done eating, the woman excuses herself to her room for the night and we make our beds in front of the dying fire. Bash insists we keep our boots on, and neither Ty nor I protest. With our bellies full and our bodies warm, it doesn't take long for us to fall asleep.

Maybe we fall asleep a bit too quickly.

CHAPTER FIFTEEN

BASH

I'm not sure what wakes me. Maybe it's the low voices, the chill from the open door, or simply instinct, but regardless, something pulls me from my dreams. At first, my brain is too muddled by sleep to make sense of anything, but slowly the world comes into focus around me. We're on the floor in the cottage. Ty rests a few inches away, his chest rising and falling evenly in sleep.

"I cannot be caught," a woman's voice insists. "If this truly is the prince—"

"It is," a sharp male voice cuts her off.

I close my eyes, pretending to be asleep, but every nerve in my body is acutely aware of the threat in the room.

"And if you want your money, you will go back to bed, shut your door, and let us do our work."

The woman must agree because a moment later I catch the clinking of a heavy bag of coins being exchanged followed by the door clicking shut. Footsteps cross the room and the woman whispers a prayer asking forgiveness before her bedroom door creaks open and closed.

I wait a moment more before easing up and taking in my surroundings. The fire is almost out, but enough of the glow remains for me to be able to take in the room. Silver moonlight peeks around the curtains, which means the night should be clear enough for me to assess the danger outside. I double check to make sure the bedroom door is closed before creeping across the room and looking outside. I can make out a couple figures standing along the trees a few yards away, their backs to turned to me.

I swallow and take a deep breath and reach for the door handle, turning it slowly so as not to make a sound. I slip into the coolness of the night, closing the door behind me. Once outside, I spot a third figure to my left near the corner of the house. Voices around the side of the house have me slinking though the dark to get a more accurate count of how many people I'm dealing with.

"—should be here any minute," a seemingly female voice is saying. "The rest were less than a half-mile out when we got word."

"Kent getting them?"

"And Malachi."

I edge closer to the corner and peer around. The two figures are easy to make out in the moonlight. They're armed and likely as skilled as those who attacked the carriage. If I move quickly I can probably take them out relatively—

"Bastion?"

I spin around and come face to face with Freya. I've barely had time to register her presence before the people around the corner pause in their conversation.

"Did you hear something?" the woman asks.

My heart thrums in my chest and I react on instinct. I grab Freya and throw her up against the side of the house.

She opens her mouth but my hand covers her lips before she can utter a sound. Footsteps near the corner as they investigate the noise. I press my body flush against hers and lean forward, bracing my arm to the left of her head. We need to dissolve into the shadows, and if anyone approaches I need to make sure she's completely covered by me. It strikes me only a moment later how close we are. Her breath is hot against my palm, her chest rising and falling against my own. As the footsteps shuffle closer, I hesitantly meet her typically blue eyes to find wide pools of silver reflecting the moonlight. Her reddish-brown curls are a little more untamed than normal, framing her face in a wild but wonderful way. Has she always been this beautiful?

She takes a shaky breath, and I realize belatedly my palm is still pressed against her mouth. I slowly lower my hand. Her lips part and something in her expression sends a shiver down my spine that has nothing to do with the chill of night. This close, pressed against her like this, I'm barely even aware of the cool night air. I force myself to focus, honing in on the soft sounds of our possible attackers instead of the softness of her body against mine.

"I don't see anything," the nearest person says, their voice a little too close for comfort.

"It's these damn woods crawling with gods know what," the other replies. "Come on, let's check the other side. See if there's anything over there."

This is my moment. I jerk away from Freya and instantly miss the heat her body provided. I shake my head. I can't think about that now. I need to get her away to a safe spot. I mouth a quick *follow me* and start to move away, but I have the urge to touch her. I need her within reach. I'm sure it's nothing more the innate need to protect, but whatever causes the desire sits beneath my skin like an itch. I reach back and grab her wrist, tugging her after me. She lets out a soft gasp that's lost to the night as she stumbles forward, struggling to keep up with my long strides.

My years of training and fieldwork have honed my senses so I can easily track all the movement around me despite the darkness. Despite needing to keep a good portion of my attention on Freya, I'm still able to get us several yards from the house without being spotted. I pull her along a walkway that leads out to what I assume is the main road. Once we've crossed over the road, I push her down behind some bushes, kneeling in front of her.

"I need you to stay here," I whisper.

She starts to nod, but pauses, looking past me. "Are they with the same people that attacked us before?"

"I'm fairly certain they are." I push up from the ground, glancing around to take stock of our surroundings. "Now stay here and stay quiet. I have to get Ty out of there." I look down at her. "Don't move unless they spot you."

"And if they do?"

I take a deep breath and meet her eyes. "Run."

Her eyes widen. I pull a sheathed dagger from my boot and press it into her hand.

"Get away safely and hide. I'll find you again. I swear it."

I can't quite make out what her expression means before I'm distracted by a noise near the house. Ty. I have to get to Ty. Gods. Why have I waited so long? He should have been my priority. Anything could have happened to him in my absence. I race back to the house, heart thrumming in my ears so loudly I have to concentrate twice as hard to locate where our enemies lurk in the dark. I pass a couple of them easily enough, but when I round the corner to the door, I find my way blocked. One of the figures from before has taken up a position directly in front of the door.

I glance around and approach them once I'm confident I won't be moving into sight of anyone else. My boots crunch on leaves and sticks and the figure turns to face me. Their eyes widen a fraction when they spot me, mouth turning up into a snarl. Their lips part, ready, no doubt, to call out for aid, but I call on my magic before they can utter a sound. With a quick jerk of my hand, I slash across their throat with a bit of concentrated wind, more effective than any blade. Terror fills their eyes as their hands fly to the line of blood pouring from their neck. Even with their vocal cords cut and their life force draining quickly, I can't let them make any noise. I cross the distance between us in three smooth strides, grabbing their head between my hands and snapping their neck. Their body goes limp in my arms, and I lower them to the ground carefully.

I look up and take in my surroundings. No one seems to be aware they've lost a comrade. Good. I take a steadying breath and open the door carefully and quietly. Ty is alone in the room, still curled up in front of the fire, sleeping peacefully. I sigh in relief and quickly make my way to him, dropping down by his side. I give him a shake and his eyes flutter open.

"We have to go," I whisper, casting a quick glance to the woman's bedroom. When I'm sure she's not going to appear, I look back to Ty, who's blinking up at me blearily, brow furrowed. "They found us."

That seems to wake Ty up a bit more and he bolts upright, looking around.

"Freya. Where's Freya?"

Jealousy bubbles inside me, but I shove it down. Now is not the time.

"She's already somewhere safe, but I don't know how much longer that will be true." I stand, moving around Ty to grab my bag from where I left it before. "Let's go."

I help Ty to his feet and he follows me to the door. I open it first, peeking outside to make sure our path is still clear. When we step outside, Ty nearly trips over the corpse I left behind, his wide, horrified eyes meeting mine.

"Did you—" he begins, but I cut him off with a sharp wave.

"I did what needed to be done," I reply, my voice much harsher than I intend. Something painfully close to pity flickers in Ty's eyes and I turn away quickly. "Come on."

We make it around the house without running into anyone else. Freya is huddled exactly where I left her, my unsheathed dagger in her hands. When she spots us, her whole body sags with relief.

"Thank the gods," she whispers, sliding the dagger back into its sheathe. Ty offers her his hand and helps her to her feet.

"Don't thank them yet," I reply. "We're not out of danger."

She tries to hand me my dagger, but I shake my head.

"Keep it in case you need it."

She swallows nervously but nods, slipping it into her own boot.

We've only made it a couple yards before a shout goes up from the house. They've likely discovered the body we left behind. The three of us exchange a quick look before we race through the forest, staying hidden in the trees but running mostly parallel to the road. Freya is the first to start falling behind despite her best efforts. Ty keeps glancing back, stumbling every time. I growl in frustration and spin around, coming to a halt. Ty nearly plows into me, his attention on Freya.

"Keep moving!" I hiss.

Ty frowns at me, but only hesitates a moment before he takes off again. I turn my attention to Freya and lunge forward, grabbing her and throwing her over my shoulder. She yelps in shock but only struggles a moment before surrendering. I take off running again, catching up and passing Ty quickly. Once we've put a fair amount of distance between us and the cottage, I set Freya on her feet and we continue, not quite running but moving quickly. When we finally come to a complete stop probably good half hour later, Ty is huffing and puffing nearly as much as Freya. Freya collapses on the ground, stretching out, and Ty is bent in half, his hands braced on his knees.

"We need to get you two some endurance training."

Ty glares up at me. "I've had endurance training, thank you very much." He straightens, shooting me a cocky half-smile. "You know I have excellent endurance."

My face warms against my will, but before I can reply, Freya sits up with a groan, drawing my attention.

"Do you think we've lost them?"

I look back the way we came. "Lost? No. Put some good distance between us? Yes." I look back at Freya and Ty. "But we should keep moving."

Ty groans and I shoot him a sharp look. He holds up his hands in faux surrender. "Fine." He sighs, rolling his shoulders. "Not like I could get back to sleep anyway."

Freya nods her agreement and the three of us resume our moonlit trek, walking this time.

CHAPTER SIXTEEN

TY

By the time the sun starts its ascent in the sky, I'm really feeling the fact I got maybe two hours of sleep. My head buzzes with exhaustion and my muscles beg for a break. At least once we put good distance between us and the cottage, Bash let us walk on the road instead of the uneven forest floor. I look over at Freya. She's sagging, her shoulders slumped forward. I'm half convinced she's sleepwalking. Bash is hiding his exhaustion better, but I know him well enough to recognize that the straightness of his shoulders and his overly intense gaze focused ahead are signs he's forcing himself to stay alert. A loud yawn from Freya has me trying to bury my own, but I'm unsuccessful.

"Maybe we should take a break," Bash suggests, glancing between me and Freya.

"Huh? What?" Freya mumbles, blinking rapidly.

I stifle a laugh. "A break would be good."

We settle along the edge of the road, and I stretch out on the ground, tucking a hand behind my head as I look up at the bright colors flooding the morning sky. Freya lies down near me, not right against me, but close enough I could reach and touch her if needed. I close my eyes with a sigh as Bash settles on my other side.

"We probably shouldn't sleep," Bash says.

I hum in agreement. "Not sleeping. Just resting my ey—" A yawn swallows my words and Bash chuckles.

"Fine, just a few minutes. Then we need to get back on the road."

"Sounds good," Freya mumbles around a yawn of her own.

A smile curls on my lips. It won't hurt to rest just a little.

"Shit!"

Bash's swearing jerks me awake, and I blink, taking in the world though a sleepy haze. It only takes me a moment to realize why he's swearing. The sun is significantly higher in the sky and the colors of early morning have faded away to a brilliant blue. I'm not sure how long we've been sleeping, but it's been a couple hours at least.

I ease up into a sitting position with a groan. Freya sits next to me, rubbing sleep from her eyes. Bash is pacing around almost frantically, and at first I wonder if he lost something. Then he sighs and runs a hand through his hair.

"I think we're safe," he mumbles. "There's no indication anyone stumbled upon us while we slept."

"How long did we sleep?" Freya asks.

"I'm guessing about three hours," Bash says, his voice heavy with guilt. "I'm sorry. I should've stayed awake and woken you earlier."

"I disagree," I say, pushing up from the ground. "We

clearly needed the sleep, you included." I offer my hand to Freya and help her to her feet. "And now that we're refreshed, we can survive a walk into town. It's better this way."

I try to force a little cheer into my voice, but I'm pretty sure I'm not fooling anybody. After literally running a couple miles or more last night, on top of walking several more, and then sleeping on the ground for two nights in a row, my body aches all over. Bash might be used to it, but Freya seems as stiff as I am.

"We still shouldn't linger," Bash says with a sigh as he looks down the road. "From what Mandy said last night, we should be able to get to the next town before nightfall if we hurry."

The prospect of walking all day seems less than ideal, but we have little choice. Bash takes up the lead and I fall into step next to him, Freya on my other side. We march in silence for a while before Freya breaks it.

"So, who exactly are those people and why do they want us dead so badly?"

Bash frowns, shaking his head, but before he can answer, Freya cuts him off adding, "You made me think they weren't as big of a deal as they obviously are, so don't avoid the question and give me any bullshit or brush me off like before. Give me a real answer."

I barely manage to stifle my laugh in time, earning a sharp glare from Bash. I bite my lip to hold it in, but I'm sure my eyes give me away.

"They're a cult," Bash answers simply, shifting the bag on his shoulder.

"A cult? Is that why they were yelling something strange when they attacked?"

Bash nods. "*Bás ad faecræft.* It's kind of their motto, their rallying cry." Bash turns his attention to Freya. "Do have any idea what it means?"

Freya shakes her head. "No. When I asked before you said it meant they wanted me dead, but beyond that I have no idea. I've never heard that language before that I know of."

"I'd be surprised if you had recognized it," I say. Freya shoots me a sharp look. "Not because I think you're stupid," I hurry to add. "Because it's a dead tongue. *I* barely know it and only learned it against my will."

Freya nods, satisfied enough with my reply. "So what does it mean?"

"Death to magic," Bash translates.

Freya's eyes go wide. "Death to magic? Like they want everyone with magic to die?"

Bash nods. "At their hands apparently, but it's more than that." He sighs. "I don't even know where to start."

"Why do they want magic dead?"

"Well, they didn't always."

I glance over at Bash, surprised by this little tidbit. "They didn't?"

He shakes his head. "The *cultas draíochta* formed around the time magic was faded to the point where it wasn't accessible to everyone. They felt robbed of magic and their initial creed was *Faecræft pro alle* or 'Magic for all.' When it became clear they'd never have access to Fae magic again, they changed their views and decided to take out those with magic so it could return to its rightful place in nature under the possession of no one."

Freya hums. "I guess I can understand that."

I halt and spin to face her. "Excuse me? Did you just say you can understand why someone wants to kill us?"

She pales little, shaking her head as she stumbles to a stop. "No! Of course not! Only . . ." She glances away.

"What?" I demand, stepping closer, hands in fists at my sides. "What can you possibly understand about the cult that wants us dead—me in particular?"

She raises her chin defiantly. "Stop putting words in my mouth! I don't understand why they feel the need to try to assassinate you—us—but I can understand why they feel cheated." Her voice softens. "I know what it's like to feel lesser because of things I was born without."

I swallow hard. "This . . . this isn't the same."

She cocks an eyebrow. "Isn't it?"

I bristle at her tone. "No, it isn't."

"So it isn't deciding who should access something based solely on their status when they're born? It isn't deciding that certain families get something based on their wealth and standing while others don't even have a chance?"

"It's more complicated than that," I grit out, trying very hard to reign in my temper.

"I know it is, and I'm not saying that everyone should be handed magic, especially not when it's weak like it is right now. All I'm saying is that I know what it's like to be considered unworthy without anything I can do to change it." She sighs through her nose and looks over at Bash. "You get it, right?"

I scoff. Bash would never—

"I do."

I spin to face him, but he's looking ahead at the road, refusing to meet my eyes, his jaw set. All the fight leeches from me and my shoulders sag with something close to defeat.

"Bash, I—"

"I don't blame you," Bash cuts me off, looking my way. "And I obviously don't agree with the way the *draíochta* is going about things, but I do understand what Freya is saying. As a child I was an outcast in my own family for things beyond my control."

"But you have magic now," I protest, gesturing to the crystal hanging around his neck.

He reaches up almost absentmindedly to twist the crystal in his fingers. "Yes, and I am forever grateful, but how much stronger would our armies be if more soldiers were allowed access to magic instead of nobles sitting back on lazy thrones, using magic for petty, useless reasons?"

His voice is filled with so much bitterness, his eyes cold. My breath is trapped in my chest, heart aching. If Bash and Freya feel this way, how much of my kingdom feels like I'm failing them?

"Hey," Freya says softly, placing a gentle hand on my arm. "We know it's not your fault."

I force myself to meet her eyes. I expect a look of pity or even anger, but all I find is kindness.

"If I could find a way to restore magic so everyone could access it, I would," I say with as much earnestness as I can muster.

"We know, Ty," Bash says, his voice gentle. "The *draíochta* are extremists. They are literally a cult I spent nearly two years trying to disassemble and eliminate. They don't speak for the majority of the kingdom—I know that for a fact. You will make a good, excellent king."

I manage a nod, but guilt still twists in my gut.

"Now we should get moving or we'll be sleeping on the side of the road again," Bash says.

We slowly start moving forward, my mind swirling with

thoughts. I need to distract myself some way. I look over at Freya.

"You'll get your crystal soon. What sort of magic do you hope to have?"

The corner of Freya's mouth tips up. "I don't have to hope. I already know."

I laugh. "You know? That's impossible. Do you mean you have a feeling?"

Freya cocks her head as she glances over at me. "No, I mean I know what type of magic I have. It's water magic." She looks back at the path ahead. "It manifested when I was a child. It was weak, so when I was forced to hide the fact I possessed magic, it faded away."

I shake my head, frowning. "No, that's not possible. You can only access magic with a crystal."

"For most people yes, but it's not entirely unheard of for those with stronger Fae heritage to have some magic. There's a reason I'm forced into this marriage, Ty," she says, her voice tight.

No, that can't be true, because if Freya's slightly golden blood is enough for her to have access to magic without a crystal then . . . I look over at Bash who once again seems very intent on not looking my way.

"Bash?"

He sighs through his nose, still refusing to look at me.

"Bash?" I repeat a little more firmly.

His jaw flexes, but his eyes remain fixed on the road ahead. "Yes, Ty?"

"Bash, do you . . . ? Could you . . . ?"

He squeezes his eyes shut for a moment before whispering, "Yes." He finally meets my eyes, guilt swimming in the deep gray of his irises. "My mother made me hide it, but when my father discovered me using wind one day, that's when he knew for sure I wasn't his. It wasn't just the color of my blood."

So many emotions assault me I can't distinguish one from another. My breath comes out in short, desperate bursts.

"Do you . . . do you even need the crystal I gave you?"

The crystal that meant something. The crystal that means *everything*. The crystal I risked everything to give him.

"Yes, I need the crystal now," Bash insists. "When magic first presents in children, it's a little wild and unpredictable, but that fades. It had faded away almost entirely by the time you brought me to the castle. I doubt I could access my magic anymore without a crystal, but even if I could, the crystal enhances magic and makes it stronger."

I swallow and nod, not exactly comforted by his words.

"Hey," Bash says, cutting in front of me and bringing me to a halt. He places his hands on my shoulders, and I look up into his eyes, furious at the tears burning in my own.

"This crystal means everything to me," he says, his voice low. "I need it, just like I need—"

He breaks off abruptly, removing his hands with a jerk as he glances quickly to Freya then at the ground. He takes a wide step back, turning abruptly.

"We're losing daylight," he mutters, marching ahead at a faster pace.

I stand frozen to my spot, watching him walk away. I glance to Freya who's standing next to me, her brow furrowed with concern as she studies me. Or is it pity in her gaze? Either way, I can't stand it. I shake my head, trying to push away the feeling of betrayal rising in me, and dash to catch up with Bash. Maybe the cult is right. Maybe magic causes more problems than it's worth.

CHAPTER SEVENTEEN

FREYA

Ty is clearly bothered by our conversation about magic, but I have a feeling there's something deeper behind his sudden shift in mood beyond the obvious. I'm pretty sure it has something to do with Bastion, given the way he won't even look at Ty. A little after noon, we stumble upon a bunch of mushrooms Bastion assures us are safe to eat. After a little persuading, Ty uses his flames to roast them, making them a little more edible if altogether somewhat flavorless. They don't fill us up, but it at least takes the edge off our hunger.

It's dusk by the time we reach the town. It's far from a busy city, but it's more than a humble village. Several merchants with carts still line the streets selling their wares, but most have already started to pack up for the night. We weave through the crowd, Bastion on high alert and as tense as I've ever seen him. He doesn't even relax when we stumble into an overstuffed tavern advertising beds to rent.

"You two go find a table while I get us some food and

somewhere to sleep," Bastion says, his eyes trailing over the rowdy crowd. His eyes land on Ty. "Stay together."

Ty offers him a false salute, and Bastion rolls his eyes.

"Make sure you get me something to drink. The stronger the better," Ty calls over his shoulder as he leads me through the crowd.

We manage to find a rickety table pushed up against the far wall. My chair wobbles when I sit down, but I'm so tired of walking and standing I can't bring myself to care. Bastion pushes through the crowd a few minutes later, balancing a tray with mugs and bowls.

"I have good news and bad news," he says, setting the tray down in the center of the table.

"Is the bad news that this is dinner?" Ty asks, scowling at a bowl of what looks to be a thick stew.

Even though the stew doesn't look or smell particularly appetizing, I bristle at Ty's reaction. "Not everyone can serve fine meals. It's a pity you have to eat poor commoner food, but I assure you, you won't die."

I pointedly eat a big spoonful of the stew, barely holding back my grimace. It's not exactly bad, but it's not great either.

Ty lifts his eyes to mine and frowns. "I didn't mean—"

"The bad news," Bastion cuts in sharply, "is that they didn't have a full room to spare."

"What's the good news then?" Ty asks, poking at his stew with a spoon.

"They had two beds left to rent."

Ty looks up from his meal. "Just beds?"

Bastion nods, swallowing bite of his own stew. "We'll share a room with a few other travelers, which I don't particularly like, but at least you and Freya will have a bed."

"What about you?" I ask.

Bastion shrugs. "I can sleep on the floor between you."

"You don't have to sleep on the floor. We can share a bed if they're big enough," Ty says, lifting a spoonful of stew eye level. "Screw this."

Ty closes his eyes and shoves the spoon in his mouth. He gags slightly but swallows. He opens his eyes and reaches for the mug of ale, gulping the entire contents before slamming the mug on the table with a gasp. I reach across the table and jab his arm.

"Ow!" he cries, jerking his arm away. "What was that for?"

"Just making sure you're still alive. Thought that tiny bite might've done you in."

Ty huffs indignantly. Bastion contains his laugh, but his eyes shine.

"I'm getting a refill," Ty says, pushing up from the table and grabbing his mug. "Do you two need more?"

I frown at him. "No. We just got—"

He waves me off and walks away. My eyes follow him until he dissolves into the crowd. Once he's gone, I turn to Bastion who's shoveling stew in his mouth.

"Has he always been this bad?"

Bastion looks up at me, arching his eyebrows. "What are you talking about?"

"The alcohol," I say, motioning to where his mug sat a moment ago. "He seems to drink a lot."

Bastion sighs, sitting up straight. "He doesn't have a prob-lem, if that's what you're getting at."

"Are you sure? Because I've only been around him a handful of days and I've seen him get pretty drunk more than once."

Something in Bastion's expression hardens and I get the idea I crossed a line of some sort.

"He doesn't have a problem," Bastion repeats, emphasizing each word.

"I only want to help him."

"If he had a problem, that would be nice of you, but seeing as he doesn't, maybe you should mind your business."

I bristle. "I think the drinking habits of my husband might fall into my business."

Bastion's eyes flash and he opens his mouth to respond, snapping it shut a moment later. He takes a slow breath through his nose before trying again.

"Look, I know Ty might seem like he has a problem, but he doesn't." I open my mouth but he holds up a hand, silencing me. "He can go long stretches of time without touching a drop, never has withdrawals, and doesn't crave it. He doesn't need it."

Bastion pauses, glancing over his shoulder to make sure Ty isn't returning. He turns his attention back to me with a sigh.

"He tends to overthink things and is prone to falling pretty deep into despair. Drinking takes the edge off and lets his brain turn off for a bit. So, yes, when he's stressed or overly worried, he tends to get pretty deep into his cups. He used to have other ways to deal with it, but I guess he's had to find different ways to cope. Let him cope."

I scowl at Bastion, but don't get a chance to reply before I spot Ty pushing his way through the crowd, a mug in each hand.

"Figured there was no point in going back up there twice," Ty says, resuming his seat and setting one mug on the table and the lifting the other to his mouth. "Not bad."

He takes a couple more big gulps and I shoot Bastion a pointed look. Bastion shakes his head almost imperceptibly and I sigh, focusing on eating. By the time I've finished my stew, Ty has polished off both his mugs of ale. He stumbles back to the bar, returning with two more. After he downs them, he tries to go back for more, but Bastion stops him.

"Come on, Bash," Ty whines. "You're no fun."

He looks at my half-empty mug, plucking it up and chugging it before I can stop him. Bastion yanks the mug away, but he's already downed most of it.

"Hey!" Ty cries, drawing several glances.

"You're done."

Ty mutters something incoherently and the muscle in Bastion's jaw twitches.

"Maybe we should head to bed?" I suggest.

Bastion nods. "Not a bad idea." He turns to Ty. "Come on."

It becomes obvious pretty quickly Ty is in no shape to walk. Bastion keeps one hand between his shoulders, guiding him through the chaos of people. When we reach the winding staircase that leads up to the rooms, Ty can't even make it up two steps without falling back, giggling hysterically.

"Go on up. We're in room three," Bastion says, looping his arm around Ty's waist to steady him as he tosses me a key with the other hand. "I'll be right behind you."

I nod and make my way up the stairs, exhaustion pulling at me more with each step. I'm relieved when I stop in front of our room. It takes me a minute to unlock the door, but when it swings open, I freeze. There are ten beds lined against the wall, most of which are occupied. Despite the glowing lanterns hanging along the wall, five of the occupants are already asleep, but three men are still awake. One is supine but the other two are sitting up. The nearest man's eyes flash with interest as they rake over my figure.

"Well, hello, darling," he says, pushing up from the bed and taking a step my way.

The other two men's attention also turn to me, the one man sitting up as he too leers at me. I swallow, wishing the dagger Bash gave me wasn't stashed all the way down in my boot.

"No need to have paid for a bed," the man continues, taking a step closer. "I wouldn't mind sharing mine."

The other two snicker and I stumble back a step into something firm and hard.

"Well, that would be inappropriate," Bastion's low voice rumbles behind me as his hand settles on my waist. "Why would she share a bed with you when she'll be in mine?"

The man's eyes widen and it's his turn to stumble back.

"I-I didn't know she was taken," the man rushes.

"So that gives you the right to harass her?"

I catch a flash out of the corner of my eye and realize Bastion has his sword drawn.

"N-no," the man gulps.

"That's what I thought."

Bastion's sword hisses as it slides back into its sheath. He leans in and I can feel his breath on my ear as he whispers, "Are you okay?"

I manage a jerky nod and he hums in reply. His hand drops from my waist, and I turn around to look at him and spot Ty leaning against the far wall. Bastion follows my eyes and shakes his head. He steps away for a moment and retrieves Ty before guiding us both into the room, kicking the door shut behind us. He lays Ty down on the bed closest to the door, making sure he's on his side, before taking a seat on the remaining bed. A moment later the lanterns are snuffed as the other men take to their beds. I take a tentative seat next to Bastion as my eyes adjust to the darkness.

"I can sleep on the floor," he whispers, leaning close enough no one can overhear.

I glance over at the men and even though their backs are to us, I'm still uncomfortable. I shake my head. The last thing we need is for them to call our bluff.

I look up at Bastion. "It's fine."

"You're sure?"

I force a smile and a nod. "Yeah, there's plenty of room for us both."

It's a lie, really. The beds aren't terribly small, but they're not really made for two adults. It will be a tight fit. Bastion arches an eyebrow.

"It's really fine."

Bastion nods and moves over to stretch out along the side nearest our roommates.

"If that changes, let me know and I'll rectify it," he says, still keeping his voice low.

I nod again and settle down beside him, facing Ty. The bed is even smaller than I thought and I can feel the heat of Bastion's breath on my neck. He shifts behind me and I turn over to double check that he's truly comfortable with the arrangement, only to come nose to nose with him. My breath catches in my throat. My mind flashes to the night before when he had me pressed up against the side of the cottage and my heart stutters.

"You okay?" he asks.

My eyes unwittingly drop to his full lips and I swallow, forcing my attention back to his dark eyes.

"Are you?" I manage, my voice a hoarse whisper.

He hesitates a moment, taking a slow breath before he nods. "I am."

I hold his eyes for a moment longer than I probably should. I can't help it. Something about having him so near has me flustered. The only time I've slept in a bed with someone was when we were doing much more than sleeping. My tired brain offers an intimate image of Bastion that I quickly force away. I can't think of him like that. The very idea has my face heating.

The corner of his mouth tips up as if he can read my thoughts. "Are you sure?"

I turn back over sharply, refusing to give in to his teasing. Thank the gods it's too dark for him to see the blush warming my cheeks. "Good night, Bastion."

I can feel the low rumble of his chuckle as he says, "Goodnight, Princess."

CHAPTER EIGHTEEN

BASH

It only takes a moment for my feeling of comfort and contentment to fade into a realization that something is off. I open my eyes and my brain takes a moment to catch up with my surroundings. That's right. We're in the upstairs of a tavern. Last night Ty drank too much and Freya . . . My heart lurches as my brain finishes registering everything. I'm not in bed alone or on the floor like I should be. I'm sharing a bed with Freya, and at some point in the night, she curled into my chest and for some unspeakable reason, I didn't push her away. No, my arm is definitely wrapped around her right now. As if sensing my awakeness, she sighs contentedly in her sleep and snuggles closer. I swallow hard, squeezing my eyes shut. I have to get out of this bed before she wakes up.

My mind whirls in panic. The way I have my arm around her makes it nearly impossible to remove it without waking her. How did we even end up this way? Usually even in sleep I'm semi-aware of my surroundings. I'm better than this. I've had to share beds before and this never happens. Well, not unless I'm completely comfortable with my bedmate and they feel mutually about me. In fact, it's so rare I can only think of one other person I would do this with, and that was instinctual, a desire to be close. Never have I ever wanted to do this with anyone else, let alone a woman. I can't feel that way about Freya. I don't feel that way about anybody ever beyond—

No. That can't be the case here. I don't do this. I don't feel these things. Whatever caused this must be the lingering need to protect. Freya is under my protection—that's why I'm in this damn bed in the first place—but most people do read into things like physical closeness because they do feel things. What if Freya wakes up and finds us in this intimate position? Will she assume I feel something for her? Does she feel something for me? I was teasing her last night to ease my own muddled feelings and discomfort at our closeness, but what if—

I will not panic. I am a trained assassin for gods' sake. I have brought down hundreds of people single-handedly in the past three years. I am stealthy. I have gleaned information that others died trying to prove existed. I have snuck into some of the most heavily guarded places in the world and lived to tell the tale. I can figure out how to free my damn arm from a sleeping woman without panicking about feelings.

I take a steadying breath and shift in the bed, scooting all the way to edge. As I do so, Freya rolls away a little and I'm able to escape. Freya scowls in her sleep, but doesn't wake. I breathe a sigh of relief and slowly peel myself from the bed.

I glance around the room and see what likely woke me. The travelers at the far end of our shared room are shuffling around, preparing to leave. I make eye contact with one of them and they nod in greeting. My attention falls to the men who gave us trouble last night. They're still fast asleep. Good. We should probably leave before they wake. I ease from the bed, deciding to wake Ty first.

"Hey," I whisper, kneeling next to Ty's bed and shaking his shoulder. "You need to get up."

Ty mumbles something incoherent and bats me away. I shake him harder and he groans, flipping over and burying his face in the bed. He's never been exactly easy to wake up in the morning, and the way I found most effective isn't exactly appropriate anymore, especially not in a shared space. I try giving him another firm shake but when that doesn't work, I shove him off the bed. He falls to the ground with a thud and a crumpled yelp. Thankfully, the noise doesn't disturb our sleeping guests, but Freya opens her eyes with a groan.

"What the hell, Bash?" Ty hisses, sitting up with a wince. He rubs his fingers on his temples. "My head is pounding."

"Maybe you should drink less," Freya says through a yawn.

Ty waves her off. "I didn't drink that much."

Freya's jaw tightens but I jump in before she can pass judgment. "We need to get on the road."

Freya shoots me a look of frustration but doesn't protest. Ty moves slowly, mumbling under his breath, and I wonder if Freya actually has a point. When we finally trip down the stairs, we find an empty tavern. A busty barmaid stands behind the counter, wiping it down with a rag that looks filthy enough I doubt it's actually cleaning anything.

"Do you have any breakfast?" I ask, sidling up to the bar.

The woman nods, casting a glance to Ty who's flinching against the light flooding in through the windows.

"I even have something that will fix him up," she replies with a nod to Ty. "I also have boiled eggs, if that will suit."

"I'll take three eggs," Freya says, taking a seat on the stool.

"Same," I say. "And give him whatever will fix his head."

The woman busies herself, placing a bowl between Freya and I with six eggs. A minute later she places a glass of grayish green sludge in front of Ty. His face tuns a matching green as he stares at the glass.

"I'm not drinking that."

"Yes you are, because I'm paying for it," I reply matter-of-factly as I pass the woman coins.

Ty glares at me as I take an egg from the bowl and peel away the shell. I take a bite of the lukewarm egg as Ty scoots the glass closer, a look of disgust on his face.

"Oh, what the hell," he mutters, grabbing the glass and gulping down a good quarter of it before slamming the glass back on the counter with a gag. "Gods! That's awful."

"Maybe you'll think twice before you drink yourself into oblivion," Freya says curtly, rolling her second egg along the counter to remove the shell.

Ty leans forward to look past me at Freya. "I don't need your sass this morning."

Freya levels him with a glare. "Well, you need to hear it from someone." She turns her glare to me. "Don't you think so, Bastion?"

"Got something to say, Bash?" Ty challenges, turning his attention to me.

I frown, staring down at the egg in my hand. "I should go out and check the perimeter."

"No," Ty shouts as I push away from the counter. "Don't you leave me with this sludge and Freya!" I keep walking. "Bash! Bastion!"

Ty is still yelling my name as the door closes behind me. I inhale through my nose and close my eyes for a moment, breathing in the crisp morning air. I lean against the wall of the establishment, trying to appear as casual as possible as I look for threats. Early rays of sunlight bathe the street in a golden glow, and a few merchants take advantage of the slow morning to get their carts set up. As far as I can tell, the street is clear of anyone that might be a risk. I pull out the map from my bag and check it over. A few minutes later, Ty and Freya stumble out, arguing.

"I'm just saying—"

"No," Ty cuts her off as the door slam behind them. "You're pushing. *Pushing*, Freya."

She huffs, crossing her arms. "Forgive me for caring."

I bite back a smile. I admire the way Freya meets Ty's fire with her own. Despite what they both think—and even what I initially thought—they work well together. Ty seems less amused, rolling his eyes as he falls back against the wall on my right.

"I can't believe you made me drink that stuff. I think I'm going to be sick."

I grin as Freya steps in front of him, cocking her eyebrow. "Remember that next time you want to drink."

"Sod off," Ty grumbles. He looks over at the map in my hands. "Figure out where we are?"

I nod, rolling the map up. "Yeah, I was pretty sure already, but now I have a confirmed path." I stick the map in my bag and lift it to my shoulder. "We're a little way off course, but not too much."

"Really?" Freya asks. "So we can finish our tour or whatever?"

"More or less," I reply, shoving away from the wall. "We

were supposed to go in an arc to the south, staying at a few estates along the way. When we left the carriage, we headed a bit to the north, which puts us off the initial course, but overall on a more direct route to the Hallowbridge estate for the ball."

Ty groans. "So we still have to go to the ball?"

"I would assume. We might arrive a day or so late, but if the soldier got his message to the palace on time, they should be aware we may be delayed." Ty groans again and I resist rolling my eyes. "When have you ever hated a ball?"

"Since now," Ty says petulantly. I cross my arms and stare him down and he sighs. "I hate being on display."

"Lies."

Freya chokes on a laugh and Ty shoots her a glare.

"Okay, I guess I don't mind when I'm on display, but I hate my whole relationship being put on display."

"So you hate being put on display with me," Freya says softly.

Ty's eyes widen and he pushes away from the wall, stepping to her. "No. That's not it. I—" He sighs again, rubbing the back of his neck. "I hate feeling like a million people are watching and waiting for me to complete a test, that I have to be perfect, that *we* have to be perfect." He meets her eyes slowly and I feel like I'm intruding on what should be an intimate moment. I look away as he takes her hands. "I don't like that you're being pressured to put on an act to please a bunch of people when you're actually pretty decent on your own."

"I—" Freya fumbles. "Thanks."

I clear my throat and Ty releases her hands, taking a wide step back. Pink colors Freya's cheeks and she turns to me.

"Would it be faster if we bought some horses? Do we have the funds for that?"

I've already done the calculations so I shake my head. "We'd have to choose between horses or shelter and food. While we could scavenge up some meals, I'd feel better if we could get you two somewhere safe to sleep at night and inns cost money."

"We could always get horses and promise payment later," Ty suggests. "I obviously have the power to make sure the debt is paid."

"And let everyone know exactly where you are?" I counter. "No. We need to keep a low profile, and after our last experience, I think it's best not to trust anyone right now."

Ty shrugs as Freya looks down the road. "We should probably get going, then. The Fae moon isn't going to wait, and we're already behind."

I take up the lead, Freya matching me step for step as a grumbling Ty follows behind. We pause at a few of the carts and procure a little food and water for the road. When Freya's eyes light up over a selection of baked buns, Ty sweeps in to purchase one for her. She smiles at him and when he returns the smile, my heart clenches, and I have to force myself to look away.

CHAPTER NINETEEN

FREYA

I've decided I hate walking, especially when I'm walking down an endless stretch of road with no protection from the sun. At least today I have some food in my belly and a stash of water. When we stop for lunch, I'm clearly not the only one ready to take the break. Ty collapses next to me with a groan, mumbling swears under his breath. Bastion rolls his eyes, having no pity for us. When we resume our journey, he pushes us a little less and we take a more casual pace. We stop a little before sunset.

"No point in going much farther tonight," Bastion says as we settle on the side of the road, pulling out our rations. "We won't make it to the next village today on foot, and it's probably best we make camp while we can still see clearly."

"I'm not going to argue with you," Ty mumbles, stretching out on the ground and tucking a hand behind his head. "If I never have to hike another day in my life, I won't protest."

Bastion rolls his eyes but doesn't say anything as he digs through his bag. I sigh and stare off down the road to where the sun dips into the horizon, coloring the sky with soft bursts of orange and gold.

"You going to eat that?" Ty asks. I look over at him and catch his eyes fixed on the bit of food in my hands.

"Yes," I say, taking a large bite to punctuate my point.

Ty doesn't seem put off, shrugging. "Figured it couldn't hurt to ask."

I finish off the last couple bites and stand, feeling restless. Ty ignores me, eyes closed as he hums mindlessly, but Bastion fixes his attention on me.

"What's wrong?" He looks around, tensing. "Do you hear something?"

I shake my head. "No, I need to do something."

Ty waves his hand through the air in a sweeping motion. "Go do it away from camp."

I frown at him as my face heats. "Not like that. I just can't sit still. I have too much energy."

Bastion nods knowingly and pushes to his feet, taking a step toward me. "We can continue your training, if you like." He nudges Ty with his boot. "It wouldn't hurt for you to join us."

Ty groans. "Why'd have to open your big mouth, Freya?"

Bastion smirks and gives Ty another kick. Ty huffs and sits up, leaning back on his palms as he glares up at me. "This isn't the way to win my affection."

I grin. "Oh, shoot. And I was trying so hard."

Bastion unsuccessfully tries to hide his laugh with a cough as Ty childishly sticks his tongue out at me before pushing up from the ground. Bastion quickly goes over some of the basics he taught me before, using Ty to demonstrate some of the stances and moves. Despite his protests, it's soon evident Ty is extremely skilled. The daylight is quickly fading by the time I get to try my hand with a dagger.

"Okay, widen your stance a little," Bastion says, placing his hands on my waist, turning me a bit.

I swallow, forcing myself to focus on Ty and his dagger rather than how warm Bastion's hands are. I adjust my stance accordingly and Bastion steps back with a nod.

"Good. Ty don't go easy on her."

Ty flashes me a wicked grin. "Oh, I won't."

I barely have time to register Ty's words before he's lunging toward me. Instinct kicks in and I dodge, spinning back quickly to face him, but he's already making the next move. I try to block his blow, but I stumble and start to fall. I reach out and grab the closest thing—Ty's arm—to stay upright, but only bring Ty down with me as we tumble to the ground. Ty clearly wasn't prepared to fall, and his whole weight lands on top of me, pushing my breath from my chest in a sharp gasp.

"That's one way to do it," Ty mumbles, his breath hot on my cheek. He pushes up onto his palms to hover above me and looks down, something intense in his eyes. "I can't say I mind it."

I frown and press my hands against his chest in an attempt to move him off me, but he doesn't budge. His grin grows and something about his attention turns almost predatory. Excitement twists in my gut before I can stop it.

"Get. Off," I mutter, shoving him again.

He chuckles but obliges, pushing up from the ground and brushing dirt off his clothes with his palms. Bastion steps forward and offers me his hand. I glare at it for a moment before allowing him to help me to my feet.

"Well, you did disarm him," Bastion says, nodding to

where Ty's dagger lies a few feet away, "but you didn't follow the instructions."

I cross my arms indignantly. "Still worked."

Bastion looks like he's barely containing an eye roll. "This time, only because it was Ty."

"Hey!" Ty protests, snapping into a standing position from where he's leaning over to pick up the dagger.

"I mean," Bastion clarifies quickly, "because it was Ty only posing a fight. It wasn't a real fight with someone who wants to kill you."

"Oh, yeah, that's true," Ty says with a nod, stepping to Bastion's side. "If that happened in a real fight, I would've taken your dagger and slit your throat before you even realized I was on top of you."

I swallow hard, but any fear I might have felt vanishes quickly as Ty's mouth tips up into a smirk and a mischievous twinkle returns to his eyes.

"As it was, I liked having you underneath me too much to want you dead. I had other ideas that might be fun to try out." My eyes widen and Ty's smirk grows into a full grin as he adds, "With your permission, of course."

Bastion grumbles something under his breath I don't quite catch and Ty shoots me a wink. My cheeks heat and I pray Ty and Bastion assume I'm embarrassed and don't guess that I'm thinking of the things Ty might actually try to do and how much I might like them.

"Let's try again," Bastion says, taking a few steps back.

Ty takes up his stance and I stumble into the position Bastion showed me before. His eyes trail over me, taking in my position and, while I know that's all he's doing, something else stirs in my stomach. Gods, I really need to work out some of my frustrations. It's been too long. There's no other possible explanation for me to be feeling this way about either of these headstrong men.

This time, I manage not to fall within the first few seconds. Ty still knocks my dagger from my hands, but I manage to hold my own well enough. After a few more tries, I'm lasting several minutes and even land a few blows of my own. My blood pumps, eager for more, but it's soon too dark to see properly. Bastion makes us call it a night.

"We should set patrols," Bastion says as we make ourselves comfortable on the ground.

"I can take first watch," I offer, still feeling too energized to fall asleep. Bastion stifles his laugh better than Ty. "What? I can take watch!"

Bastion studies me carefully while Ty shakes his head.

"Freya, Freya, Freya," Ty mutters, not even bothering to hide his amusement.

"What?" I demand, glaring at Ty. "I can take a watch. Just because I can't fight off someone on my own doesn't mean I can't be alert looking for them."

"I don't think—"

"She's right," Bastion says, cutting Ty off.

Ty shoots him an incredulous look. "You can't be serious."

He ignores Ty, turning his full attention to me. "You have to stay awake. You start to doze off, you wake me immediately. You hear a single thing, you wake me. I don't care if you think it might be nothing. Understood?"

I nod, words sticking in my throat. Bastion studies me for another moment and then nods sharply.

"Good."

Ty looks between Bastion and me, eyes wide.

"Bash . . ."

Bastion shakes his head but doesn't look at Ty as he

stretches out on the ground. "She can share duty tonight, and we can get some more sleep." He tucks a hand behind his head and closes his eyes. "Wake me in a couple hours, even if you're not tired yet." He cracks an eye open and looks over at me. "Got it?"

I nod but realize he may not be able to see me very well in this light at that angle. "Got it."

Ty looks one last time between me and Bash before shrugging his shoulders and lying down. I watch them for a moment, half expecting them to change their minds and make me go to sleep instead, but neither do. After a few minutes, they're both solidly asleep, breathing even. Only then do I allow myself to smile. They trust me and they don't think I'm useless. I could almost get used to this.

CHAPTER TWENTY

TY

Freya must do a decent enough job on her watch, because when Bash wakes me a couple hours before dawn he doesn't look quite as exhausted as he should. Good. He needed the rest. It takes me a little while to shake sleep from my brain, but I'm soon alert and eager to move. By the time the sun rises, I'm fully awake and ready to get back on the road. I wait until bright colors paint the sky before waking the other two. Freya is rumpled and adorable until I point it out, then she turns into a grumpy, glaring beast, but I'd like to think she's at least a little pleased on the inside.

Once we get on the road, I'm wishing I'd been able to get in a little more sleep. It doesn't take long for my legs to feel heavy and my head fuzzy. When a passing merchant with a wagon offers us a ride into Brushwake, the nearest village, I'm more than happy to accept his offer and am silently thrilled when Bash deems it safe. I curl up between crates of eggs, sleeping soundly until Freya wakes me with an elbow to my ribs.

"That was uncalled for," I grumble, rubbing my side.

"We're here," Freya replies, clearly not bothered by my pain.

Sending her one last glare, I pull my gaze away and look around. I was expecting a smaller town like the one we stayed in before, but this location is thriving, bordering on being a full-fledged city. The roads are crowded with people and merchants selling anything and everything imaginable. The wagon jerks to a stop at the end of a busy street, pulling into an empty space between two carts.

"This is my spot," the driver says, stepping down from the driver's seat and rolling his neck.

Bash stands first. "Thank you. Are you sure we can't pay you for your trouble?"

The man shakes his head. "Not necessary. I was headed this way and had the space."

Bash offers the man a thankful nod and steps from the wagon, extending his hand to help Freya disembark before helping me. We elbow our way through the crowd as the man goes about unloading his wares. When we reach the main square of the town, the crowd spreads out, and it's a little easier to navigate. It doesn't take us long to discover that this town has multiple places to stay the night.

"Let's split up and get the lay of the land," Bash says, keeping his voice low as he leans toward me. "We can figure out which place is least likely to swindle us, if nothing else."

I nod, glancing over at Freya who's a few feet away examining some jewelry on a nearby cart. "One of us should probably stick with her, don't you think?"

Bash shrugs. "Honestly? I think she's better suited for this crowd than you are."

I open my mouth to protest but snap it shut when I see the gleam in Bash's eyes. "Ha ha. Fine. Split up we shall."

Bash relays the plan to Freya, and we weave through the crowd. Even as I browse stalls and chat with the merchants my eyes keep searching for Freya. I find myself wandering back to the jewelry cart and let my eyes travel over the goods. It's decent enough jewelry, but it's nothing compared to things I can offer her. Yet, these simple things made her eyes shine. Suddenly I have the urge to find a little something to gift her. I know we don't have much money to spend on frivolous things, but surely I can find something.

I'm examining some small wooden figurines at another booth when Freya's delighted laugh breaks through the chatter of the crowd. I frown and look up, unsettled I'm unable to find her immediately. When I do, however, I'm less than happy. She's at what looks to be a flower merchant's cart, and the merchant is young. And handsome. Very handsome. Like handsome enough that, were the circumstances different, I would likely be over there looking at him the way Freya is. Nope. Nope. Before I even realize what I'm doing, I'm marching her direction.

"No, I insist," the merchant is saying, holding out a white flower. "I simply wouldn't be able to forgive myself if I let you walk away without a token."

Freya smiles softly, dipping her head, a blush coloring her cheeks as she accepts the flower. "Thank you. I appreciate it."

The merchant's smile is wide, charming. "The pleasure is quite mine."

"Freya," I say loudly as I sidle up next to her. "There you are."

Freya startles and looks over at me, her delighted expression falling into a scowl as she shifts away from me. "What do you want, Ty?"

I offer her a grin and step closer so our arms brush. "Thought I lost you in the crowd." I look down at the flower she's twirling in her fingers. "What's that?"

Her eyes brighten again but before she can speak, the merchant speaks up.

"It's a white villifloria, commonly known as a honey floria because of their sweet smell." He smiles, looking at Freya. "It deserves to go to someone equally sweet."

Freya's eyes sparkle as she returns to the smile.

I hum, nodding my head. "How much did that little weed cost?"

Freya hisses my name in reprimand, but the merchant only laughs. "Not a thing." His attention shifts to Freya, his eyes twinkling. "I can't help but to offer pretty flowers to pretty ladies."

I scoff. "Doesn't seem like great business practice."

He grins, flashing rows of perfect teeth I want to knock from his face. "My father would agree with you. My name is Gil, by the way," he says, extending his hand.

I accept it reluctantly, giving him one firm shake. "I'm Ty."

"Gil was just telling me about the Freckled Hen," Freya says, nudging me with her elbow.

I narrow my eyes at him. "Was he?"

"He was," Gil says. "Or rather, I was. I've had to stay at a couple of the inns here in town, and that one is by far the best. A few other chaps and I stay there and often spend a few hours down in the tavern playing dice games for extra money. You'd be welcome to join us, if you'd like."

"Well, I think we may have other pl—"

"Sounds wonderful."

I jump at Bash's voice coming from right behind me and Freya swears under her breath. Gil looks a little surprised as well, but recovers quickly, his former cheer returning.

"More of your traveling party, I assume?" he says with a nervous chuckle, looking to Freya.

"Unfortunately." Freya sighs. "This is Bastion."

"Nice to meet you, Bastion!" Gil says, holding out his hand.

Bash looks down at the proffered hand, sniffs, and turns to me. "We should secure a room if there any are left."

Gil deflates as he drops his hand. Freya mouths *sorry* as I bite back a grin.

"Yes, we definitely shouldn't hang out here wasting our time."

As we start to walk away, Gil calls after us. "I hope to play a game with you later!"

I'm about to tell him to shove his dice where the light will never see them when Bash replies, assuring him we'll be there. He pushes me further down the road before he leans in, giving his explanation.

"We're low on funds, so if we can make a bit playing with merchants like him, we should."

I can't deny Bash has a point and resign myself to the fact that, like it or not, I'll be seeing Gil later tonight. At least I can wipe that smile from his face by taking all his money.

It turns out the staff at the Freckled Hen is friendly and accommodating. They have one room left, and it's private, thank the gods. According to the owner it only has one bed, but he claims it's large enough to fit at least two people and that there's enough space for a third person to put together makeshift bed on the floor. The food is more than decent and the ale is some of the best I've had outside the palace. I soon discover that Kitty, the lovely young barmaid, likes a little flirtatious attention and doesn't charge me as much for my ale as she does everyone.

We quickly settle into a game of cards with a party of middle-aged men. Bash and I do a good job balancing our draws, losses, and wins in a way where we come out on top without being obvious. I'm not keeping close track, but I'm sure we're doing well by the way Bash nods after each hand. I have a feeling Freya is bored, however, if her constant sighs are anything to go by.

Gil comes in about an hour or two later with a couple other young men, and he motions us over to a larger table. He needlessly explains the rules of their game—it's honestly so incredibly basic—and we join in the "fun." Luck is not on my side and I lose several games in a row. Bash wins a few, but I'm pretty sure he's using his magic to cheat just a little, tipping the dice in his favor with an almost imperceptible wind.

"It's all right! You'll get the hang of it!" Gil encourages after I lose yet another round. I literally bite back a sharp retort, the tang of blood from my cheek filling my mouth.

After a few more rounds, I realize that one of the young men that came with Gil keeps casting me what can only be described as furtive glances. I relax back in my seat a little and decide to show him a little extra attention. On one round he's ahead, but when I bite my lip and meet his eyes, he fumbles his turn. I shoot him a wink and take my turn. I actually win that round. A few rounds later, my wiles have helped me win a decent stash of money.

I'm so caught up in the game, I barely notice when Freya leaves my side, moving around the table to look over Gil's shoulder. Gil glances up at her with a wicked grin, saying something too low for me to catch his exact words, but whatever he says makes Freya smile. Gil looks my way and says something else and Freya laughs. Before I can rise out of my seat, Bash's hand is on my thigh.

"Steady," he whispers, keeping his head down so no one else at the table knows he's said anything.

My blood boils as Freya leans in closer, her head practically propped up on Gil's shoulder. I clench my teeth and order another drink, gulping it down. Freya shakes her head at me, but I have no idea why she's disappointed in me. I'm not the one throwing myself at a stranger. I order another drink because if I have to sit here and watch my fiancée act like this in public, I need something to take away the sting. But I can't tamper down my feelings forever.

CHAPTER TWENTY-ONE

FREYA

Here I was thinking we had actually grown closer the past couple of days, but judging by the way Ty keeps flirting with the barmaid and Timothy, Gil's friend, I was clearly mistaken. Ty clearly doesn't care about me at all. Everything between us recently must have been little more than the convenience of proximity and the lack of other choices. That's fine. I can only take so long being ignored. In a moment of vindictive frustration, I cross over to Gil. When I look up, Ty is barely containing himself and something about that exhilarates me. I lean in toward Gil and allow the tips of my fingers to brush his forearm. I'm not very good at flirting, but I do my best, following Gil's lead. Ty keeps glaring at me as he downs more and more ale, but so far he's done nothing to convince me to come back to his side. Maybe I need to step my flirting up a notch.

"I've never met someone who was so good at playing dice." A lie. I could pull up a dozen people more skilled than him. Bastion is obviously one of them. I wonder if they realize how much they've lost to him tonight. "Perhaps you could share some tips?"

Gil's entire face lights up and he shifts in his chair so he's closer to me. Any barrier I had between us is gone. He's too close and something inside me screams he's invading my space, but I won't back out. I did put myself here. Ty started this ridiculousness for whatever reason and I can play the game. I barely contain a flinch when Gil places a warm hand over mine, tugging me so I'm pressed flush against him.

"Perhaps you could join me for a drink and game up in my room. It will be quieter there, and we'll have more . . . privacy to discuss it further. I can show you a thing or two."

My mind whirls, trying to find a response that declines but is also polite. A chair scrapes loudly against the stone floor and I only realize that the sound belongs to Ty when he suddenly appears hovering over us, fists clenched.

"She won't be going anywhere with you."

Irritation flashes across Gil's face as he pulls his attention from me to Ty. Gil looks intimidated for a moment, but his hand tightens around my own as he straightens in his seat.

"Last I checked she was her own person," Gil challenges, though his voice is weak.

"She is mine," Ty snarls, emphasizing each word.

I twist and look up at Ty. His face his lethal and, even though he's supposed to be keeping a low profile, he looks every bit the deadly prince he is. All his soft edges are gone, and he looks truly dangerous. The air around us heats and crackles with Ty's magic, and I'm wondering how deep of a hole I've dug myself. But even then, I'm in this deep, might as well keep digging.

"Oh, so now I'm yours?" I challenge.

Ty's eyes snap to mine and I shrink away. I've never seen him this angry.

"Yes. Mine." He turns his focus back to Gil. "She will not be going with you."

"We have to be up early in the morning for travel, anyway," Bastion cuts in, standing.

Gil swallows and clears his throat, his eyes darting between my two escorts. Bash chooses that moment to stretch, the edge of his shirt lifting to show one of his daggers tucked into the waistband of his pants. Gil pales slightly as he eyes the dagger, lifting his palms in apparent surrender as he shakes his head.

"I don't need the trouble."

"Good choice," Bastion says while Ty snaps, "Come on, Freya."

I narrow my eyes at Ty, but the look in his eyes says he's not going to accept being challenged any further. I grunt and straighten with as much defiance as I can, tripping over a chair behind me. Ty is quick to catch my elbow before I fall to the ground. Bastion must sense we need a moment because he mumbles something about settling out the game and securing the area. Ty tightens his grip on my arm and practically drags me to our room. As soon as the door snicks closed, I jerk away and turn on him.

"What the hell was that?" I demand, putting as much distance between the two of us as the small room allows.

"Me?" he yells, thrusting a finger into his chest. "You're upset with *me*? You were the one ready to sneak off with that cretin and do gods know what. Did you forget that you're *my wife*? Or in all this role play did you let that fact slip your mind?"

"I'm not your wife yet," I snap, crossing my arms.

Ty crosses the distance between us in two swift strides. He stops barely an inch away, so close I'm nearly cross-eyed looking at him.

"Give it a couple weeks. There's no way out of this and you *will* be my wife. Like it or not. You. Are. Mine."

Tears burn my eyes but I won't give him the satisfaction of seeing me cry. I fight them back, clenching my hands at my side.

"I may be your wife in a few weeks," I continue before he can say anything else cruel and break my resolve, "but that doesn't make me your property. If you think that I've forgotten for a moment that my life has been ripped away from me and I have no control over any of this, you are so wrong. My dreams have faded to nothing all because of the color of my blood."

"I have no control over that. I also have no say. I had a life before you," Ty says, his voice carefully controlled. "But it doesn't change anything, and you throwing yourself at every handsome peasant won't be tolerated."

I laugh but it's without any humor. "You were the one flirting with that barmaid. And Timothy."

He blinks at me. "Who the Hell is Timothy?"

"Gil's friend." He stares at me, raising his brows. "The man you literally winked at?"

He waves me off with an annoyed grunt. "I was merely trying to win the game and get some cheap ale."

"Right. Like you wouldn't have taken them to bed had they offered."

He shakes his head. "Not with you right there."

"But if I hadn't been there, you would have?"

He opens his mouth, leaving it wide for a moment before snapping it shut.

"What I thought. You can have your dalliances, but I'm to be kept under lock and key. I guess I'll have to be more discreet."

Ty's eyes flash and the room suddenly feels warm. "You will do no such thing."

"Because I'm not allowed any happiness?"

"That's not—Argh!" He turns to punch the wall before spinning back to face me. "Stop flirting! Don't touch other men! Or women, if you fancy them as well. Just stop! Look at me and only me! Why is that so gods-damned difficult?"

Ty takes a bold step toward me and I stumble back, my legs bumping hard against the bed.

"Most people would kill to have me in their bed."

Fresh hate flashes in my chest. "So because you're reasonably attractive and are royalty I should be *grateful* for this opportunity and spread my legs for you and only you?"

"Yes—NO! That's not—Gods! Why do you have to be so difficult? You're mine and I am yours. It's our fate and the sooner you accept that—"

I'm tired of being controlled. The anger heats inside of me and spills out in molten words I mean to keep inside.

"I hate you. I hate you so much."

Ty's nostrils flare. "Well, right now, I'm no so fond of you, either."

The tears I've been containing break free in a small sob. Ty's face falls and suddenly something about him seems softer.

"Freya—"

He reaches toward me but I duck away from his touch.

"No. Get out."

Ty's face hardens again as his hand drops to his side, tightening into a fist.

"We're supposed to share this room tonight. You can't kick me out."

I lift my chin. "Watch me."

"Fine. You want me to leave?"

I nod sharply.

"Very well." He lifts his hands in surrender as he takes a step backward, but his eyes hold a hateful fire. "I'll leave then. If someone comes in during the night and slits your throat or . . . or worse, there's no blood on my hands."

He spins on his heel and stomps to the door, throwing it open with more force than necessary.

"One last thing."

He pauses just outside the door but doesn't turn to face me. "What?"

I cross to the door but stay well inside the room. "I'm not your property and I would appreciate not being treated as such."

Ty spins back around, his mouth gaping and eyes wide, almost frightened. But that's all I register before I slam the door in his face and lock the bolt.

CHAPTER TWENTY-TWO

BASH

Gil and his crew are reluctant to finish settling our winnings, but it doesn't take them long to see sense, especially when I pull out one of my daggers to clean some pesky dirt from under my fingernails while I wait. Despite Ty's glowering, we made out pretty well, so there's a chance we might be able to upgrade our travel to something more efficient than walking. To give Freya and Ty a little more time to work out the tension between them, I do a quick perimeter check. Once I'm satisfied that everything looks as safe as possible, I head back upstairs, only to find Ty sitting outside our door, his head in his hands. I sigh and sink down next to him.

"Please don't tell me you got us kicked out of our room."

"She hates me." Ty raises his eyes to meet mine and I realize he's been crying.

"Oh, Ty," I whisper, wrapping an arm around him and tugging him closer. "What did you do?"

"I fucked up. I fucked up so badly, Bash," he mutters, burying his face in my chest.

I clear my throat, trying not to think about how good he feels in my arms, how familiar and welcome. "Any details on how you fucked up and maybe a solution so we don't get stuck sleeping in this drafty hallway?"

Ty groans and tilts his head back to look up at me. His eyes are swimming with so much emotion I almost drown.

"I don't know how to communicate with her," he murmurs. "Everything with you was so easy and everything with her is so hard."

My heart stutters but I force myself to focus. "You make it harder on yourself, you know."

"I know. I *know*. It's just . . ." He sighs, collapsing back against my chest. "She's so amazing and perfect and I really do want her. And I thought she wanted me. Then I had to go and be myself and now she thinks I hate her, but I don't. Not even a little. I mean, yeah, at first I wasn't happy about it, but I had my reasons. Now, though, I think I'll like being married to her, but if she doesn't want me, then it's all pointless, isn't it? She'd rather have someone like Gil."

He spits Gil's name like it disgusts him, and it probably does. Honestly, I wasn't a huge fan of how openly he was flirting with Freya, but Ty could've reacted much better.

I sigh and tighten my grip around him. In everything I imagined about coming back to this position as his guard, I never expected to have to talk him though dealing with his feelings regarding his fiancée and helping to mend their relationship.

"I'm pretty sure she's not actually interested in Gil."

Ty scoffs. "Seemed like she was."

"Of course it did, because you fly to jealously before common sense. You let your emotions take hold and you view everything through their lens."

He makes a sound between a sigh and a groan, but I continue before he can interrupt.

"Those emotions are good, don't get me wrong, but I know you, Ty. You've put up a shield to protect yourself and you stopped processing emotional things for so long you've simply forgotten how to handle them. You can tell Freya all day that you want to marry her, but unless you actually show her, she has no reason to believe you. She has no reason to stay devoted to you, beyond simply being bound to you by force."

Ty is very, very still. I'm not even sure if he's breathing, and when he speaks, his voice is so small and broken.

"You're right." He pulls back and meets my eyes. "But the last time I let myself feel and gave myself over to hope, everything was ripped away from me. I can't go through that again, Bash."

I take a steadying breath and look away. I can't stand the pain in his eyes, and I'm likely about to cause him more.

"I think, maybe, you two should sit down and communicate everything."

Ty flinches so slightly that if I weren't holding him I wouldn't have noticed. "Everything?"

"Everything." I steel myself and look back at him. "You two will soon be married, and I think you need to get it all out in the open. She deserves to know, especially since she's likely to hear someone else's version at some point. She should hear it from you first."

He hesitates a moment but finally nods with a heavy sigh. "You're right. Of course you're right." He tilts his head back and gives me a look that can be described in no better way than puppy eyes. "But you'll talk to her tonight, right? Get our room back?"

I bite back a smile. "I should leave you in the hallway."

"You really want to sleep in the hallway?"

"*I'm* not the one that got kicked out of the room. Freya's very reasonable and I don't think she'll make me suffer the consequences of your actions."

Ty sits up, taking his welcome warmth with him, a small smile playing on the corner of his lips. "You wouldn't leave me out here alone."

I arch an eyebrow. "Wouldn't I?"

"And shirk your duty to guard me? Not a chance." His joy slips. "But can you talk to Freya? Please?"

He looks so desperate, so lost. There's no way I can deny him anything.

"Of course." Ty pulls further away as I push up from the ground. "Maybe you should go take a walk while I do. Sober up a bit, but don't go far."

Ty gives me a small nod and allows me to help him to his feet. After he disappears down the stairwell, I knock tentatively on the door.

"Go away, Ty!" Freya yells, her voice unsteady and clearly upset.

"It's me. Bastion."

There's silence for a moment before footfalls head toward the door. Freya cracks it open just enough to look out at me, her bloodshot eyes searching past me.

"He's not out here," I say, stepping back so she can easily see the empty hall. "He's taking a walk. I only want to talk for a moment and maybe add some clarity."

Her chin trembles and I can tell she's holding back tears. "Do you really think things can be any clearer? He only wants to control me and name me among his possessions. He doesn't really want me. Not really. Not when there are other options available. I mean, he could have anyone, so why would he want me?"

Her voice cracks slightly on the word 'want' and something in me cracks with it. I swallow and straighten.

"I really think he does, but"—I glance down the hall toward the sounds rising from the tavern below—"I'd rather talk inside."

She hesitates only a moment before nodding and opening the door wider. I follow her inside and shut the door behind us. Suddenly I feel very trapped, and I take a moment to steady myself by looking around the room. It isn't large, just a small amount of unoccupied floor space, a table with a wash bowl on top and a waste bin below, a couple wall lanterns, and a medium bed up against the wall. I'm examining the wash bowl when Freya clears her throat behind me. I turn to find her glaring at me, arms crossed.

"Are you going to explain?"

I nod and run my tongue across my lips. "Yes. I— Honestly, I'm not sure sure where to begin, but I can assure you that Ty does really want you, and not just because he *can* have you."

She scoffs. "Right. That's why he was flirting with anything that moved tonight."

"When Ty flirts, it's not always to get someone into bed. Sometimes he uses it as a defense mechanism, as a way to manipulate those around him." She looks less than convinced. "Like tonight, did you notice that every time he showed Gil's friend, Timothy, any attention, Timothy fumbled his turn? And when he flirted with the barmaid she gave him free, or at least very cheap drinks?"

Her brow furrows a little so I power on, taking a small step closer to her.

"I understand how it looked from your perspective, but I promise you, he didn't see his actions in the same way you did." I look away. "He likes you and wants you. He's told me himself."

"Then why does he keep doing things that push me away?"

I look back at her, meeting her eyes, and take a steadying breath. "Ty has been through some things in the past few years that have affected him more than he might let on. Like I said before, he uses flirtation as a defense mechanism. He also uses sarcasm and pushing people away. He's been hurt, and honestly he's still healing. He can't take being hurt again."

She opens her mouth to speak, but I hold up a hand, silencing her. "I'm not excusing his actions. He's screwed up and I am positive he will screw up again. You need to decide if you can forgive him and move on, or if there will always be this barrier of distrust between you. Whichever path you choose, however, keep in mind that you still have to marry him and be bound to him for the rest of your life."

She draws a deep breath and sits down on the edge of the bed. "You know," she says, her voice barely above a whisper. "This isn't exactly easy for me, either."

I ease down next to her. "I know. Or, at least, I can imagine. It—it isn't easy for any of us."

She shoots me a quizzical look. "Even you?"

I swallow and hope my emotions are carefully trapped where they should be. "Even me."

She holds my gaze for a moment before nodding. "I guess I can try to move past this, but he cannot keep treating me like a disposable thing, to enjoy when it suits him and toss away later. I don't want a relationship like that with my husband. It's not fair to me."

I nod. "I agree. You deserve a true partner. We can keep him in check together. Gods know I've had years of practice."

The corner of her mouth tips up into a small smile, and I almost return it.

"Okay. Fine."

"Good." I push up from the bed. "So, I guess I can fetch him and let him know he can sleep in the room?"

"Sure, but he's sleeping on the floor."

I swallow hard, looking at the small floor space and then the bed. "The floor? So you and I—"

"Can share the bed." She arches an eyebrow. "We've shared before. It's not a problem, is it?"

I shake my head, maybe a little too quickly. "No, it's fine. It's—fine. I mean, Ty will be right there, so it's . . ."

"Fine?" Her eyes twinkle with mischief, and the corner of my mouth twitches, threatening to let another smile loose.

"Yes, fine." I take a step closer to the door. "I'll go let him know."

I'm halfway through the doorway when she calls out to me.

"Bastion?"

I pause, but don't turn toward her. "Yes?"

"How was Ty hurt? Who hurt him?"

My heart seizes and I inhale sharply, not expecting the question. My grip on the door handle tightens almost painfully.

"I did."

"What?" I can hear the shock in her voice. "How? Why?"

I still can't face her. "It's not entirely my story to tell. You'll have to ask Ty."

She's quiet behind me before whispering, "Okay."

I start to take another step, but stop, glancing at her over my shoulder. "And, Princess?"

"Yes?"

"Call me Bash."

She cocks her head, that tentative full smile finally breaking free. "Does that mean you'll finally start calling me Freya?"

I grin shaking my head. "Yeah, no. I think 'Princess' fits you better."

Her beautiful blue eyes shine with surprised delight as she laughs, but I leave, closing the door before she can respond. Getting closer to her is a mistake, but somehow I can't stop myself. If I am to remain Ty's personal guard after his marriage, I'll need some sort of friendly relationship with Freya as well. I'm just thinking ahead, preparing for the future.

It doesn't take me long to find Ty. He's outside leaning against the side of the building, eyes closed and head tipped back with his hands shoved in his pockets. Even though new moon is only a day away, there's more than enough moonlight to highlight his features. He's beautiful. My heart stutters and I shove the emotions away and walk toward him. I'm a couple feet away when he opens his eyes and rolls his head toward me.

"Did you smooth things over? Will she let me in the room?"

I nod. "Yes, I cleaned up another one of your messes."

He shoots me a sloppy smile. "You've always been good at that."

"I can't keep doing it, though."

His smile falls away and he sighs. "I know." He pushes

away from the wall with his elbows, keeping his hands in his pockets. "I appreciate it, though."

I turn and start to walk back toward the door, calling over my shoulder. "You get the floor."

"No! Come on!" he says, rushing to catch up with me. "I need the bed."

"Maybe you should've thought about that before you pissed off Freya."

He groans. "I can't take another night on the ground."

I turn to him with a grin as I open the tavern door. "Maybe it will help you learn your lesson faster."

He scowls at me and I can't hold back my laugh.

"You are far too amused," he grumbles.

I shrug as we move inside. "Maybe I like seeing her take you down a peg or two."

We shoulder our way through the crowd and make our way up the stairs. When we get to our room, Ty hesitates, his hand hovering over the door handle.

"Should I say anything to her?"

"I think another apology might help." He nods and I add, "Though you two need to have a good talk soon."

He sighs. "I know. Not tonight, but . . . soon." He looks up at me. "I promise."

When we enter the room, Freya is already in the bed, her back to us. When Ty apologizes she doesn't react. He sighs and we ready ourselves for bed. Ty, as agreed, takes the floor and I slide into bed with Freya. When she shifts her position so she's close enough I can feel her warmth, I wonder how I'm going to survive the night.

CHAPTER TWENTY-THREE

TY

I'm really tired of waking with aching limbs and a pounding head, but at least this morning I know that both are my fault and I deserve them. I groan and roll over, glancing at the bed Freya and Bash shared last night, but there's only one body curled under the covers. Bash must be off doing guard things. My muscles complain and my head swims as I ease into a sitting position. I close my eyes and roll my neck, wishing I could go back to last night and make better choices.

"I hope you feel terrible."

I wince. I swear Freya's talking much louder than necessary.

"Well, wish granted," I mumble, opening my eyes to look over at her glaring at me from the bed. "I feel horrible." I tilt my head, pulling on what charm I can manage first thing in the morning. "And not just because I have a headache and I'm sore from sleeping on the ground for the millionth night in a row. I really do feel bad about how things went down last night."

Her fierce expression falters enough that I feel a glimmer of hope. I push up from the ground and take a tentative step toward her.

"I mean it, Freya. I messed up and didn't convey myself very well. I—I don't share well. I never have." I tip my head and offer her a smile. "Part of being a prince, perhaps. Never really had to share." She doesn't smile, so I clear my throat and continue. "I really am sorry."

She sighs and looks away. "I'm sure you are, but I don't want to go through this again and again, hoping that each time is the last."

I swallow and nod. She has a fair point. Bash is right that I need to explain everything to her, but now isn't the right time. It would be too rushed and hurried. I need time to explain it carefully, and she deserves time to process what I have to share. But I know I need to give her some sort of explanation.

"Have you ever been out in the cold for an extended period of time?" I ask.

She looks confused but nods slowly. "Many times, but what does that have to do with anything?"

"Well, you know how when you're in the cold, especially in the ice and snow, your fingers start to freeze?" She nods again, and I continue. "They tingle at first as a warning, but eventually they go numb until you can't feel the cold anymore, until you can't feel anything at all. It can make some tasks difficult, but you adapt because you have to. In some ways it's kind of nice because you can almost pretend you aren't freezing, but it's also dangerous because if they stay that way for too long, irreversible damage can occur. When you come in from the cold and the feeling starts to come back to your fingers, it starts to hurt again. The longer you've been in the cold without feeling, the longer it takes to warm up and the more it hurts. You have to fight to keep your hands near the heat because instinct is to stop the pain."

Freya watches me carefully, latching onto every word. I take a steadying breath and take a step closer to her.

"The last couple of years I've been in the cold, letting myself go numb to stop feeling the pain of everything I was dealing with. In the process, I've done damage I may not be unable to undo, but now that you're here, the warmth is coming back. I'm starting to feel things again, and in some ways it hurts. A lot. I keep falling back into the bad habits I formed over the past couple years, even though I know it will do more harm than good. I'm thawing, albeit slowly, but I'm happy I get to do that with you."

I pause, taking a deep breath as I stare into her eyes. "I really do want to make this thing work—you and me—and I'm sorry for everything I've said and done that seems to prove otherwise."

Her gaze softens even more. "I want it to work, too, but —"

"No buts," I say, closing the distance between us so I'm inches away. "Please. I promise I will sincerely try to screw up less." My eyes search her face, looking for some sign she's willing to forgive me. "What do you need from me? I will get down on my knees if it means you'll take me seriously."

The corner of her mouth twitches like she might smile. "I don't know if that's necessary."

A smile tempts my own lips as I take a half step back and drop to my knees. I look up at her and something in her expression shifts. Something that tempts hope.

"I'll do anything to gain your trust again, Freya, to prove

to you I'm in this. Do you need me to follow you around on my knees to prove my point? Because I'll do it."

A smile slips free and she shakes her head. "As much as I like the idea, no. If you're really willing—"

"I am. I swear it."

"—then I am too."

Full hope blooms in my chest, but before I can act on it, the door opens. Bash looks mildly surprised. I'm not sure if it's because Freya and I are talking civilly or if it's because we're awake or if it's because I'm on my knees. Probably the last one. I scramble to my feet, face warming.

"Good, you're up," he says, closing the door behind him and, thankfully, choosing not to comment on my previous position. "Despite the disaster that was last night, we managed to make some decent winnings. Enough that I was able to secure us some horses for the remainder of our trip."

Freya visibly brightens and my heart warms seeing her excitement.

"Horses? You got us horses?"

Bash nods, looking away from her to let his eyes wander around the room. "They won't be winning any races, but they'll get us to Lord Brackbill's estate faster." He focuses his attention on me. "With the cult still looking for you, I'd be much more comfortable getting to a more secure location, and we need to make up time or we'll miss the Fae moon."

I nod, crossing my arms. "I agree. Plus, I'm over sleeping on the ground."

Freya mumbles something under her breath that sounds a lot like, "stop pissing me off, then," and I catch Bash hiding a smile. I'm not sure how much I like them getting along if they're going to team up against me.

"Well, let's not dawdle then," I say, sitting down on the

ground to put on my boots. "Does this place have any decent breakfast?"

Bash shrugs. "Porridge and the like, I suspect."

I make a face as Freya says, "I don't suppose there are any bakeries or bread carts?"

Hmm. I could go for a nice baked bun. I turn to Bash in anticipation of his answer, but freeze. Bash looks . . . soft and his expression almost looks . . . affectionate? I frown and follow his gaze to Freya, but all she's doing is pulling on her own boots. Bash must feel me looking at him, because his attention snaps to me and his face turns back to his expressionless norm, save for a slight coloring of his cheeks. That's odd. I shake my head and finish lacing up my boots.

"I can't say I examined every cart out there, but I'm sure we can find something."

"Well, good, because I'm on team bread for breakfast," I declare, popping up from the ground.

Freya hums in an agreement and I smile. A few minutes later, we're roaming the streets in search of delicious food. It doesn't take long before we all have warm breakfast buns heavy with icing in our hands. Bash evens finds a vendor selling blessedly strong coffee. Once we've finished our breakfast, Bash takes us to meet our new horses. They're older, but they have plenty of life left. It doesn't take us long to get saddled up and on the road.

It's been a while since I've ridden so long, and I'm a little sore after a couple hours, but it's manageable. Freya makes for a good distraction. She's so free. She keeps tilting her head back, letting the wind catch her hair, the sun warming her face. She looks like an angel. She catches me watching her, and I grin sheepishly, offering her a shrug. She laughs and she shakes her head at me. Yes, I could definitely love this girl.

We make good time, but according to Bash we're still too far out to make it to the earl's tonight. Once night starts to fall, we stop and make camp. The way Freya lights up when Bash offers to let her take first watch has my stomach twisting in the strangest ways. I love seeing her happy, and I decide I want to do whatever it takes to keep her that way.

The next morning we wake to gray clouds hanging over us, but it's not until after noon when the rain starts. At first it's little more than a mist, but it doesn't take long before it's a full downpour. Bash does what he can with his wind magic to keep us dry, but there's only so much he can do. I always stay warmer than most thanks to my magic, so when I notice Freya shivering, I ride up next to her.

"Share my horse with me?"

Freya's wide eyes meet mine. "W-what?"

"You're shivering. You're clearly cold. I can keep you warm."

She rolls her eyes. "What a l-line."

"It's not a line. It's the truth. My magic keeps me warm and it can keep you warm, too, if you'll let me help you."

She hesitates for a moment and I think she's going to decline. I'm surprised when she nods.

"Yeah?" I say, sitting up straighter.

She shakes her head at me, but I catch a hint of a smile. "Don't make me regret this."

We stop our travel to get situated, Freya sitting in front of me so I can wrap my arms around her while I steer my horse. Bash watches us carefully, and I have to try hard not to think back on happier times when I shared my warmth with someone else.

"Ready?" I ask once Freya gets situated. She nods and we're soon off again. After a minute, Freya leans back against me with a contended sigh.

"You are warm."

I chuckle. "Told you."

"Don't let it go to your head."

"Too late."

Freya groans but I'm pretty sure she's smiling. "Great. Your head gets any bigger it won't hold the crown."

I let out a full blown laugh. "It's a risk I'm willing to take."

Freya shakes her head and I tighten my arms around her slightly. I rather like having her in my arms.

Despite our best efforts, we're still thoroughly soaked by the time we reach the estate of Lord Brackbill, the Earl of Hanclover, and even I'm fighting off shivers. It doesn't help that night has fallen along with the temperature. A confused servant answers the door when we knock, and they hurry to alert Lord Brackbill while another servant promises to take care of our horses. Bash follows the servants from the room, and I resist the urge to protest his departure.

It doesn't take long for the earl to arrive. He's a stout older man I've always enjoyed, so I offer him the best smile I can given the circumstances.

"Your Highness!" Lord Brackbill says, rushing toward us, a near-panicked expression on his face as he wrings his hands. "We weren't expecting you!"

"It's fine," I say as reassuringly as possible as the man comes to a stop in front of us. "We had to take a rather unexpected route. We've arrived later than expected. Or are we early? I'm afraid I've lost track of the days."

"A day later than expected, but we received word that

there was an attack that delayed your journey. I am quite pleased to see that you are doing well."

"Well, we are a bit wet," I say with a shrug like I'm mildly inconvenienced at best. "And we've lost our clothes."

The earl's eyes widen almost comically. "Oh! I am sure we can wrangle you up something decent to wear. Right, Berkley?"

I turn and nearly jump when I notice the servant standing in the corner of the room, still as a stature.

"Of course, sire," the man says, inclining his head. "I will have the staff look through what we have available for our guests."

"And make sure there's something for Ba—my guard as well, if you will," I add quickly, thinking of how poor Bash is downstairs with the staff in his own dripping clothes.

Berkley offers me a nod. "Of course, Your Highness."

He disappears and Lord Brackbill ushers us into a sitting room with a roaring fire. A maid offers us steaming cups of tea as Freya and I huddle near the fireplace.

"Hopefully this will tide you over a bit. I've already eaten dinner, but I've asked the kitchen to warm you up some food. Would you rather have it in your room or full service?"

"Our rooms are fine," I say, offering the earl a smile. "Thank you." I pause before adding, "And make sure my guard—"

"He's taken care of," the earl says with a knowing smile. "In fact, I've directed my staff to arrange it so his room is connected to yours. I assume he's acting as your valet on this trip?"

I swallow my surprise and manage a nod. "Yes, he is. I appreciate your forethought."

"Of course," he replies, waving me off. "It's an honor and my duty to make you as comfortable as possible."

We fall into a comfortable silence until a servant arrives to let us know our rooms are ready. Freya's room, it turns out, is also next to mine, though her room isn't directly connected. I still like the idea of having her close. When I enter my room, Bash stands inside, already changed into dry clothes.

"They brought you clothes," he says nodding to a pile laid out on the bed.

"Thanks," I say, already shucking off my wet shirt.

Bash clears his throat but looks pointedly away. "Do you need assistance?"

I laugh. "Hardly." I look over my shoulder at Bash and smirk, waggling my eyebrows. "Unless you're offering?"

Bash sighs and shakes his head. "You need to stop that, Ty."

His words feel like ice water dumped over me. "I know."

I pull on the dry shirt and make quick work changing the rest of the outfit. Bash scoops up the discarded items and lays them on a drying rack near a fireplace in the corner of the room.

"Anything else?" His voice is forced and cold, almost distant.

My shoulders sink. "Bash, I—"

A knock on the door interrupts us and I growl as Bash goes to answer the door. I'm expecting one of Brackbill's servants checking in or bringing dinner, but I'm surprised to see Freya standing in the doorway.

"I was wondering if now would be a good time to talk?" she says, her fingers fiddling with a small bow on the front of the nightdress she's been given. She raises her eyes to Bash. "Unless now isn't a good time?"

Bash takes a step back. "Now is a perfect time." He turns to me. "I'll be next door if you need me."

Before I even have a chance to protest, he slips through the door connecting our rooms. I sigh and turn my full attention to Freya.

"Well, come inside and close the door. Let's talk."

CHAPTER TWENTY-FOUR

FREYA

After I close the door, I turn to face Ty. I take a steadying breath, trying to figure out how to start.

"You always knew your future spouse would be chosen for you, right?"

He blinks at me. "Of course I did."

"Then why do you fight it? Why did you hate me so much at first?" I ask, my voice barely above a whisper, which is good given the way it cracks against my will. "Am I that disappointing?"

"Freya, no. I . . ." Ty sighs and collapses into one of the two large easy chairs near his crackling fire. "How do I explain this? I did always know, yes, but there's so much more to the story." He gestures to the chair across from him. "You might as well get comfortable. It won't be a quick explanation."

I sink into the chair as Ty gnaws on his bottom lip, brow furrowed in thought.

"When I was a young boy, my governess used to tell me the

histories and myths behind Elodia, but she told them in such a way they sounded like magical stories. Like fairy tales. Of course, among those stories was the tale of Queen Vascha of the Fae and King Harraque of Elodia binding their magic. She made it sound so wonderful that they brought magic to humans through the power of love. When I asked if I would have that one day, she told me yes, that fate and magic had worked together to create a perfect soulmate for me, I had only to find her."

I startle at the word "soulmate," but Ty doesn't pause, plunging ahead with his story.

"She promised me I'd never have to worry about a broken heart because my marriage, and thus my love, was set on course already. She assured me I was quite lucky. For many years I believed her. Even as I neared my teen years and saw some of my older peers starting relationships and falling in love—or whatever version a young man on the cusp of adolescence can call love—I held tight to her words. When I saw heart after heart get broken, I felt safe, secure in the fact that such a fate would never befall me."

He closes his eyes and leans his head against the back of the chair. He stays silent for a moment as if deciding how to proceed. When he speaks again his voice is softer, almost lonely.

"When I first started feeling attraction and desire, I was able to push it aside, willing to wait for my soulmate. I questioned my mother and father on their progress, and they assured me they were searching tirelessly across our kingdom and beyond to find me my someone. As time passed, I grew frustrated with my situation. I no longer felt fortunate; I felt alone and lost. By the time I turned fourteen I was done waiting. I was tired of being forced to dance with girl after girl and entertain visitor after visitor only for them all to fail the blood test."

"So you gave up waiting and began sleeping around?"

Ty opens one eye and peers over at me, the corner of his mouth lifting slightly. "Not quite, but I did start pursuing girls for my own, uh, personal satisfaction." He opens his other eye and stares up at the ceiling. "Around age fifteen I came to the conclusion that I was equally attracted to all genders, so no one was left out of my advances, though more girls flocked to me than anyone else. I never went all the way with any of them. I got quite close, to be honest, even going as far as to get others off, but a piece of me was waiting for my soulmate before I surrendered fully to the bliss of sex. Honestly, I longed for a relationship that meant something, one with a real connection, more than I wanted sex by itself. Then I turned seventeen."

Ty pushes up from the chair so rapidly I jump, not expecting the motion. He paces back and forth in front of the fire, shaking his head.

"I didn't ask for what happened that night. I didn't see it coming, though I had dreamed of it many times." He pauses, scowling as he glances off to the side. "I thought it was fate telling me it was okay, and for so long it was."

He exhales slowly and turns to me, pain etched on his face. I'm about to reach out to him when he moves with a jolt and falls back into the chair, leaning forward with his elbows balanced on his knees and his hands clasped in front of him. His eyes stare off past me, unfocused.

"After a celebratory birthday feast, a friend and I escaped the chaos into a garden." His voice is so quiet I can barely hear him above the crackling fire. "We were quite close and I'd had a crush on him for some time. He apologized for his lack of a gift, and I was about to tell him his friendship was gift enough when he . . . he kissed me." His eyes shutter closed. "It was meant to be a quick brush of lips, I'm sure, but when he went to pull away, my lips chased after his. Our kiss escalated and, before I knew it, I was drawing him back inside, up to my room. It was a perfect night.

"We woke the next morning in my bed, tangled together and blissfully content. We knew it had been a mistake, but neither of us regretted it. For a while we pretended like we were still friends who just happened to fall into bed together every night. We pretended it was nothing. But every day I fell more in love with him, and he with me, until we were totally and irreversibly in love with each other."

He sighs, shaking his head and looks up at me. Tears well in his eyes and everything about his expression is broken. My own heart shatters.

"We were fools. We somehow convinced ourselves that Fate indeed meant for us to be together, and that was the reason no match had been found. He has very magical blood, perhaps even more golden than yours. We made plans that we would be bound together when we were both twenty-one, and it would be our blood that kept magic alive."

Ty makes a sound somewhere between a laugh and a scoff as he shakes his head.

"Of course, there would be the matter of an heir, but we figured we'd come up with a solution at a later date. I let myself believe our lie because I loved him and I was so incredibly happy."

A tear slides down as his cheek, and I feel tears burning my own eyes as I whisper, "Then I was discovered."

He nods. "We were in bed together when the messenger burst in with the news."

"I'm sorry, Ty."

"It wasn't your fault you were born with the right blood, but I hated you anyway. I tried to refuse to go out to meet you, but my mother forced me. My . . . lover was made to stay behind as punishment for my behavior, though he typically went everywhere with me, even before we started our relationship. I was furious with my situation and became even more so when I discovered that we weren't headed to an estate or a castle or anywhere of import but merely a—"

"—nothing farming village in the poorest part of Elodia," I finish for him. "And your wife-to-be was no more than a poor, dirty, fat peasant with zero prospects who didn't even know the difference between a salad fork and a shrimp fork."

Ty's forehead scrunches as more tears fall. He licks his lips and draws a shaky breath.

"When you stepped out of your house to greet me, a piece of me instantly saw you as the answer to my fairy tale, but another larger part had already tasted a happily ever after that was nothing like you in the slightest."

His voice breaks into a soft sob and he drops his head into his hands. I rise and kneel down in front of him, placing a hand on his knee.

"I'm sorry, Freya," he sobs, his voice muffled by his hands. "You deserve better than me." He looks down at me with swollen eyes. "I'm used and broken, and you're so wonderful. I think I might be falling in love with you. I *know* I am. I can offer you what little I have left of my heart, but I'm not sure if it will be enough."

I rise up enough so I can brush a quick kiss on his cheek.

"If you want to give me any piece of your heart, no matter how small, I'll treasure it and keep it."

He reaches out and tucks a stray strand of hair behind my ear as he stares down at me in wonder. "I don't deserve you."

I smile softly. "And here I was assuming you hated me because I got in the way of your long line of lovers."

He laughs, and it sounds almost genuine. I push up from the ground and resume my seat.

"Well," he drawls, his eyes brightening a bit, "I did have lovers—you know that well enough as some of them tried to kill you—but they came after we met."

"After?" I can't keep the shock from my voice.

He nods guiltily. "When I returned from meeting you, I tried to resume my previous relationship. I insisted that I would never love you like I loved him and that we didn't have to stop. He disagreed and we fought. In the end, we decided that it would be better to break things off instead of dragging it out. It shattered me and nearly destroyed our friendship. I buried my sorrow with drink and sex and he . . . well, he coped in his own way. We only recently found our way back to each other and mended our friendship, but things, understandably, will never be the same."

I hesitate, the question on the tip of my tongue before it finally falls out. "It was Bastion, wasn't it?"

Ty's eyes widen and he swallows hard before nodding. "Yes." The corner of his mouth quirks up. "I didn't hide his identity very well, did I?"

I smile softly. "I read between the lines. Besides, I've seen you two together and it's clear you're more than friends. At least now I understand why he hated me so much when I arrived at the palace."

Ty starts to nod but stiffens, sitting straighter in his seat. "I won't dismiss him," he says, his voice hard. "I promise there won't be anything else between me and him, but I won't cast him away. He means too much for—"

"Ty, I would *never* ask that of you."

He blinks at me. "Really?"

A laugh bubbles out of me at his bewildered expression. I rise and cross to him, kissing his forehead.

"Really, Ty."

In one smooth motion he rises, pulling me into his arms.

"Thank you," he whispers, burying his face in my neck. "Thank you, Freya, I—"

He draws back and stops short. He runs his tongue across his lips as he glances to my mouth. When his eyes meet mine, there's a question there—a question I didn't even know I had been waiting for. I answer by pressing my lips to his.

CHAPTER TWENTY-FIVE

BASH

They need their privacy. I know this. Yet I find myself listening at the door. My heart constricts painfully as Ty tells our story. I'm not sure when I start crying, but my cheeks are damp by the time he's done. I loved him so much. I still do. I'll never stop loving him. I tried, but it was pointless.

Taking a shaky breath, I make my way to my bed and sink down on the edge. I wait, listening carefully for Freya to leave. Each second that passes without her departure I feel more lost. Ty is no longer mine. I know this. But the thing that's odd is it's not just knowing this is the final nail in the coffin of losing Ty. It's that I'm somehow mourning the loss of Freya as well. Knowing they're together and happy makes me feel even more alone than I thought possible.

Freya leaves too soon for me to believe they did anything more than kiss. She doesn't seem like the kind of girl who would let someone take her to bed only to leave the moment the deed is done. Or maybe she only left because dinner was delivered. I know because a plate of my own arrives via a servant shortly after. Either way, they crossed an intimate line tonight, and there's no going back.

They are together and I am alone. I'm happy for them. I really am.

I'm fine.

I'm fine.

I'm . . . fine.

I'm . . . not fine.

CHAPTER TWENTY-SIX

TY

Even though Freya and I did little more than kiss—some excellent, top-notch kissing—I wake feeling more satisfied than I have in years. I roll over in bed, tucking my hands behind my head, and grin up at the ceiling. If she can kiss like *that*, I can only imagine how amazing she'll be in bed. If we hadn't been interrupted by dinner arriving, maybe I'd have found out, though, if I'm entirely honest, I want my first time with Freya to be over-shadowed a little less by my past. That doesn't mean I can't think about what might have been.

I slip one hand beneath the waistband of my sleep pants, my body already eager and waiting. I draw on my experience from last night and let my imagination free. My hand picks up speed before I can feel an ounce of guilt thinking of Freya like this. I tilt my head back, breathing hard, on the verge of what is promising to be an amazing orgasm.

"Ty?"

"Shit!" I swear, jerking my hand from my pants and

yanking a blanket over me. I shuffle into a sitting position, my face hot, and try to look as casual as possible. "Uh, morning, Bash. Bastion. Bash."

Bash's mouth twitches and his eyes twinkle. "Morning, Ty. Tybalt. Ty."

I groan, grabbing the blanket to hide my face. "Can we pretend that—"

"Nope."

I groan again and peek around the blanket. I don't even know why this embarrasses me. It's not like Bash hasn't seen me like this before. It's not like he hasn't participated before. Somehow this feels very different. Bash folds his arms across his chest, cocking an eyebrow.

"Would you like for me to come back later so you can finish?"

My face feels ever warmer as I shake my head. My erection is already waning.

"Okay, then, let's get you ready for the day, shall we?" Bash uncrosses his arms and reaches for something sitting on the dresser. "Lord Brackbill was kind enough to provide you with some additional clothing options for travel until you can reach your next destination where you will hopefully be able to get some custom-tailored apparel."

I frown. Why is he acting so formal again?

"This is what he suggested for breakfast," Bash continues, extending what looks to be a high quality pair of breeches and tunic. "Shall I dress you?"

"Do you really think I need your help?"

He cocks his head. "With dressing or what you were doing before I walked in?"

"Bash," I hiss through gritted teeth, a little relieved that he's back to joking.

He gives me a shit-eating grin. "That didn't answer my question."

I sigh through my nose. "I really don't need your help with either." I push my back the blanket and swing my legs over the edge of the bed. "But if you insist, I guess you can assist me"—His grin widens—"with *dressing* so I can be done faster. Then can you check on Freya?"

His smile tightens, something else flickering on his face, but he's quick to hide it.

"Freya?"

I nod, standing and stretching. "Yeah. Just check in on her?"

He glances off to the side, his smile entirely gone. "I can. I thought you two had talked things over."

"We did, and things are good." A soft smile pulls on my lips at the memory of last night. "Really good."

His jaw flexes as he nods. "Did you two . . . ?"

I shake my head quickly, though I'm not entirely sure why I feel the need to deny it. "No. We talked and kissed a bit —some really good kissing—but that's it."

"Did you want to do more?"

"I—"

"You know what?" He offers me a tight smile that doesn't even remotely reach his eyes. "I don't need to know. I don't *want* to know."

I take a step toward him, my stomach twisting with guilt. "Bash."

He shakes his head. "It doesn't matter. Let's get you ready for the day, Your Highness."

"Bash." Another step closer.

He holds up the tunic and gives it a shake. "We don't want to keep Earl Brackbill waiting."

I take another step and he swallows. I start to reach out to place my hand on his arm, but he takes a wide step back, squeezing his eyes shut.

"Please, Ty," he says, his voice tight. "Don't." He opens his eyes and I nearly stagger back a step at all the emotion in their depths. "Please. Let me do my job and nothing more."

I hesitate, taking a moment to fight back emotions of my own. "All right." I force a smile. "I would appreciate your assistance in dressing."

Bash's shoulders sag with relief as he steps closer. "Thank you."

BREAKFAST WITH THE EARL IS A COZY AFFAIR. SINCE THE EARL'S wife died over a decade ago without providing an heir, it's just the earl himself. Instead of putting on airs, he has us take breakfast in a homey breakfast nook, even inviting Bash to join us, which doesn't feel odd since his manservant Berkley joins us as well. Honestly, if the other nobles could be as decent as Lord Brackbill, I wouldn't mind them half as much. Even though Bash has been made more than welcome he seems a little stiff, but Freya is relaxed, shooting me shy smiles across the table.

After several days in less-than-ideal conditions, we take the morning slowly, in no rush to resume our journey. Since we're already behind, however, and have limited time to complete our tour before the Fae moon ceremony, we leave a little before lunch, the earl sending us on our way with bags packed full of provisions. If we were following our original pathway, we would have gone a little south to the house of a minor duke, but since we're behind schedule we take a more direct path to the Hallowbridge estate. Thanks to our horses, we make it to a small village a little before nightfall, securing a room at an inn that, sadly, has a separate bed for each of us.

The night is fairly uneventful. It's comfortable, even. Freya and I still have a ways to go before we're where we need to be to become the successful pair ruling a kingdom together, but we're much closer. Bash also seems to have accepted everything and is as back to normal as can be. And yet, I feel like there's something hanging over us, ready to drop at any moment.

When we reach our destination the following evening, we're met with a flurry of activity. We've managed to manipulate our schedule so that we arrive on our normal day, and everyone seems quite relieved. And by everyone I mean practically anyone with even a snip of noble blood on this side of the kingdom. Given the pompous nature of said nobles, Bash is once again relegated to the serving quarters, leaving my side before I've even stepped through the large door of the estate, but at least I have Freya. She gives me a gentle, knowing smile, and takes my hand in hers. I show my appreciation by giving it a small squeeze before we're ushered off to our separate rooms to prep for a stuffy dinner.

Since the ball is supposed to serve as our main debut as a couple, we have to endure a couple nights of hobnobbing first. This means dinners and small talk tonight and tomorrow that will more than likely make me want to rip my hair out. I can only imagine how it will make Freya feel. Once I've taken a soothing bath and am dressed for the evening—in new clothes of my own that were made in anticipation of my arrival—I slip down the hall to Freya's room.

She answers after one knock, looking flustered and wearing only her shift.

"Are you all right?" I ask, stepping into the room and closing the door behind me. "Why aren't you dressed?"

"I'm sorry. I really don't want to mess this up again, but . . ." She bites her lip and shakes her head. "I don't know what I'm supposed to wear, and even if I did, I'm not sure how to put half of it on. It's all far more complicated than what I usually wear, even around the palace."

She gestures behind her where several dresses and layers of what I assume are undergarments lay scattered across her bed. I'm assuming much like my own attire, these were made custom for her using measurements sent ahead by my mother and Liege Greengrass. I furrow my brow and step closer.

"I think this one would be a good dinner dress," I say, pointing to a dark yellow silk dress with white lace. "At least, it looks similar to ones I've seen other ladies wear to dinner before." I take a step to the side, stopping in front of what look to be a collection of torture devices poorly disguised as ladies' underthings. I'm more accustomed to removing them than putting them on. My cheeks warm slightly. "As for these, um, I'm not sure."

Freya steps to my side. "I'm pretty sure I know what I'm supposed to wear with that style of dress, but I'm not sure if I can manage to put them on myself." She looks at me through long lashes, a light blush coloring her cheeks. "I don't suppose you could help?"

I swallow, wondering if the room feels as warm to Freya as it does to me. "I . . . well, I could try, but, um, I'm not very good with hooks and buttons and"—I gesture vaguely—

"things." I scratch behind my ear. "I don't suppose they offered you a maid?"

She shakes her head. "No, and when I asked for one, the servant that escorted me here mumbled apologies and said she'd see what she could work out, but that was"—she glances at a small clock sitting on the bedside table—"nearly twenty minutes ago. I'm not holding out hope she'll be back."

I hum my agreement. I look back at the masses of clothing, debating if I should give it a try anyway, when an idea hits me.

"I know! Bash could help!"

Freya's eyes widen. "What?"

"Bash," I say, already walking to summon a servant to her room so they can fetch him from whatever corner he's been shoved into. "He's helped me into some rather odd outfits before." And out of them. "I'm sure he'd be better at this than me."

"Ty," Freya says, her voice tight as she hurries after me. "Are you sure that would be appropriate?"

I'm already ringing for a servant before she poses the question, so it's too late to debate my solution. Instead, I dig in, turning to her with a smile.

"It'll be fine. I don't think it's all that uncommon for royal guards and valets to help with these sorts of situations." I honestly have no idea what the proper protocol would be here. "If anyone has a problem with it, then maybe they should have made sure you had a proper lady's maid in the first place."

Before Freya can relay any more of her worries there's a knock on the door. I answer, the servant stumbling back a step and falling into a bow. Obviously she wasn't expecting me. When I ask for Bash to be sent up as quickly as possible, the servant doesn't hesitate to scurry away. The moments waiting for his arrival stretch with awkward silence, and I'm beginning to debate if I've made the right choice. When Bash's firm knock sounds through the room, I can't get the door open fast enough.

"Hurry, come in," I say, ushering Bash inside and peering out into the hall to make sure the coast is clear.

Bash doesn't hesitate to step inside the room while I hurriedly secure the door behind him.

"Is everything okay?" he asks, his eyes darting between me and Freya, his hand resting on the hilt of his sword.

"What? Oh, yeah, we're fine. Well, we're safe. Freya needs assistance."

Bash relaxes a little, his hand dropping to his side as he turns to her. "What kind of assistance?"

Freya's cheeks are bright pink. "I—" She shoots me a sharp look. "Ty, this was your idea."

I chuckle somewhat nervously as I bite my lip. "Uh, yeah, I guess it was."

Bash crosses his arms and levels me with a glare. "What harebrained idea did you come up with?"

I hold up my hands defensively. "It's not that bad. Freya needs help dressing."

In all the time I've known Bash, I don't think I've ever seen him more horrified than he is in this moment.

"You cannot be serious."

"They didn't give me a lady's maid," Freya rushes to explain. "Then they left me with all this." She gestures to the bed and Bash's wide eyes follow. "I don't know how to manage half of this. Of course, if it's trouble . . ."

"Nah, he can handle it. Right, Bash?"

I shoot him my most winning smile, but my gut is

twisting and sloshing. This is a horrible, *horrible* idea, and Bash looks like he would rather be anywhere else. But then he schools his features and straightens, marching over to the bed to examine the clothes. After a moment he clears his throat and turns to face Freya.

"Do you have any idea what to do?" he asks, his voice steady and calm.

Freya shakes her head. "I mean, I know where some of the pieces go, but there's no way I can get them into position or lace them up on my own."

Bash sighs, his shoulders sinking in resignation. "I can't say I know anything about how this works, but I can fasten a hook and pull a string."

Freya brightens. "Really? You don't mind?"

"I didn't say I didn't mind, but I'll do it."

"Great!" I say, clapping my hands once and taking a step backward. "I guess I'll leave you two to it."

"Stop right there, Tybalt Adrian Shadowmoss!" Bash snaps, pointing a finger at me. "You cannot leave me in the room alone to undress and dress your fiancée!"

I wince, knowing he's right. "She's technically already undressed." Bash levels me with a glare. "Fine, but what exactly am I supposed to do? Surely you don't want me to watch?"

"No!" Freya jumps in, looking nearly as horrified as Bash had moments ago. "Just"—she scans the room frantically, finally settling on a chair in the corner—"read a book. Over there."

I sigh with relief. Read a book. I can do that. I glance at the clock and both Freya and Bash follow my gaze.

"How much time do we have?" Bash asks.

"Maybe fifteen minutes before we're expected in the

drawing room?" I reply with a grimace.

Bash inhales slowly through his nose, giving me a look that says I owe him, before he turns to Freya with a forced smile.

"Let's get started then, Princess."

CHAPTER TWENTY-SEVEN

BASH

This is Hell. It's the only explanation for the situation I am in right now. I have no idea why Ty seems to have so much confidence in my skills as a dresser. I have never even taken clothes off a woman, let alone tried to dress one. And yet, a rather embarrassed and flustered Freya stands in front of me in little more than undergarments. When she looks up at me through her ridiculously long eyelashes, biting her lip in the same nervous way Ty does, I nearly have to leave the room to collect myself.

"If you have somewhere else you need to be, you don't have to help me. I'm sure I can figure it out on my own."

She sounds helpless and almost contrite. I straighten, shaking my head.

"No, it's fine." I look at the piles of clothes, hoping my cheeks aren't as flushed as they feel. "You'll have to guide me a bit, though, where you can."

Her head bobs in agreement and she picks up one of the items. "Let's start with this."

It doesn't take long into the process for me to become very frustrated and upset with the count and countess. There is absolutely no way one could dress themselves in these ridiculous tangles of layers without assistance. They wanted her to either embarrass herself by not dressing properly or to be late to dinner after struggling to dress herself. Likely both. I do the mental math on how much of a problem we might have on our hands if one of them had a little accident.

"There, that isn't too tight, is it?" I ask, tugging the final laces on a corset.

She looks at me over her shoulder, a wry smile on her lips. "No, which means it probably isn't nearly tight enough." Her smile slips before she forces a weak one back. "It takes a little more work to get me to what most consider a 'proper' figure for a lady."

If I was angry before at the horrible behavior of the nobility, it's nothing compared to the fire of hatred heating my veins now.

"Your figure is more than fine," I say before I can stop myself. Her eyes widen in surprise and I hurry to add, "What I mean is that you're beautiful exactly as you are and anyone who says otherwise is either jealous or severely visually impaired."

"He's right, you know," Ty calls from where he's perched on the arm of the easy chair reading a book.

Freya's blush returns as she shakes her head. "I'm nothing compared to—"

"Nope!" Ty says, bouncing off the chair and closing the book with a snap before tossing it in the chair. "I'm not going to let you compare yourself to anyone."

Freya's expression softens. "Thank you." She glances at the clock. "But we really should hurry."

Those last couple of layers slip on easily enough, and Freya quickly fixes her hair into what will hopefully be acceptable to everyone in attendance tonight. Freya studies herself in the full-length mirror, turning and examining her appearance from every angle. Her brow is furrowed and I'm not sure what she sees, but what I see is the most startling attractive woman in the entire kingdom. She really is beautiful, and if they don't agree they're fools. I'm about to say as much when a satisfied smile slips onto her lips, and she turns to me.

"Thank you, Bastion."

"Bastion?" I arch an eyebrow. "I thought that was behind us."

She giggles. "Bash, then."

I shoot her a wink. "That's better."

I don't even need to glance at Ty to know the bewildered look he's giving me. I can feel the heat of his eyes. No one besides him calls me "Bash." I ignore him, focusing entirely on Freya.

"You're very welcome, but if you don't hurry, you're going to be late." I glance at the clock and wince. "Well, later."

Ty steps to my side, shaking his head. "I'm the fucking prince. *I* decide when it's time to arrive and they can get used to that." He offers his arm to Freya. "Shall we?"

Freya smiles and steps forward to accept his arm, but pauses, looking back up at me.

"I really do appreciate your help."

Before I can register what she's doing, she's on her tiptoes pressing her lips to my cheek. It's the quickest brush of her lips on my skin, but it heats me through my core. All I can do is blink at her as she gives me a shy smile, linking her arm with Ty's. Ty shoots me a grin and wink and leads her out of the room. I stand frozen for longer than I care to admit, staring at the closed door. I lift a trembling hand to touch where Freya's lips brushed moments before. I swallow hard and drop my hand into a fist. It meant nothing. It was a thank you and nothing more. I need to keep my head clear. I need to focus. I have things to deal with far more important than the fluttering in my gut, and one of those things is handling the slight toward Freya.

Summoning my resolve, I head directly down to the servant's quarters to locate the head of house, Mr. Barry, a nervous, balding man who always seems to be sweating.

"You'll have to excuse me, but I have a dinner to look over," he says, trying to dodge around me, but I'm quicker, easily blocking his way.

"Now, see here," he huffs, scowling up at me. "You cannot come in here from the palace and mess up how everything is done and organized. We have a system."

I hold up my hands in surrender. "And I don't want to. I want His Highness to have a good time here, so I have no intention of keeping you from your work."

"Then please move so I can go about my business!"

"Hm, now I'm afraid I can't do that until we discuss how poorly your household is staffed."

The man's face reddens with fury. "Pardon me? My household is *not* poorly staffed!"

"Then I suppose it was merely an oversight that Her Highness wasn't provided a maid to help her dress tonight?"

Mr. Barry very purposefully looks away, a muscle twitching in his jaw. "We do not have an endless supply of maids."

"Surely you have at least one? Due to your shortsightedness, I had to step in and help her tonight, and I'd rather—"

"What!" he declares, his full attention snapping to me. "Why, I never! How incredibly improper!"

"I agree. It was incredibly improper for you not to supply her with a lady's maid and to leave me as her only choice."

For the first time, he looks contrite and flustered, stumbling back a step.

"I expect the issue can be rectified immediately so I don't have to help undress her as well?"

Mr. Barry's eyes widen to a level I've never seen on a human before, and I have to call upon my training to keep my delight hidden.

"After all, if word got back to the palace that your household is ill-equipped to host royal visits to the point that it lead to perceived impropriety, I can only imagine—"

"It will be addressed!" he squeaks. "I will find someone as soon as dinner is over but as it is"—he glances past me down the hall—"I really must get back to the dinner."

"But you promise to find a servant to help her tonight and for the rest of our stay here?"

He looks back up at me. "Yes. Yes. I promise! Now, may I go?"

I step to the side and wave my hand for him to pass. "By all means. I do apologize for the interruption."

Once he's scurried off to do whatever it is heads of households do, I head outside. I'm sure the premises are secure, but going through a basic security routine is soothing. Plus, after my evening I could do with some fresh, cool air. There's only a sliver of moon tonight—a reminder we're just under a couple weeks away from the Fae moon—but plenty of sparkling stars light the sky. It's so beautiful I can't bring myself to go back inside. I'm sure I'd only be in the way.

I'm not sure how long I've been outside when a familiar laugh carries across on the night breeze. Without meaning to, I follow the sound to where Ty and Freya are hidden away in a side garden. I stay well in the shadows so as not to disturb them, but I move closer. Ty should know better than to come out here where there's no protection.

Freya laughs again and Ty tugs her closer.

"Shhh," he whispers with a grin. "You're going to get us caught."

"We wouldn't want that," she murmurs so quietly I barely catch her words from where I'm standing. "That dinner was dreadful."

"I know. I know. But you know what else I know?"

"Hmm, what's that?"

"A way to make the night end better."

Ty pulls her into a kiss and I know I should look away, but I can't. I'm captivated by the two of them. When they separate, both breathless, they look so happy, so content. My chest constricts painfully. I had that once. Or at least I thought I did. It's funny how life hands you things only to rip them away. Broken hearts never truly mend; the scars last forever.

Swallowing hard, I force myself to give them privacy. I don't go far, however; I still have a job to do. After a few minutes, they go back inside and I'm well and truly alone again. This time it hurts.

CHAPTER TWENTY-EIGHT

TY

Escaping after-dinner activities isn't exactly easy. Everyone wants a moment of my time, of my attention, but the only person whose attention I crave is Freya's. My eyes keep searching for hers and every time they meet my heart flutters. We escape once into the garden and I steal several furtive kisses before we're forced back into the droll company of all these nobles. I want nothing more than to finish what we started in the garden, and I find it very difficult to focus on anything else. The very moment we can get away, I grab her hand and we flee. We stop midway to our rooms, and I press her against the wall, kissing her with almost crushing force. She gasps into my mouth and nips my lip.

"Ty," she gasps, half laughing. "We need to—"

I cut her off with a bruising kiss before pulling back, eyes bright. "I know."

I pull her the rest of the way to her room, kicking the door closed as my hands fumble to undo the buttons of my dinner jacket. I groan in frustration when we're interrupted by a knock on the door.

"Don't answer. They'll go away," I mutter.

She laughs against my lips, giving me one last kiss before walking toward the door. She pauses, her hand on the knob, turning back to me and mouthing *hide.* I grin but obey—I am a good boy after all—ducking behind a changing screen as the door creaks open. I struggle not to laugh as Freya assures a timid sounding maid that, despite the problems that occurred before dinner, she's fine undressing for the night. The maid sounds less than convinced, arguing in the politest way possible. I snicker into my jacket to smother the sound. Bash must have really made an impression. When the door finally clicks shut, I step out, grinning at Freya.

"Well, I think it's safe to say I'll have no problems in the morning," she says with a light laugh.

"Indeed," I say, stepping close enough to wrap my arm around her waist and tug her against me. "Now, where were we?"

It takes longer than I'd like to tear away all her fancy layers. When I literally rip off the more complicated layers, I swallow her initial protests with kisses and she surrenders willingly, no longer caring about the bits rolling across the floor. When she's bare before me she stretches out across the bed, her arms almost subconsciously covering her exposed skin. I bite my lip, shaking my head as I crawl over her.

"You. Are. Beautiful," I whisper, punctuating each word with a kiss a different place on her body. With each one, she inhales slightly, and I want to draw more sounds out of her. I trail my hands over her flesh, relishing every tiny little gasp, moan, and whimper. My fingers and mouth map every inch of her, taking their time to explore, to memorize her every curve as she trembles and shudders beneath me.

"Ty," she gasps out, my name on her lips sending shivers through me. "Please. Please!"

"Please what?" I murmur as my mouth finds a sensitive place on her neck, drawing out another moan.

"Please," she begs again, arching beneath me, my own body responding with a plea of its own. "I need you."

I chuckle, pulling back from her enough to remove what few clothes I still have on. She watches me with interest, pupils blown wide and lips swollen. I love her like this. I could see her this way every day for the rest of my life and never tire of the view. I slowly join her on the bed again, relishing all the places our bodies touch, each spot sending a fresh surge of desire and need through me. I press my lips against hers before pulling back and looking down into her eyes.

"Are you sure about this?" I ask, my voice rough. "Are you sure about me?"

"Yes, Ty," she breathes, not even hesitating a moment. She pushes up enough to press a kiss against my lips. "More than anything, I want you."

I practically sag with relief, before one more thought invades my brain.

"And it's safe? I mean, child-wise?"

She looks up at me confused for a moment before she breaks out into a laugh. "Yes, Ty. I take a monthly tonic."

"And that's enough?"

She smiles, pressing a kiss to my lips that fills me with heat. "Yes."

I huff a small laugh of my own. "Then what are we waiting for?"

Before I can let any more doubt flood my brain, I push into her. A sharp cry of pleasure escapes her lips, and I almost come right then and there. I'm nowhere near ready for this to be over yet, however, which is something I've missed over the past couple years. I've forgotten how much better it feels to be with someone who means something, to have emotions involved along with the physical urges. I actually care about how she feels and it fuels me. It isn't just about me and my pleasure alone. Her pleasure *is* mine. Every needy gasp, every wanton moan, every hungry sound might as well be coming from my own mouth. I relish how responsive she is, letting it drive me.

I'm not sure how long we last, but when I feel her clench around me, her mouth a beautiful gaping thing as she cries out, I follow close behind. Breathing hard, I collapse, half beside her, half on top of her, burying my face in her neck and offering shaky kisses as my soul returns to my body.

"You are incredible," I whisper, pressing a kiss beneath her ear.

She turns her head, her eyes meeting mine. "You aren't too bad yourself."

I seal that affection with a chuckle and kiss, and slowly peel myself away from her. With a groan I push up into a sitting position.

"Are you leaving already?"

I don't miss the disappointment in her voice, and I turn to her with a reassuring smile. "No, I'm a proper gentlemen." I push off the bed, shooting her a wink. "I'll help you clean up, and then I'd like to hold you awhile."

A few minutes later, we're both a little less sticky and gross, and the top blanket for the bed sits in a discarded heap in the corner. She's slipped into a nightdress, but the only thing I've bothered to put on is my underwear. We're stretched across the bed, Freya snuggled on my chest, her loose curls tickling my nose.

"You probably shouldn't stay here all night," she mumbles, sounding half asleep already. "If the maid finds you, it probably wouldn't be good."

I chuckle. "Maybe not, but I can promise you it's not the worst rumor anyone could spread. After all, this time next month we'll be properly married."

She hums, snuggling closer. "Still."

I sigh, pressing a kiss to the top of her head. "Five more minutes."

It's probably closer to ten when I finally leave the bed, tucking in a sleepy Freya and plucking up my shirt from the floor. I slip it over my head, but decide I'm too worn out and exhausted to dress any further. I ball up my trousers and jacket and tuck them under my arm with my boots before slipping out into the hall, a wide smile on my face. I think the hall is empty until a figure steps out of the shadows. My heart stutters to a stop before I register who it is.

"Bash," I say with a light laugh. "You scared me! I thought —"

Before I can get out another word, Bash is grabbing my arm so hard it will bruise and jerking me down the hall. He throws open the door to my room, shoving me inside. I stumble forward, nearly falling over as my clothing tumbles to the ground. I right myself and spin around to face Bash.

"What the Hell?"

"Exactly," he snaps. "What the Hell were you thinking?"

He's mad, well and truly mad. In all my years of knowing him, I'm not sure I've ever seen him quite this furious. This is the Bash that kills.

"Bash, it's okay. No one saw."

"Are you sure? Because I saw you leave that room like you didn't have a care in the world. Anyone could've seen. Anyone. You know better. You're not that careless."

Frustration and anger bubble up inside me and I take a bold step closer to him. "I'm the prince and she's my wife—or she will be soon. I can sleep with her if I want."

He laughs but it's bitter and harsh. "You are not that stupid. Please tell me you aren't that stupid."

"I don't see what the problem—"

"Exactly!" he yells, throwing his hands in the air. "At least half these people are looking for any reason to throw away you or her or both of you, and if the wrong person had seen you tonight, you would have handed them the reason wrapped in a tight little bow."

Blood rushes from my face as some of my anger dissipates. He's right. I know I didn't do anything wrong, but it could be so easily twisted and used against us. I take a deep breath and meet Bash's eyes. I'm ready to admit my mistake when I notice something I didn't before. Beneath the fury and anger is something I missed entirely. Pain. Bash is hurting.

"You will be an amazing king, if they let you," Bash continues. "And Freya will make an amazing queen." His voice breaks slightly and I catch the hint of tears shining in his eyes. "But you have to be careful. If they catch you . . . If they catch you . . ."

Suddenly, I'm no longer in this room. I'm back in my own bed in the castle, two years ago. A messenger is barging into my room and Bash is scrambling away from me. I'm in my parents' private quarters receiving a tongue lashing from my mother and sharp, disappointed glances from my father. I'm yelling back at her, defending a silent Bash who stands beside me, shaking and refusing to look up from his feet. I'm in a corridor with a bloody lip and cracked, bloody knuckles standing over a sneering nobleman's son in an attempt to protect Bash's honor. I'm standing in the courtyard, rain pouring around me, holding a letter explaining Bash is gone and he may not be coming back.

"Bash, are you—"

"I'm fine," he snaps, the tremble in his voice undermining the harshness. He turns his back to me. "I'm fine, Ty. I'm always fine. I—I have to be."

Tears burn my own eyes as I step closer, placing a hand on his shoulder. He flinches beneath my touch but doesn't pull away.

"Bash, please look at me."

He spins to face me and I'm not prepared for the look of panic and desperation shining in his eyes. His eyes flick over my face and a tear escapes as his resolve shatters. Tears of my own soon follow.

"I'm sorry," I croak out. "I'm sorry for everything."

It's not enough. It will never be enough. Bastion Shamblefoot was the best thing to ever happen to me, but I have little to no doubt I was the worst thing to ever happen to him. I can't fail Freya the way I failed him. I hold his eyes and for a moment we let the emotions out we'd been holding in. Bash, as expected, is the first to recover. He breathes deep, taking a wide step back as he wipes the tears from his cheeks. His expression steadies as he shoves everything back to wherever he keeps it. He straightens his shoulders and gives me one sharp nod, returning to the stoic, trusted guard he plays so well.

"Be careful, Ty," he says, his voice low and controlled.

"For both your sakes." He attempts and fails a smile as he adds, "I only have so many places I can bury the bodies should some accidents needs to occur."

He's gone before I can formulate any sort of response, and I know there's no point in chasing after him. No one can disappear as quickly or as efficiently as Bash. Drained and exhausted, I collapse on the bed and let nightmares pull me away.

CHAPTER TWENTY-NINE

FREYA

I expect the day leading up to the ball to be torture, but with Ty by my side it isn't half bad. Unfortunately, by my side during the day is all I get from him. A shadowy look appears in his eyes any time we might have a chance to sneak off alone. He assures me he definitely wants a repeat of our intimate time together, but since most of the nobles still seem decidedly set against me, he doesn't want to give them any more reason to hate me. Ty helps me navigate the crowd and social engagements to find those who actually seem supportive or at least open to having me as Ty's bride, and by the time the night of the ball arrives, I think I may have even made a couple of friends.

When I head to my room to get dressed for the ball, I lose some of my confidence when I see the dress waiting for me next to the full-length mirror. It's absolutely marvelous and I can easily see why Gregorian Greengrass is considered the highest in fashion. They started the design before I left the capital, but they had to finish up some of the detailed work, sending the dress along after us. Now as I stand staring at the work of art, it doesn't feel like it should belong to me.

For one, the rich shade of purple is one reserved for the highest nobility, typically only royalty since it's made from some rare and expensive dye. For another, the material is the softest silk known to mankind, another expense not afforded the majority of Elodia even among the nobility. Add in the plethora of diamonds and gems stitched into the fabric with what I'm assuming is thread made from actual gold, and it's too much. If that isn't enough, I'm to have enough accompanying jewelry to pay an entire village's wages for a year at least.

When my maid arrives, however, I have no choice but to allow her to dress me in all the finery. Like many of the other dresses made by Liege Greengrass, this one is fitted tightly to my curves, making it difficult to sit while she tugs and weaves my hair into an intricate design, pinning everything in place with more gold and gems. When she leaves the room with a bow, I take a deep steadying breath and turn slowly to the mirror. It takes me a moment to register the young woman staring back is indeed me. I take a step closer, looking for myself in the reflection. Is this really what I look like? Is this who I've become?

I'm so lost trying to find myself, I don't hear the door open and am startled by a sharp inhale behind me. I spin around, cheeks flushing, to find Bastion—Bash—standing a few feet away, his eyes wide and his mouth open. I look away from the intensity in his gaze.

"Do I . . . do I look okay?" I ask, nervously twisting one of the rings on fingers. "I know it's all a bit much, but—"

"I've never seen anyone more beautiful."

The stark honesty of his confession has my eyes jerking

to his. He swallows, struggling to reign in the emotion flickering across his face as he steps closer. He hesitates a moment before taking my hands into his. My breath catches in my throat, and I can't look away from his stormy gray eyes.

"You will be the most beautiful and powerful woman in that ballroom tonight, and I don't want you to forget that. Many of the people down there will try to make you feel lesser, like you aren't worthy, but you're ten times more worthy than any of them. When they try to manipulate you through snide comments and sharp glares, because they will, just remember they're jealous and all of them want nothing more than to be you."

As he talks, his thumbs trace over my knuckles and I find it very hard to breathe and it has nothing to do with my corset. The way he's looking at me tells me he means every word and more. I'm not sure how to handle the sudden emotions warming my chest or the swooping of my stomach.

"Bash," I whisper, my voice catching in my throat.

He must realize how close we're standing and he drops my hands, jerking back a step, color flooding his cheeks.

"I'm to escort you to Ty," he says, looking away. "He's waiting near the ballroom but didn't want to go in without you."

It takes me a moment to adjust to the abrupt change in Bash and the conversation, but I manage a nod.

"Thank you."

Bash motions for me to take the lead, and I leave the room, Bash following behind a few paces. When Ty spots us arriving, he lights up, eyes trailing over me.

"You look amazing," he whispers, drawing me close to

kiss my cheek. "Almost as amazing in this dress as you'd look out of it."

My cheeks warm as he leads me inside the ballroom. An attendant announces our arrival and everyone turns their attention to me. I recognize a few friendly faces in the crowd, but most people are eying me with disdain. I swallow, wanting to shrink into myself, but Bash's words float back to me. He's right, I realize, meeting the sharp gaze of a countess. They're jealous, at least to an extent. Using this knowledge to empower me, I straighten my shoulders and wear my new status as confidently as I can.

Ty guides me through the crowd, introducing me to more nobles and helping me avoid the ones who seem likely to cause the most trouble. Occasionally he leans over and whispers little secrets about the nobles that have me hiding smiles behind my hand. Like the time Lord Barrington lost his toupee in a windstorm during a hunt or when Lady Calloway got so drunk she mistook a vase in the hall for a chamber pot. He humanizes them in a way that makes them much more bearable.

"I don't suppose Her Highness would give me the privilege of a dance?" asks Lord Falloway, a stuffy earl from the north.

My heart leaps into my throat. I knew this was a ball which means dances, but I'm not sure I'm prepared to actually dance.

"Now, now, don't you think I should be the first to dance with her?" Ty teases, slipping a hand around my waist.

The earl chuckles. "Of course. You are right, Your Highness." He glances to me, then back to Ty. "But perhaps after you?"

Ty's smile has a sharp edge as he replies. "If she's amiable, but you'll have to ask her." He gives me a meaningful look as he adds, "She's not my property after all."

My heart flutters and I almost miss the earl asking my permission for a dance. I turn to him, my face warm, and manage a weak smile.

"Of course. I would be delighted."

"And it seems a new song is starting now, so if you'll excuse us," Ty says, steering me toward the dance floor.

We take up positions in the center of the room, and my nerves swell and twist in my stomach.

"Ty, I don't know—"

"Don't worry, Freya," Ty whispers, pulling me close so the warmth of his breath tickles my cheek. "I've got you and I'm not going to let you go."

My heart flutters and I resist the urge to kiss him in front of all these people. Luckily the music starts up and I'm thoroughly distracted trying not to stumble over my feet and Ty's. Ty keeps true to his word, however, and keeps me upright and looking competent. By the end of the dance, I can admit I'm enjoying myself. Of course, the dance ending means I have to dance with others now, but every time the music stops, Ty is right there, pulling me back into his arms, no matter whether he was dancing with someone else or not.

I relax and find enjoyment in each dance, even with the men who have wandering hands, knowing I'll end the night with Ty. After dozens of dances my feet are aching and I'm ready for a break. I give my thanks to the young lord I just danced with and turn to find Ty standing off to the side balancing two glasses of sparkling wine in one hand and a plate of food in the other.

"I saw a delightful garden out that door," he says, nodding

to an exit at the back of the ballroom. "I thought we could pop out there and refresh a bit."

I practically sag with relief. "That would be nice, thank you."

I follow Ty outside, and we make ourselves comfortable on a stone bench just out of reach of the glowing ballroom light. We can still hear the hum of conversation and the music, but it's quieter and much calmer. A breeze blows trails over us and I shiver.

"Here," Ty says, shirking off his jacket. "Take this."

I shake my head, plucking up a sugared berry from the plate and popping it in my mouth. "I don't want you to be cold."

"I'm fine," he says. "Remember, I run hot."

I bite back a grin. "Okay, if you insist."

He grins, standing. "I insist." He drapes the jacket around my shoulders and resumes his seat. "I can't have you freezing to death at a ball in our honor."

I laugh and meet his twinkling eyes. His grin grows before he clears his throat nervously and picks up one of the glasses.

"To us," he says, raising his glass.

I lift my own glass. "To us."

We take a sip and I find myself watching Ty closely, taking in every little movement. Even though there's not a lot of moonlight tonight, I can still make out all his features. I've always thought he was handsome, but lately, something has changed. He's more attractive to me, somehow. That's when it hits me like a boulder—I really am in love with Ty. Truly, deeply in love, or, at the very least, I'm falling very hard and very fast and will be very soon.

Ty tilts his head, his brow furrowing as he studies me. "Are you okay?"

I swallow, working to steady my racing heart. "I'm fine." I force a small smile. "I just . . ."

Ty places his hand on my knee, and even though there are layers of fabric between his palm and my knee, I swear it sends a rush of warmth up my spine.

"Yes? You can tell me anything."

I take a deep breath and release it slowly. "I . . . think I love you."

Whatever Ty was expecting, that clearly wasn't it. He inhales sharply, eyes going wide as his hand drops. My heart plummets into my stomach.

"I mean, I'm not . . . You don't have to . . ."

"No, Freya," Ty says quickly. "Don't take it back. Please, don't take it back."

I force myself to meet his eyes. "But you don't love me?"

He takes a shaky breath, glancing off to the side. "I'm not sure." He looks back to me and the corner of his mouth tips up into a smile. "Maybe?"

He sighs and stands, walking a couple paces away to stare out over the garden. I'm not sure if he wants me to follow, so I stay seated, stomach twisting.

"I loved once and I loved hard," he says his voice so low it's almost a whisper. "And I want to love again." He looks at me over his shoulder, his expression sad. "I want to love you."

"But you don't."

He's quiet a moment and my hope shatters. Then he steps toward me and extends his hand. I place my palm in his and pulls me to my feet. He slips his arms around my waist and looks down at me so we're almost nose to nose.

"I think that's the problem, Freya. I *do* love you, but I'm afraid of what admitting it would mean."

Hope flutters back to life. "It would mean you can still have your happily ever after."

A smile twitches on his lips. "Would it?"

"I'm not going anywhere, Ty," I whisper, reaching a hand up to caress his cheek.

He leans into my touch. "Promise?" he asks, desperation and fear in his voice.

"I promise."

The words are barely out of my mouth before his lips are on mine. After the intimacy of last night, something as simple as a kiss shouldn't affect me this way, but it feels different. It's like my whole world has shifted in the most amazing way. I press closer to Ty as he holds me flush against him. At some point, Ty's jacket falls from my shoulders, but I don't notice the chill of the night. Even though there's a whole ballroom of people not far away, it feels like Ty and I are the only people in the world. We're in our own bubble, safe and happy.

Until that bubble is shattered by the world outside.

CHAPTER THIRTY

BASH

I'm careful to keep my distance during the ball. I nearly gave everything away when I first saw Freya in her ballgown earlier. Now she's safely in Ty's arms where she belongs. I'm not technically invited to the ball, but good luck to anyone trying to keep me out. I stay well hidden in the shadows. I doubt even Ty knows I'm here. I take note of everyone Freya and Ty dance with, and while there are a few men whose fingers I would like to remove for touching Freya in ways she clearly doesn't appreciate, everything stays calm.

A little after midnight, Ty and Freya slip outside. I take up a position in the doorway, far enough that they have their privacy, but close enough I'm nearby should they need me. I can't quite make out what they're saying, but whatever it is appears to be emotional. Freya seems upset, but I can't see Ty's face. Then Ty's pulling her into his arms and they're—

I force my eyes away, looking over the crowd of dancers. When I look back out they're still kissing. It shouldn't hurt as much as it does. It shouldn't hurt at all. And the confusing thing is I'm not sure if it hurts because it's Ty or because it's Freya. It would fit with my luck that I fall for the only two people I can't have.

I'm wallowing in my own pathetic misery when I notice movement out of the corner of my eye. My senses go on full alert and I'm stepping out into the garden before I even register my movements.

"Ty, get back inside!" I yell, already drawing a dagger from my belt.

Ty pulls back from Freya, eyes hooded and love-drunk. "What?"

I rush forward, pushing him behind me as I narrow in on the figure—no figures—approaching through the shadows of the garden. "Get Freya inside."

"Um, Bash," Freya says, her voice trembling.

"What?" I snap, not looking at her, my eyes trained on what appears to be six well-armed people in masks heading our way.

"Bash!" she calls again, her voice more urgent this time.

I spin to face her, hoping Ty has his wits about him enough to keep his eyes on our approaching attackers. I'm ready to snap at her again when I take in her wide, terrified expression, but she's not looking where I was. She's looking in the opposite direction, where at least a dozen more people are closing in. We're surrounded.

I swear under my breath, taking stock of our surroundings as Ty and Freya slink closer to me so we're all practically touching. Ty doesn't have his sword, not even an ornamental one. Why would he have brought a weapon to the ball? Even I left my sword behind in favor of daggers hidden on my person. It should have been safe.

"Here," I say, passing Ty one of my daggers while I grab a second one with my left hand. Ty accepts the dagger without taking his eyes off the approaching people. I turn so Ty and I are shoulder to shoulder so no attackers are behind both of us while Freya hovers nearby. I withdraw another dagger so I have one in each hand. Being ambidextrous has its advantages.

"What's the plan?" he whispers. "We each take half?"

"You get Freya inside, and I'll take care of them."

"You can't—"

"I can," I hiss, "and I will. I won't be able to concentrate with her—you—in danger."

I feel Ty's nod more than see it. "Fine."

Before we can discuss it any further, the attackers make their move. Ty grabs Freya, pulling her toward the door while I do my best to ward off everyone I can. A couple of intruders cut between Ty and the door, but he takes them out quickly. I force myself to focus on the ones attacking me. I call for my magic, but it's slower answering than usual. The delay allows one of my opponents to land a blow on my chin, but I retaliate by jamming a dagger in his chest. I take two more out, dodging a few more blows.

"Freya!"

Ty's cry from behind sends ice-cold terror through me. I spin around in time to see a hefty, masked figure hauling Freya away over his shoulder while two others fight Ty back. Everyone else seems to be retreating to follow Freya's abductor. I flick a dagger and lodge it in the throat of one of Ty's assailants, allowing him to overpower the remaining one. I rush to his side, only noticing then the gold and red soaking the side of his tunic.

"You're hurt."

"I don't care about me," Ty says, wincing as he presses his hand to his side. "We have to get Freya."

"I'll get her. You go inside and get that looked at."

"It's not deep and—"

"No, Ty," I cut him off, my voice firm. "We don't have time to argue. Get inside. Now."

He makes a noise that sounds close to a whimper as he looks off into the darkness where she disappeared. I place a reassuring hand on his shoulder.

"Go inside. Get help. I'll bring her back. I swear on my life."

He hesitates only a moment before he nods. He staggers toward the door, and I make sure he makes it inside before I leap into the darkness. They only have a minute or so lead on me, but it makes it difficult to find them. I'm almost frantic when I hear Freya's voice. With renewed vigor I race around the main building to where Freya is fighting off her abductors. I don't know where she managed to get a dagger, but she's brandishing it wildly in the air while they circle her like she's a wild cat.

"Stay back," she says, stumbling a little. "I won't hesitate to slit your throat."

Someone chuckles. "I'd like to see you try."

Her hand trembles. "I have training."

"I'm sure you do," someone else says, amusement in their voice as they move in closer.

I slink forward and Freya's eyes fall on me. I shake my head and hold a finger to my lips. She gets the point and turns her attention back to the others, her shoulders straightening.

"I really wouldn't come any closer."

I inch forward, staying in the shadows, but I'm close

enough now I can easily use my remaining daggers and magic to take out most of these people.

"You really think you can take us?" a deep voice taunts.

Freya lifts her chin, a smirk playing on her lips. "Maybe not, but I don't have to."

"And why is th—"

He doesn't get a chance to finish before my wind magic is slicing his throat open. Everyone else spins around, searching frantically, but by the time their eyes find me, I've already taken out two more—one with magic and one with a throwing dagger. They organize quickly, rushing me. When I reach for my magic again, it's not there. It doesn't feel blocked, more like when it's empty from overuse, though it shouldn't be that way. Not already. I adjust quickly, relying only on my weapons.

The fight dissolves into a blur of activity. I react instinctively, not even taking time to think over my movements. I slash and stab. I snap someone's neck before kicking someone else down and crushing their skull beneath my boot. The coppery tang of blood saturates the air. I don't pause until they're all dead, and I'm standing in a sea of broken and bloody bodies, breathing hard.

"Bash?"

Horror washes over me. Freya. Gods. Freya just witnessed me at my worst. I take a shaky breath, keeping my back to her. I can't face her. What kind of monster am I to her?

"Bash?"

She doesn't sound scared. She sounds . . . concerned? I turn toward her slowly. She's not far away, but she's well out of my reach. She probably doesn't want to be any closer to a killer like me.

"You—you killed them all." Her words are barely a whisper on the wind.

"They touched you," I say, my voice level as I fight to keep my face expressionless. I swallow hard, daring to take a step closer. "No one is supposed to touch you."

When she doesn't flinch or step back, I take another step toward her.

"No one's allowed to touch me?"

I shake my head once. "No."

Another step. I'm barely a foot away, but she's still not moving away. I'm covered in the blood of at least a dozen men. She should be frightened, but the look on her face is closer to awe than fear.

"Except Ty?"

I inhale sharply, freezing in place, my jaw tightening. Something close to anguish rises in my chest, but I push it away.

"Except Ty."

This time she's the one to take a tentative step closer, and I have to force myself to hold my ground.

"What about you?"

My eyes lock on her and I don't think either of us are breathing. She closes the distance, stopping a breath away. "Can *you* touch me?"

My lips part as I look down at her. She's so wide-eyed and innocent, but she just watched me slaughter all these people and she's not scared. She's not running away scream-ing. Her dress is torn and bloodied. Her hair is a mess, pins falling everywhere. And yet, she's never been more beautiful to me. I want to pull her against me. I want to kiss her. I want to feel her heart beat in time with my own. But there are boundaries that must be maintained. Lines that cannot be crossed.

"Only with your permission. Only to help you. To treat you." My eyes fall to her arm where there's blood. Beautiful gold-tinted blood. "You're hurt."

She blinks rapidly like she's waking from a dream and follows my gaze to her arm. "Oh," she whispers, lifting her arm so it catches the starlight. "I guess I am."

I carefully take her arm in my hands, keeping my touch gentle. "May I?"

She nods, biting her lip. I turn her arm over, leaning forward to examine the wound, catching whiffs of lavender and mint mixed in with the metallic scent of blood. I force myself to focus. The cut isn't deep, already clotting, but I don't hesitate to rip part of my shirt to wrap around her arm.

"We'll have to get it cleaned up more inside and put a proper bandage on it, but that will do for now. Are you hurt anywhere else?"

Freya shakes her head. "I don't think so. A few bruises maybe, but nothing severe."

She still looks so small and yet so fierce. I reach out and tuck an escaped lock of hair behind her ear. Her eyes widen, but not with fear. Surprise. Then her expression softens, her eyes brightening.

"Let's get you back inside," I say, turning as I attempt to ignore how hard my heart is pounding in my chest. I need to get her back to safety and put some distance between us.

"Wait," she says, placing her hand on my arm.

I pause, looking at her over my shoulder. "Yes?"

"Are *you* hurt?"

I furrow my brow, turning back to face her. "What?"

"Are you hurt?" she repeats, her eyes scanning me over.

"No. I'm fine." At least, physically. I took a couple minor

hits but nothing that broke skin. I don't think so, anyway. I'll check later.

"Are you sure?"

"Why are you worried about me?" I snap, the harsh words escaping before I can stop them.

Freya stumbles back a step before straightening and looking me defiantly in the eyes. "Because I care about you for some gods forsaken reason, you idiot."

I know what I do next is foolish. I know it's wrong. I know I shouldn't do it, but I can't help it. I close the distance and look down at her, lifting blood-stained fingers to trace her cheek. Her eyes meet mine, pupils blown wide as my hand settles under her chin, tipping her face up. Her lips part and my thumb brushes her bottom lip, drawing a soft inhale from her. Heat and desire pool in my gut, and I lean almost imperceptibly closer to her, aching to press my mouth to hers.

"Freya, may I—"

"There they are!"

I jerk away from her so fast I nearly trip over my own feet and a couple dead bodies. Ty and a few other nobles, all properly armed, are headed our way. Thank the gods they showed up before I could make a fool of myself. They swarm around us, a few of the men searching the darkness for anyone who may have escaped my slaughter.

"Is this everyone?" Count Hallowbridge asks, his eyes roaming over the piled bodies.

"I believe so," I reply with a nod.

The count meets my eyes and swallows once. Twice. "And you killed them all?" I nod once and his eyes widen with the fear Freya should've shown. "So, the rumors are true."

"The rumors don't tell the half of it," I say. "Now, if you

don't mind, I'd like to get inside and clean up. Her Highness also needs proper medical care."

The count nods, taking a step back, seemingly happy to put distance between us. "Of course. My men will dispose of these . . ." He pauses, paling as he swallows, seemingly searching for the word that is least likely to make him hurl. ". . . bodies."

He turns to discuss something with one of the noblemen who came out and I pause before heading inside. I meet Ty's eyes and motion with my head toward the estate. He nods, looking from Freya to me and I nod. The message is clear. I need to talk to him and he'll find me as soon as he gets Freya settled.

I head inside and make my way to the servant quarters I've been given. I shed my clothes and use the wash bowl provided to wash away as much blood as I can. As I clean up, I check myself for injuries. Some decent bruises are forming on my sides and back, but I've had worse. I've slipped on a new pair of pants but haven't yet pulled on my shirt when Ty enters, clearing his throat. I snatch up my shirt and tug it on before turning to face him.

"No need to dress up on my account," he says, attempting at humor, but his weak smile quickly falls away. "Are you okay?"

I nod. "I'm fine, but, Ty, something is going on. Something not good."

"Yeah, Bash, I kind of figured that out when a cult tried to abduct my fiancée. At least I assume it was the cult."

"I'm sure it was. They were wearing the same masks as before. But that's not all. There's something potentially worse."

Ty shakes his head and sinks down on the edge of my cot. "What could be worse?"

"Use your magic."

Ty frowns up at me. "What?"

"Just use your magic."

"Okay," Ty says, holding out his hand. "I don't see what . . ."

He trails off, frown deepening as he stares at his hand. After a moment a weak flame flickers to life, disappearing into a wisp of smoke seconds later. Ty lifts panicked eyes to mine.

"What's happening?"

"Magic is weak. I don't know if it's something the *draíochta* put in place before their attack, but I doubt it. It doesn't feel like it's been tampered with. It could be the proximity to so many magic-using nobles watering it down. Or . . ."

"Or my father's dying. Really, truly dying," he whispers, his voice cracking.

I sink down next to him, pulling him against me. "Maybe not. We don't know enough."

Ty raises his tear-brimmed eyes to mine. "Magic is dying with my father, Bash. We've known that. We've been biding our time, and now the time is up."

"You and Freya will fix it. We have less than two weeks until the Fae moon. We get the crystal tomorrow."

Ty shakes his head. "Today. It's past midnight. We get it today and head out as soon as possible. This evening if possible."

"Are you sure?"

"We can't risk missing the Fae moon ceremony and if my

father—" His voice breaks but he recovers quickly. "If my father is dying, I should be there when he—"

"Of course. I'll make the arrangements."

I stand and Ty stands with me. We walk together through the servant halls, but when we go to split, Ty turns to me.

"Thank you for saving her, Bash."

"It's my duty."

"I know, but she means so much to me. I can't lose her. I already lost you and it hurt like Hell. I can't lose her, too. I wouldn't survive it."

My heart seizes. I wish I could tell him he doesn't have to worry about me always being there to protect her because I feel the same, but I can't. Instead, I manage a smile and nod.

"Anything for you."

Before he can say anything else, I turn and walk away as quickly as I can. I have plans to put into action.

CHAPTER THIRTY-ONE

TY

Every time I close my eyes I either see Freya getting kidnapped and murdered by the cult, Bash getting stabbed and bleeding out, or my father dying alone in a dark room, calling out for me. It doesn't help that every time I move the wound in my side aches even though it's not that deep. It bothers me a little less after I discard my sleep shirt so the bandages can breathe, but then I'm cold. Eventually, I give up on sleep and lie in bed, staring up at the ceiling until Bash comes in to wake me. I'm sitting up, blinking at him through bleary eyes before he's even two steps into the room.

"I take it you didn't get much sleep last night, either," he says with a sigh.

"Nope," I mutter, rolling my neck and scooting to the edge of the bed.

"I think I'll feel better myself once we get back to the palace." He heads over to the wardrobe and starts pulling out what I'm wearing for our temple visit. "I've made arrangements for body doubles to take your and Freya's places tomorrow morning while we leave tonight taking an alternative route."

"What? No," I say, sliding off the bed. "You can't use doubles for us. That puts someone else unnecessarily in danger."

He turns to me, his expression hard. "It's not unnecessary if it saves your life."

I shake my head. "I won't agree to it."

"You don't have a choice."

Anger heats my face as I clench my hands into fists at my side. "I'm your prince."

"You're my charge, and it's my job to do whatever it takes to protect you, no matter whether you like it or not," he says, refusing to back down. His expression softens a fraction as he adds, "It also protects Freya."

My anger dissipates, my shoulders slumping. Seeing her carried off last night was one of the most terrifying experiences, and I have no desire to relive it in any form.

"Look, Ty," Bash says with a sigh, "you and Freya have escaped capture, and likely death, three times now since leaving Rosana. Your luck is bound to run out eventually and I don't want to push it." His eyes fall to my bandaged side before looking back up. "You're already wounded. Next time it could be a killing blow. With magic being unpredictable . . ."

"I get it," I concede. "I don't like it, but I get it." I smirk at Bash. "You have to be the one to tell Freya."

"Nope," he says, turning and snatching up a shirt and handing it to me. "Your fiancée, your problem."

I slip the shirt over my head, careful to hide a small wince from Bash as the movement pulls at my wound. "Your plan, your problem."

Bash levels me with a look, which I return.

"Fine," he grumbles. "We can tell her together."

"Deal."

"Now, let me get a look at your wound. Don't think I didn't see you wince."

I roll my eyes but know there's no point in arguing. Several minutes later, Bash has checked and redressed my wound, and I'm downstairs guzzling as much coffee as possible. Freya arrives shortly after, practically collapsing into a chair.

"Here," I say, handing her a cup of coffee with sweet cream.

She cups her hands around the coffee and inhales its rich aroma. She takes a sip and looks up at me with a tired smile. "Thank you." She takes another sip and cocks her head. "You know how I take my coffee."

I shrug, not bothering to hide my smile. "I pay attention to things sometimes."

I take a seat beside her, sipping my own coffee. We sit in comfortable silence until Bash comes and lets us know our carriage is ready. The morning is foggy and cold, which seems a bit too foreboding for my taste, but I choose not to believe it's any sort of sign beyond bad luck in weather. The majority of the nobles will stay in bed until noon, most likely, so our travel party is only made up of the three of us and a handful of guards.

Given the threat made on our lives last night, Bash is allowed to ride in the carriage with Freya and I—or at least that's the excuse I use to keep him near. We explain our departure plan to Freya, and while she argues a little, she seems to understand the need for the rush and body doubles. We spend the rest of the couple hour ride to the Temple of the Divine in companionable silence, too weary for conversation. When we arrive, an elderly man, who I assume is the man in charge judging by his floor-length crimson and gold robes, and a group of acolytes dressed in black meet us at the gate.

"Welcome, Your Highnesses," the priest says, briefly bowing from his waist. "I am Father Malikin, head priest here at the Temple of the Divine."

"Thank you for allowing us to come, Father," I say as Bash helps Freya down behind me. "Your service to the kingdom in this time is invaluable, as you well know."

"We are happy to play our part, Your Highness. We have everything prepared for you, but we do ask that you leave your soldiers outside as our temple is a place of peace."

I glance over my shoulder at my escorts. Since these men were provided by the count and I don't know any of them personally, I honestly don't mind leaving them behind. However, given the current attacks, it seems unwise to throw all caution to the wind.

"Of course, but may I request that my personal guard accompany us if he leaves his sword outside?"

I gesture to where Bash stands. The priest eyes him for a moment, and I'm pretty sure he knows as well as I do even if Bash leaves his sword outside he still has a litany of weapons hidden on his person. I'm afraid he's about to decline, but instead he offers us a tight smile, inclining his head.

"Of course, Your Highness."

Bash hands his sword to a very timid acolyte and the priest leads us inside. I haven't been to many temples of my own free will. They always have a stuffy feel to them, and this temple is no exception. The walls are lined with floor-to-ceiling paintings depicting gods and saints, and it feels like they're all passing judgment on me. When we veer off from the main halls, it's a relief.

The priest unlocks a large oak door and leads us down a long, wide corridor lined with crystals on display in nooks along the walls. Many of them give off a weak glow, humming faintly of magic, while others seem little more than rocks. I wonder if they all once held great magic and are merely a hard-to-ignore statement on how magic is dying as we speak or if their magic was simply spent long ago and they now sit on display as relics. When we reach the end of the hall, we're greeted by another set of heavy oak doors, these guarded by two acolytes.

Father Malikin says something to them too low for me to hear, but the acolytes nod. They each pull crystals on chains from around their necks and take up positions on either side of the doors. It's only then I notice the crystal-shaped holes hidden in the intricate design carved around the edges of the doorway. They press their crystals into the notches, whispering what I assume are either prayers, spells, or both, and the crystals shine with a brilliant white light. Father Malikin steps forward, withdrawing a key from his pocket that looks like it was carved from another magical crystal, and inserts it into the keyhole. A loud, resounding click echoes down the hall, and he pulls the door open.

The room we enter doesn't look nearly impressive enough for the level of security, but I know that what's hidden here is more valuable than everything else in the temple combined. The walls stretch at least three stories to the full height of the temple, lined with shelves bearing locked wooden boxes and precious books. A few neat desks sit along the edges of the room, but the majority of the tiled floor remains clear and open.

But none of the other things matter, for it's what sits in the center of the room that is the most valuable. On a pedestal beneath glass, a stone the size of my fist rests on a pillow of deep purple velvet. My breath catches in my throat as I slowly approach the stone, drawn forward by its importance and the soft hum of its magic calling to mine.

According to pictures in record books and paintings decorating the palace, the crystal was once a brilliant blue, but years of ceremonies have stained it with a thick coating of golden Fae blood mixed with the red blood of humans. Even still, the crystal is beautiful, both everything I always imagined it would be and yet nothing like I expected.

"That's it?" Freya whispers, her voice full of awe as she steps to my side.

"I assume," I reply, not taking my eyes off the crystal as one of the acolytes who unlocked the room lifts the glass, placing the crystal, pillow and all, in a wooden box held by the other.

"This is Father Finnick," Father Malikin says, drawing our attention back to him. "He will be the one to perform your ceremony."

It's only then I realize there's another man in the room, dressed in deep blue robes. Standing next to Father Malikin he looks young, but I suspect anyone next to Father Malikin would look young. At a closer glance I notice graying strands in his brown beard and hair, but his face doesn't have any truly noticeable age lines. Yet, he still manages to have a wise look in his amber eyes. He could tell me he's anywhere from age twenty to fifty and I'd probably believe him.

"You aren't performing the ceremony?" I ask, addressing Father Malikin but keeping my attention on Father Finnick.

"Alas, my old bones do not do well with travel anymore,"

Father Malikin replies with a shake of his head. "Father Finnick is more than educated on the ceremony and the procedures needed."

"I have made it my life's mission to study and understand the histories and practices surrounding magic in Elodia," Father Finnick offers with a small smile.

I study both men for a moment before nodding. "Very well." I offer them my most winning smile. "Who am I to argue?"

"We may, however, need to discuss the best way to get you back to the capital safely," Bash says, stepping forward.

"Ah, yes, it has reached our ears the *cultas draíochta* is rising again," Father Malikin says.

"Unfortunately. They have already attempted multiple attacks." He glances over at the acolytes standing nearby. "Is it safe to discuss matters here?"

"There is no place as safe as the vault," Father Malikin says. "All here can be trusted."

Bash turns to Father Finnick. "We are using decoys set to leave tomorrow. I have already made tentative arrangements for a decoy for you to accompany those for their Highnesses. Would you be able to ride to the palace on your own and are you skilled in any weaponry?"

"To the first matter, yes, I am quite skilled in riding. I grew up riding horses from a young age," Father Finnick replies. "As for the second, I'm afraid my knowledge of any sort of weaponry, or any combat for that matter, is rather weak."

Bash nods once. "I will make sure you have a guard or two to accompany you to the capital via the most direct route. It would be best if you wore common clothes for travel and saved your robes until you are securely in Rosana.

If you could provide a spare set of robes for your decoy that would also be ideal."

"Of course. I can manage that."

"Now that travel is settled, I believe there is one more reason for your visit," Father Malikin says, motioning for the acolytes. They slide a long wooden box from one of the shelves and approach slowly. Father Malikin opens the lid and withdraws a slim crystal the length of my palm set on a gold chain.

"For you, Your Highness," he says, extending the necklace to Freya with a dip of his head.

Her eyes widen for a fraction of a second before she inclines her head and accepts the crystal. "Thank you."

She looks to me and I give her an encouraging nod. She swallows, hesitating a moment before she slips it over her head.

"It may take some time for your magic to activate," Father Malikin explains, "but you're welcome to try to call on it now, if you'd like. Magic is strong here, so it may help strengthen yours."

Freya takes a deep breath, closing her eyes. The crystal reacts to her inner magic with a soft, violet glow. She opens her eyes, holding out her hand. She furrows her brow in concentration and a moment later a couple water droplets hover above her palm. She wiggles her fingers and the droplets dance and twirl. A blink later and they're gone. She looks over at me and grins, eyes bright. Pride swells through me, and I'm tempted to pull her into a kiss.

"It bodes well for your match that you are already able to wield the magic," Father Mailkin says with a pleased nod. "And while Fire Magic and Water Magic may seem opposites,"—he nods to us each in turn—"history has shown that wielders of such magic often have high compatibility, so this is an excellent sign for your union as well."

My lips tip into a smile, and I reach and take Freya's hand in my own. She meets my eyes and warmth floods me at the gentleness in her eyes.

"We should get back as soon as possible so we can finish our preparations for our return to the palace," Bash says, clearing his throat and bringing me back to everyone else.

"Of course. We won't keep you any longer," Father Malikin says, inclining his head.

Bash leads the way out of the room and the priests and acolytes follow behind us, locking doors as needed. When we arrive back outside, we find Father Finnick's horse loaded and ready to go. With extra eyes on us, Bash takes a seat outside the carriage with the driver and his absence is keenly felt. I don't like not having him by my side. Freya must sense my mood and opts to sit beside me instead of across from me. As we ride, she rests her head on my shoulder, and at some point we relax enough we both drift off, sleeping almost the whole way back.

CHAPTER THIRTY-TWO

FREYA

Despite sleeping most of the way back from the temple, I'm exhausted most of the afternoon and through dinner. When Ty finally declares we're heading to bed because we have any early departure in the morning, I'm relieved. Of course, I don't actually get to go to bed since we're absconding into to the night in an attempt to trick the *draíochta* who want us all dead, but I think socializing is more exhausting than running away from a cult.

When I get to my room, I find a neat pile of clothes on my bed with a note on top written in sharp, precise handwriting.

I took the liberty of packing everything you needed for your journey or made arrangements to have things sent ahead. Put these on and use the back hallways to get to the stables without being spotted. Ty and I will meet you there.
—Bash

I've barely finished reading the note when my maid knocks on my door. I quickly hide the paper beneath the clothes and allow her in. If she thinks it's odd I only need her help unfastening everything and don't want her help getting into my night clothes, she doesn't show it. Once she's gone, I go to slip into the clothes Bash left and am startled to discover that it's not a dress like I expected, but rather a loose white shirt and a pair of brown breeches. Even the boots he's laid out on the floor are knee-high men's riding boots. It won't be the first time I've ever worn clothes like this—you don't grow up on a farm without donning pants at least a few times—but it's been ages. I dress quickly, relishing how comfortable this outfit is in relation to the clothes I've been wearing lately. I tuck my hair up under a hat Bash also left for me before I follow his instructions, slinking through the back halls until I find my way out into the crisp night air.

Once outside, it takes me a minute to orient myself, but once I do, I make quick time getting to the stables. Our horses are packed and ready to go, but no one is here. At first I think I'm either early or have the instructions wrong, but then Bash steps out of the shadows, startling me.

"Gods, Bash!" I hiss, my hand flying to my racing heart. "Are you trying to kill me?"

The corner of his mouth twitches like he wants to smile. "Actually, quite the opposite. Otherwise I'd be in bed right now instead of trying to sneak you to safety."

I huff, crossing my arms to fight against a breeze.

"Ah, here," Bash says, stepping forward and extending a dark cloak.

"I don't want your cloak," I say, shaking my head. "You need it."

This time his mouth does turn up a bit. "It's not mine. I got it for you but didn't leave it with your other clothes because I thought it might be easier to sneak out in fewer layers."

"Oh."

"See," he says, reaching over to his horse, withdrawing another cloak, and clipping it on. "This one is mine, and this one"—he steps closer, draping the first cloak over my shoulders—"is yours."

He carefully fastens the cloak under my chin and looks up to meet my eyes. His smile slips a little as he drops his hands to his sides, but he doesn't step back. He's so close I can feel his warmth. We haven't been this close since last night right after he rescued me. Right before he almost kissed me. Or at least, that's what I think he was about to do. And I think I might've kissed him back thanks to the emotional nature of the moment. I *almost* want to kiss him now. Thankfully, he clears his throat and takes a wide step back.

"So," I say, glancing to the horse, desperate for a distraction, "it looks like we have plenty of supplies."

Bash nods, rubbing the back of his neck. "Yes. I think the count may have felt a little guilty about the whole attack business and gave us a bit of everything. Clothes, food, money, you name it, we've got it. He even gave us a couple tents and proper bed rolls." His eyes drop to my arm. "We even have more bandages and medicine should we need them."

When he lifts his eyes back to mine there's a hint of something similar to last night there. I wish I could understand what it is.

"Bash, about last night," I start.

"What about it?" he asks a bit too abruptly, his body tensing.

I hesitate. Maybe I shouldn't bring it up again. Maybe I should let it lie. It's probably all in my overactive imagination.

"I only wanted to say thank you," I say instead. "I'm not sure I said it last night."

He looks surprised for a fraction of a second before he schools his features, giving me a sharp nod. "Of course. It's my duty to protect you."

Before either us can say anything else, bootsteps crunch behind us and we both spin to see Ty strolling our way through the dark.

"'Bout time," Bash grumbles, walking over to his horse and pulling out another cloak. He tosses it to Ty. "Put that on or you'll freeze."

"Doubt it," Ty says, but he fastens it anyway.

We waste no time mounting our horses. Bash leads us out via a small road that winds around the back of the property. We ride in silence, the sounds of night coming alive around us. It doesn't take long before exhaustion catches up with me and I'm nearly falling off my horse. We're probably two or three hours into our journey before Bash lets us call it a night. For the sake of time we agree to only set up one tent. Once it's ready, Bash checks Ty's wound and seems satisfied enough that the ride didn't do any further damage.

"I'll take first watch," Bash says, holding the tent flap open for Ty and I to enter. "Then Ty can take second."

"I'll take third, then?" I ask, fighting back a yawn.

Bash shakes his head and I glare at him. "I thought—"

"We won't be here long enough for three shifts," he cuts me off. "We'll need to be on the road in just a few hours. I want to be moving by first light."

"Is that necessary?" Ty asks around a yawn of his own. Bash levels him with a look and Ty raises his hands in surrender. "Fine." He turns to me. "Come on, Freya, let's get what sleep we can or it will be an exceptionally long day tomorrow."

It turns out even with the handful of hours I manage to sleep, the next day is still remarkably long. There's barely a hint of light when Bash wakes me up, thrusting a mug of strong coffee into my hands. I sip down the bitter drink while he and Ty pack up the camp. We're on the road a couple hours before our doubles would be. I say a quick prayer to the gods that they'll be okay. I really don't want anyone to die in my stead.

Our journey is monotonous, broken up by occasional stops so Bash can check Ty's wound and re-bandage it with more medicine. During one break, we pass around a flask of ale while we down some dried meat and crackers. We ride well past sunset, setting up only one tent again, but this time Bash lets me take first watch. Unfortunately, I barely make it two hours before I need to wake him.

The next day is a little better. Bash doesn't insist we start quite as early. According to him, we're making good time and should arrive at our next destination well before nightfall. A little before noon, our scenery turns into bright rolling grounds and farming country that makes me ache for home. Not much later a large estate appears like a speck in the distance.

"Wait, we're heading to Langsworth Manor?" Ty groans once we're close enough for us to make out the grand details of the main house.

Bash doesn't even bother looking at Ty as he replies, "Where else did you expect us to be headed?"

"I don't know, but there *have* to be at least a dozen other places we could stay."

"Not that meet the expectations for your tour while also providing enough variance and security to keep the *draíochta* at bay."

I glance between the two of them. "Why don't you want to be here? Is whoever lives here that bad?"

"No," Bash says, a hint of a smile on his lips, "they're just family."

I raise an eyebrow, looking at Ty. "Family?"

"Yeah," he says with a sigh. "Pretentious, pushy family. The Duke of Brexington is my father's cousin, and, even though he's a bloody duke for gods' sake, he still insists most people call him Prince Alexander." Ty delivers the title with a dramatic eye roll.

"Is he a prince?"

"Well, technically. If anything were to ever happen to my father's direct line—basically me—and my uncle were to die or pass on the throne, he'd be next in line. But it's so pretentious. Like take your dukedom and be happy with that for gods' sake, and definitely don't try to pawn your daughter off as a bride to her fucking cousin."

"And there's the real reason he doesn't want to be here," Bash says with a grin.

"His cousin?" I ask.

"Klarissa," Ty says, making a face.

Memories of some of the other noblewomen rise up and my stomach twists with nerves. Very few of them have been pleasant, and I hope Ty's reaction doesn't mean I'm about to receive more of the same treatment here. Especially not the kind of treatment that got me pushed off a cliff.

"She tried for a marriage contract?"

"Yes, well, her father did. I'm not sure how much she had to do with it. I highly doubt she was on board. There was some nonsense about keeping the bloodline strong by having her matched with me. Even though her blood is even weaker than mine, her father argued that our child"—Ty gags dramatically—"would have a better chance of having magical blood. Thankfully, that got shut down quickly by everyone."

By the time we ride up to the front of the estate, servants are already lining up outside to greet us. As we come to a stop, the door opens and out marches a man who is undeniably Ty's relative. I've only ever seen portraits of the king, but this man has the same general face shape and warm brown skin. He holds himself like a man who owns a kingdom, too. Honestly, he holds himself like a prince. Next to him stands woman with light brown skin and straight shoulders wearing a sharp expression. But I don't focus on either of them very long, my attention going to the elegant young woman who exits the house last. Her brown skin is a shade or two darker than Ty's, but she has the same golden-brown eyes, which are currently studying me a bit too intensely. I'm suddenly very aware that I'm still dressed in men's riding clothes and nothing near a formal dress. She, however, looks immaculate in rich blue silks, her dark hair twisted into a high bun and decorated with silver and blue gems that match the jewels adorning her ears and neck.

"Don't worry," Ty whispers as he helps me dismount, hands lingering on my waist longer than necessary. "They won't attack you in broad daylight, and they're too polite to say anything too rude to you yet." He winks at me and I barely hold in a laugh as he turns around.

"It's excellent to see you again!" he says a little too cheerfully.

"And you, my boy," the duke says in a tone that borders on belittling. "I've heard you've had a terrible time with assassins and whatnot. Thank the gods we run a tighter ship here."

Ty's grin is tight and false as he nods. "You have no idea how pleased I am to be here." Ty slips an arm around my waist, tugging me forward. "And I'm even more pleased to introduce you to Freya, my fiancée."

The duke's cheerful expression slips for only a moment before he clears his throat and forces the smile to return, bowing slightly from the waist.

"A pleasure indeed to meet you," he says, straightening.

"Dear," the duchess says, placing her hand on her husband's arm, "I imagine our royal guests would love to go inside and rest and refresh a bit before dinner."

"Ah, yes. Of course. We have additional guests, as you may know, joining us for dinner and you will want to be at your best. Your rooms have been prepared so you can rest as much as needed. A servant will come get you when it's time for dinner."

Ty nods and we start to move forward into the house when Klarissa steps forward, her eyes fixed on me.

"Actually, I was rather hoping you could meet me for a tea once you've had a chance to recover a bit from your journey." A lethal smile slips onto her lips and I find little comfort as she adds, "I think we have some things we need to discuss between just us ladies."

I glance quickly at Ty who is staring at his cousin with a furrowed brow. When I look back at Klarissa, she's clearly awaiting my answer. I force a weak smile of my own.

"Yes, of course. I look forward to it."

"Excellent. Now, let's stop dawdling on the steps like

traveling merchants and get indoors," she says, spinning on her heel and marching inside.

As we move to follow her, Ty leans over to whisper in my ear. "I don't know what she has planned, but I can send Bash with you."

I shake my head. "I'm sure I'll be fine." I look over at Ty. "I will be fine, right?"

Ty shrugs as we make our way up a large, winding staircase. "She's never killed anyone over tea before."

I'm about to ask if she's killed anyone any other way before when I notice the twinkle in his eyes. I elbow him as discreetly as possible and he chuckles.

"You'll be fine. As annoying as she can be, you can trust her."

However, his words of reassurance do little to calm my rising nerves.

CHAPTER THIRTY-THREE

FREYA

Unlike our previous stay, I'm treated like the soon-to-be princess that I am. In addition to immediately receiving a lady's maid, I'm given a full set of rooms including a sitting room, washroom, and bed chamber. There's even a wonderfully warm bath waiting with oils and soaps galore, and the moment I step out, my maid is ready and waiting with a warm towel and a fresh change of clothes. I vaguely recognize the dress as one that was given to me as a replacement for my lost clothes. I assume it was one of the arrangements Bash made, which makes me all the more grateful to him. I delay as long as possible, but eventually I call for a servant to take me to tea with Klarissa.

I try to make note of the long winding path we take, but I'm pretty sure I'm going to get lost if I try to make it back on my own. The servant takes me to a tea room situated at the corner of the estate. The walls and ceiling are made of glass, giving the same feeling as being in the actual garden surrounding the room but without the chill of the wind. A scattering of potted plants and blooming flowers add even more to the garden feel. In the center of the room Klarissa sits as a small table loaded with a decent selection of tasty delights on a tiered tray. A servant stands nearby next to a tea cart, ready to serve the tea.

"I hope I didn't keep you waiting," I say, easing into the chair across from Klarissa.

"Not at all. I've only just arrived myself." She waves her hand like it truly isn't a bother. "Please, do fill up your plate and enjoy as much food as you'd like. I know I fully intend to, and I don't even have the excuse of traveling for days."

She nods to the servant to fill our teacups as she places a couple tea sandwiches and some mini tea cakes on her plate. I follow her lead, trying not to seem overly eager at the mouth-watering delights.

"I hope you like this tea blend," she says, as the servant moves from filling mine to hers. "It's one of my favorites, made from some herbs from our very own garden." She twists in her seat to look up at the servant. "Thank you, Madeline, that will be all. We'll ring if we need anything else."

"Yes, miss," the servant says with a bow, setting the teapot next to a bowl of sugar and jar of cream on a small cart and leaving the room.

"Good, now we can talk properly." She glances at my plate and teacup. "Feel free to add whatever you want to your tea, and please, eat."

As if to punctuate her point she plucks up a small tea cake, popping the whole thing in her mouth. Despite the fact that shoving an entire cake, mini or not, in your mouth should be considered unladylike, she still somehow manages to look proper doing it. I add a touch of cream and sugar to my tea before obediently plucking up one of the tea sandwiches and take a small bite. My eyes go wide as flavor bursts across my tongue.

"Delicious, right?" she says, dabbing her lips with a cloth napkin. "Papa stole the chef from some other noble family—the Stoneswallows, I think?—and I've never been more grateful for anything in my life. Just wait until you taste the roast duck he's preparing for dinner. It will almost make up for the dull conversation of Penelope."

She rolls her eyes with disdain and I can't keep myself from asking, "Penelope?"

"Yes," she says, taking a delicate sip of her tea. "Lady Penelope Merriworth is the daughter of the Earl of Nexelby, and she is the drollest person you'll ever meet. Her parents aren't much better, if I'm honest, but since Penelope is closer to my age, we've often been shoved together at events and whatnot."

"That sounds . . . dreadful," I say, hoping my tone is correct even though I don't really understand her plight.

She sighs. "It truly is, but that's why I've asked you to this tea. I'm hoping you can help me."

My eyes widen with surprise. "You want me to help you?"

"Yes, well, it would be a mutually beneficial situation. I want you to bring me to the palace as one of your official ladies-in-waiting."

I blink at her a moment, eating one of the small cakes as an excuse to gather my thoughts.

"So you're not upset that I'm marrying Ty and you aren't?"

She barks out a laugh, nearly choking on her tea. "Gods, no! I have never been happier for one of my father's marriage plots to fail. You can have Ty all to yourself. Believe you me, I don't want him. Not in the slightest. I know him far too well. We might only be cousins—second cousins, actually—but we're barely two months apart in age and were treated very much like siblings from the ages of seven to fourteen. Let me tell you, once you've heard someone belch the entire first verse to our kingdom's anthem, it's really difficult to see them in any sort of romantic light."

"He belched the anthem?"

Her eyes brighten with mischief. "Yes, and he wasn't nearly as young as you are thinking. Go on. Guess."

"Nine?"

"Thirteen! He was thirteen, which isn't exactly the peak of maturity for young royals, but definitely old enough to know that doing it at a very formal ball wasn't the right time."

We laugh together for a moment before she sobers. "I know magic is in danger. I may not have strong magical blood or incredible skill, but I can feel how much weaker it is than normal."

She reaches out her hand and hovers her palm over one of the small potted plants near her chair. I wonder what she's doing until I notice the leaves quivering slightly before they twist upward, the stalk stretching slowly. After growing maybe two inches, it stops and Klarissa pulls her hand back with a sigh.

"I used to be able to make it come to a full bloom with little effort," she says, her voice weighted with sadness. She raises her eyes to mine and offers me a small half-smile that doesn't quite reach her eyes. "Honestly, I'm happy you've found each other, and not just for the sake of magic. I know I haven't seen you together much, but from what I've heard, you're good for each other."

I frown at her. "What you've heard?"

"I'm excellent at keeping my ear to the ground, following the gossip and rumors. Nothing ever happens here, so I have to live vicariously through everyone else. Which brings me back to my original proposition: let me join you at the palace. I know better than anyone how catty and atrocious the other nobles at court can be when they don't like you. I'll use my social talents to find out where any threats are coming from so you can avoid them and keep you updated on all the rumors surrounding you. I can even use my influence to sway things in your favor. I spent much of my childhood in the palace and know its social politics like the back of my hand."

"What's in it for you? I mean, surely you aren't offering to help me out of the goodness of your heart, no offense."

"I think, perhaps, offense should be taken." She laughs. "But, no, you're sharp. I like that about you." She takes a sip of her tea. "What's in it for me is that I get away from Langsworth Manor in the middle of nowhere Brexington. I get to go where things are actually happening. Better yet, it gets me out from under my father's thumb. Just because his attempt to get me to marry Ty failed doesn't mean he doesn't have dozens of backups, far too many involving dodgy men twice my age. I want a chance to live my life on my own, to find my love match, if such a thing exists, and, if things go well between you and me, maybe I can even make a new friend. So, what do you say?"

I consider her for a moment. "When would you come?"

"I would need to pack and take care of a few things here, but I could easily join you in Rosana in a week or two."

I hesitate a moment, but there's not much to think about. Having an ally could be useful. I shrug, offering her a smile. "I honestly don't see why not, so sure."

She squeals, clapping her hands together once. "I knew you'd be reasonable. Thank you, Freya. You have no idea what this means to me." She regains her composure, straightening in her chair. "Now, in exchange for your kindness and cooperation, I will regale you with stories of Ty from childhood."

She grins wickedly over her teacup, and I lean in closer to make sure I catch every word.

CHAPTER THIRTY-FOUR

TY

Freya is spending far too long at tea with Klarissa. Any time I've been trapped into any sort of luncheon, tea, or event with her, I've always found a way to escape as quickly as possible. But for some unknown reason, Freya has been gone for close to two hours now.

"Stop pacing or you'll wear right through the floor," Bash says with a sigh from his chair in the corner.

At least one perk of being here is that Bash doesn't mind sticking closely. Probably because everyone here knows all of our history, and because he knows all the secret servant pathways in and out of every room so he can move about without being spotted.

"I'm concerned," I retort, crossing my arms and glaring at Bash. "Honestly, you should be more concerned as well. Freya's life could be in danger."

Bash rolls his eyes. "I highly doubt your cousin—"

"Second cousin."

"You didn't call her that when her father wanted you to

marry her, but fine, *second* cousin, is out to murder your fiancée. If anything, Klarissa is warning Freya away."

My eyes widen as fresh new horrors present themselves. "That's worse! You see how that's worse, right? What if they become . . . friends?" I shiver dramatically for effect.

"Would you feel better if we went and waited in Freya's room so you know the second she returns? That way you can interrogate her immediately."

"Yes!" I say, pointing at Bash. "That. Let's do that."

Bash blinks at me. "I was kidding."

"Well, I wasn't. Come on. Let's go."

Bash sighs and pushes up from the chair, mumbling something under his breath that sounds treasonous. The hallway is clear and we make it to Freya's room without being spotted. I make myself comfortable on Freya's fainting couch while Bash wanders around, surveying the rooms.

"Freya has a jar of biscuits next her bed," he calls from the bedroom. He pokes his head out, holding up what looks like a rectangular shortbread biscuit. "Why don't you have biscuits in your room?"

I shrug. "I don't know. Maybe they're poisoned biscuits and they're trying to take her out quietly while leaving me alive."

"Nope," Bash says, his voice a little muffled by the biscuit he just shoved in his mouth. "Perfectly fine."

"You have crumbs on your shirt."

He looks down and brushes the crumbs off his chest before glancing over his shoulder. "I'm going to try another one to make sure they're all safe."

I bite back a smile as Bash disappears into the bedroom. I'm about to call out to him to bring me one when the door opens. I jump up off the couch and Freya, who clearly wasn't expecting me, lets out a startled gasp, her hand flying over her heart.

"Ty! You scared me!" She steps further into the room, shutting the door behind her. "What are you doing in my room?"

"I'm checking on you," I say, striding across the room, hands clasped behind my back. "Bash is here, too."

As if summoned, Bash steps out of the bedroom, munching on another biscuit. Freya raises an eyebrow at him and he shrugs.

"Your room has biscuits," he says. "And Ty wouldn't shut up about needing to check in on you."

"I wanted to make sure Rissa didn't eat you alive," I add defensively.

Freya scoffs at my concern. "She was actually quite pleasant." A smile curves on her lips. "She had all sorts of stories to tell."

My eyes widen in horror. "You can't believe a word she said!" I cry out frantically, waving my arms as if I can erase everything Klarissa shared from Freya's memory. "She's a pathological liar. It's a problem. We're considering ways to find her the help she needs."

Bash chuckles, stepping to my side. "You can believe every word she said."

The traitor. I smack his chest with the back of my hand, glaring at him.

"I'm sure she embellished, at the very least," I amend, offering Freya a smile to override the less than charming memories Klarissa shoved into her brain.

"So the thing with Lady Darkmeadow's cat . . . ?"

"Was an accident. How was I supposed to know fur caught on fire so quickly? Cats should be more fire retardant than that. Besides, he was entirely unharmed and the fire was put out before the poor creature even realized it had been aflame."

"And the Earl of Braxberry's shoes . . . ?"

"Were that way when I found them."

"And I'm sure you didn't actually belch the anthem at a very formal ball?"

I grin. "Now that one I'm proud of."

She rolls her eyes, walking away from me, but I follow her.

"Do you know how much work it took to be able to belch the entire first verse while carrying a tune? It's not my fault the sparkling wine was the best way to achieve the effect I wanted so I had to wait for a formal event to sneak some."

She looks over Bash who lifts a shoulder in a half-shrug.

"It was relatively impressive."

Oh, so now he's back on my side. Freya seems less than impressed, however, shaking her head and turning back to me.

"Either way, I had an enjoyable tea, and you have no reason to worry."

"I have plenty of reason to worry if Rissa is sharing my deepest, darkest secrets," I mumble.

"I would like to rest now, so if you don't mind, leave."

She gives me a playful shove. I glare at her, mouth opening to protest, but Bash steps forward, tugging me toward the door before I can get a proper word in. I grumble the whole way out, but the last thing I see before the door closes is Freya smiling at me affectionately. Maybe Klarissa actually did me a favor.

Tonight's dinner is the absolute worst and we're still only in the pre-dinner drinks portion. Okay, maybe that's a bit of an exaggeration given what happened at the first dinner on our tour, but the way that Freya and Klarissa are practically attached at the hip has my nerves acting up. Every time Rissa leans over and whispers something in Freya's ear that has them both looking over at me in pure glee has me wanting to rip Freya away and find some sort of magic that erases memories. Since this is a formal affair, Bash has been regulated to hiding in the shadows and isn't even in the room to defend me. But the worst part is that with Rissa and Freya smooshed together in a corner gossiping, I'm left chatting with the Earl of Nexelby and his daughter Penelope, who are possibly two of the most boring people in the world. When we're called into the main dining room, I can't escape their company fast enough.

Unfortunately, during dinner I don't fare much better. Even though Freya is given a seat next to me, Klarissa is on her other side, allowing the gossip and lies to continue. Fortunately, the dinner is less cozy, forcing us all into conversations with everyone at the table so the worst of the Ty-bashing has to at least pause a bit. Unfortunately, that includes not only the Merriworths, but also Lord and Lady Stillweather and Lord Gillington.

"So, Freya," Lady Stillweather says, leering at Freya over her wineglass. "How are you adjusting to life beyond peasantry?"

I tense, ready to come to her defense, but Klarissa is the first to speak.

"I believe she should be addressed as Lady Freya at the very least—Lady Brambleberry if we're being truly proper."

She pauses, looking over at Freya. "That is your current last name, isn't it? Brambleberry?"

Freya nods. "Until I marry your cousin, that is."

Lady Stillweather inhales sharply at the reprimand, her eyes going cold as she looks between Freya and Rissa. "I wasn't aware she was a proper lady, given she was likely born in a barn."

"Actually," Freya says, her voice dripping with lethal sweetness, "I was born in a farmhouse. They're quite different, but I assume you've not traveled enough to know that, despite the fact you look more than old enough to have gotten some travel in."

I manage to keep from laughing, but I have to hide my grin behind my wine glass.

"Well, I never!" Lady Stillweather exclaims, her face turning red.

"To answer your question—at least I assume it was a question, even though you didn't phrase it as one—yes, she should be addressed with the title of Lady," I jump in. Lady Stillweather turns her ire to me, and I meet it with a charming smile. "Her entering into a formal engagement with me was enough to raise her status. Actually, as my fiancée, she outranks you, so I believe you should actually call her 'Princess Freya'. Hmm. Yes, I like that. Address her that way from now on."

Freya's cheeks take on a delightful pinkish glow, but she's smiling softly. Klarissa is grinning like a cat. Lady Stillweather's eyes widen and I think she's about to burst a blood vessel when the duke cuts in.

"Lord Stillweather, how go things in your province? I heard it's turning out to be a good year for wine."

Everyone seems settled by the shift in conservation, so I

don't fight it. Besides, I am a little interested to find out how the wine harvest is faring. The rest of dinner passes without much more trouble, which is boring but overall good. As we're leaving the dining room for more drinks, Klarissa insists that us young adults take ours together in a separate room. Given the near disaster at dinner, no one objects. Of course that means Penelope is tagging along.

"Don't worry," Klarissa whispers conspiratorially to Freya as we head into the drawing room. "Penelope is such a light-weight. One glass and she'll be out cold."

As we settle around the room, Klarissa heads to a drink cart in the corner and withdraws a couple bottles of champagne from buckets of ice and holds them up.

"Tonight we're celebrating!"

"Celebrating what?" Penelope asks, her face pinched in an ugly scowl.

Rissa rolls her eyes, motioning to me and Freya with one of the bottles. "Them, obviously."

Penelope frowns. "But—"

"If you're going to be a spoil sport, head over and join the adults as they pass their judgments. We, however, are cele-brating!"

A loud pop sounds through the room as Rissa removes a cork from one of the bottles. Penelope flinches and a small laugh escapes me before I can stop it.

"And you can come into the room, Bastion," Rissa calls out as she pours champagne into flutes. "I know you're out there, and the way you're slinking about in the shadows is practically shameful."

Before she's even done speaking, the door creaks open and Bash slips inside, eyes twinkling. Penelope seems prop-erly disgraced to be joined by a servant, but if Freya's surprised Bash has been allowed in, she doesn't show it. A few moments later, we each have a glass in our hands and we're celebrating away. True to promise, Penelope doesn't last past the first round, drifting off in an armchair in the corner. The rest of us keep at it until both bottles have been drained, as well as some other spirits we find in the drink cart. The further into the night we go, the more childhood secrets we spill—some of them even Rissa's—but eventually the late hour and alcohol catch up with us.

CHAPTER THIRTY-FIVE

FREYA

After-dinner drinks are a delight once Penelope falls asleep, but it quickly becomes clear that Klarissa and Ty can outdrink us all. By the end of the evening only Bash and I are sober enough to walk in a straight line, though Ty definitely seems worse off than Klarissa.

"I'll go find someone to help the girls to their rooms, if you can get Ty upstairs," Bash says with a sigh.

I look over at Klarissa and Ty in the corner where they're giggling over literally nothing. At least this time he's drunk because of too much fun and not because he was trying to avoid something or drown out the world.

"Do they do this often?"

"Often enough for there to be protocol in place."

I sigh and push up from my own chair. I'm a little tipsy, but I stopped drinking long enough ago that I'm mostly sober.

"Fine. I'll meet you upstairs."

It only takes a moment for us to wrangle them, and soon

I'm tripping up a back staircase with Ty's arm slung over my shoulder.

"I've been in love with you for, like, ages," Ty slurs.

I chuckle and his forehead scrunches as he frowns.

"No, I'm serious, Frey."

"Right. Ages as in a couple weeks?"

He shakes his head so hard he almost topples over, taking me with him. We're only saved by the wall to our right, which we slam into hard enough to send the air whooshing from my lungs.

"Don't you remember the first time we met?"

Now it's my turn to scowl. Of course I remember. One, it wasn't that long ago, barely a couple years. Two, you don't forget royalty inviting themselves into your town and life. Three, we just discussed this a few days ago.

"We were nineteen." He pauses. "Well, *I* was nineteen. Just turned it. You were seventeen."

I nod. "I remember. I was forced to have my blood tested by a stranger and then a meeting was arranged between us. I was incredibly nervous, but when we finally met, it didn't even matter. You took one look at me and frowned. You muttered something under your breath to your guards and stormed from the room. You left the next morning."

Ty licks his lips. "Yeah." He grins, tilting his head. "You do remember."

I roll my eyes. "Obviously. We've already had this conversation, remember?"

"Yeah, I know, but you need to know that's when I started falling in love with you. I didn't really tell you that before. You were so pretty and . . . different. Yes, different. You weren't like the girls back at court. It was refreshing."

"You stood there staring at me. You barely spoke a word

to me. No, you *didn't* speak a word to me. You just spoke in my presence."

"I know. I know. I was stupid. And mad. I still had this idea that I'd somehow get out of an arranged marriage with a stranger and I'd get to be with Bash. Still thought you were pretty."

"Thinking someone is pretty doesn't equal love, though." We come to a stop outside his room, and I shift his position so he can lean against the wall while I open the door. "Come on. Let's get you into bed."

"No!" he yells, his eyes meeting mine desperately. He shakes his head, clutching his hair in frustration as he staggers back. "You don't get it." He stumbles to the wall, pressing his forehead against it. "I wasn't in love with you yet, but I was falling. Oh yes, Frey, I was already plunging off that cliff headfirst into love, even if I didn't realize it yet."

He sighs and sits down on the floor, leaning back against the doorframe.

"We didn't just up and leave you, you know," he continues after a moment, tilting his head up to look at me. "We left people behind."

"Yes, you left a few soldiers to blend into the village for my protection. I know." I sigh and lean down, grabbing his arm and pulling him to his feet. "You need to get into bed."

"Yeah, and a couple others to watch you and report back."

I feel like a cold bucket of water has been dumped over my head, and I freeze halfway through the doorway. "What?"

Ty nods. "There was a girl about your age. She was supposed to be your friend and make sure you were okay. Like really, really okay."

My stomach plummets. Only one girl befriended me around that time. "Cora?"

Ty's eyes widen and brighten as his grin returns. "Yes! Coooooora." He sighs contentedly, closing his eyes as he leans his head against the doorframe. "She would write me letters and tell me all about you. Even though you were so far away, I got to know you. As much as I hated you, a piece of me fell for you so hard that I knew there would never be anyone else for me. Well, other than Bash, but we know how that worked out."

I struggle to process his words. Cora and I were close. So close. Closer than close. To know that she was only that close to me to spy on me hurts. It really hurts.

"I was so jealous of her. She got to be with you and dance with you and touch you. Meanwhile, I was trapped in the palace."

I swallow hard. "She told you everything?"

Ty's eyes blink open and he frowns. "I'm sure she kept some details to herself. She only shared enough that I could get to know you."

I nod, trying to think of what to say next. Thankfully, Bash chooses that moment to return so I'm saved a reply.

"Bash!" Ty cries out, a sloppy smile on his face.

Bash looks at me and cocks an eyebrow. "Did he somehow get drunker while I was gone?"

I shrug, trying to act causal, but something must show on my face because he stiffens, his brow furrowing.

"Are you—"

"Let's get Ty to bed," I say, cutting him off quickly and walking further into the room.

Bash studies me for a moment but slowly nods. He hoists Ty up from the ground and slips an arm around his waist, directing him to the bed. Ty flops back on the mattress, fully clothed.

"You should at least take your boots off, you heathen," Bash mutters.

Ty laughs. "I love you, too, Bash."

"I know, Ty. I know."

Bash helps Ty unlace his boots, but I can't be in the room any longer. I also don't want to go to my own room yet. Instead, I stay outside Ty's closed door, my arms wrapped around myself thinking about Cora. She wasn't technically my first kiss, that was Matthew Hornway, but she was the first kiss of significance. She was a lot of important firsts. I wonder how much of our relationship was a lie.

"He'll have a headache in the morning," Bash mumbles as he slips into the hall, closing the door behind him.

He turns and takes me in. Under his caring gaze, my lip trembles and a tear falls free. Without a moment of hesitation, he crosses to me in two quick strides, gathering me into his arms.

"What happened, Freya?" he whispers into my hair as I dissolve into his chest, craving the comfort and security he offers.

I can't seem to find an answer. I clutch his shirt and sob while he traces gentle circles on my back.

"What I can do? How can I help? Please, let me help you."

After a moment I manage to compose myself, and I draw back to look up at him. He lifts a hand and tucks a loose strand of hair behind my ear.

"Did Ty say something? He can be a rambling fool when he's happy-drunk. You shouldn't pay him any mind."

"Did you know about the letters?"

Bash's scowl deepens. "The letters? What let—" His eyes flash with recognition and he takes a step back, raking a hand through his hair. "*Those* letters."

"So you know about the letters from Cora?"

He nods slowly.

"What did they say?"

He shrugs, shaking his head. "I never had any interest to read them. All I know is that Ty hoarded them away from anyone else. I was honestly gone most of the time he was receiving them. I do know he reread certain parts."

"What sorts of parts?"

Bash shakes his head, turning away. "I . . . just things like your favorite color and your favorite flower." He turns back to me. "I remember one of the first letters mentioned how you loved almond cake with strawberries, which also happens to be Ty's favorite. He went on a ridiculous rant about that as if you daring to like the same cake as him was some sort of travesty or insult."

His expression softens and he takes a step back toward me. "But the letters never said anything bad or invasive that I know of. Is that what you're worried about?"

"It's stupid," I mutter, wiping a tear away with the back of my hand.

"No," he says quickly, reaching out and taking my hands. "Nothing that upsets you like this is stupid. You can tell me what's wrong if you want."

"Cora and I were . . . close. *Very* close."

He holds my gaze, waiting for me. I see the moment it clicks, his mouth forming a small "o".

"You were lovers." I nod. "And now you're wondering how much of that was her and how much of that was Ty pushing her to get to know you."

I nod again, a strangled sob escaping.

"I don't know all the minute details of the arrangement, but she wasn't asked to do anything but casually befriend you. Ty would never have asked her or pushed her to get closer to you than she would have on her own. She was simply placed in your village to be near you. Any relationship beyond friendship you formed would have been her own decision."

"You can't really be sure about that, though. We only met because of Ty."

"How you met didn't necessarily affect your relationship. You and Ty were forced together and now you love him, right?"

I swallow and manage a nod. "Yeah, I suppose."

"See," he whispers. "It was real."

"But—"

"No more," he cuts me off gently, pulling me toward my room. "Get some rest and in the morning when Ty is sober, you can talk this through with him. He's the one who read the letters and who knows exactly what was said and the details of the arrangement."

I sigh and allow myself to be led to my room. Bash opens the door for me but doesn't enter himself. I hesitate a moment in the hall before sighing and stepping into the room.

"'Night, Bash," I say wearily, exhaustion catching up with me as I turn to him.

He smiles softy at me, hesitating only a moment before leaning forward to brush a kiss on my cheek. "Goodnight, Princess."

A smile twitches on my lips at the nickname.

He turns to leave but pauses, looking over his shoulder at me. "I wouldn't stress too much about it. I'm sure Cora really loved you. She would have been a fool not to. I can't imagine how anyone doesn't fall in love with you. It's impossible to resist."

I've barely processed his words before he's gone.

CHAPTER THIRTY-SIX

BASH

I open Ty's door with a bang. He swears, shooting up in bed, only to lie back down immediately with a groan.

"Could you be a little quieter, please," he mumbles.

"Nope," I yell, throwing the curtains wide open so plenty of morning light floods the room.

He swears again, wincing as he drapes his arm over his eyes. "Surely I'm not needed for breakfast yet."

"You were needed for breakfast five minutes ago," I counter. "Now get up, get dressed, and go apologize to Freya."

That has his attention. He sits up, swinging his legs over the edge of the bed.

"Why do I need to apologize to Freya?"

"You don't remember?"

He shakes his head slowly, his face scrunched as he thinks last night over. After a moment he sighs, scrubbing hand down his face. "I mentioned the letters, didn't I."

Even though he's not really asking a question, I nod. He frowns, shaking his head.

"But why would that upset her?" I arch an eyebrow at him, and he looks away sheepishly. "Okay, I know it's a *little* invasive, but nothing was ever said that was overly personal or anything."

"That's what you need to tell her when you apologize for being invasive." He opens his mouth to argue but I cut him off. "Get out of bed and dress so she doesn't have to suffer through breakfast alone, giving you something else to apologize for."

Ty groans but slides from the bed without further argument. Despite his protests, I check his wound, and I'm pleased to see that it's healing nicely. Another day or two and it will be little more than a faint scar, if it scars at all.

While Freya and Ty enjoy their breakfast, I pack and ready our horses for travel. The day is a little on the cold side, but it won't be bad weather for traveling. We're able to get on the road fairly quickly, keeping a decent pace. Things seem a little awkward and stiff between Ty and Freya, leaving me to believe they haven't had a proper conversation yet, but I suppose they haven't had much time alone yet. Hopefully they'll find time soon because I'm not sure how long I can stand the tension between them.

DESPITE MAKING GOOD TIME, WE DON'T QUITE REACH OUR next destination before night falls. We make quick camp, setting up only one tent and taking turns for the watch. The next morning we get on the road quickly, arriving our destination a little before noon. Freya and Ty are immediately whisked inside while I'm barely allowed to dismount my horse. When I try to enter through the servants' entrance in the back, I'm stopped by tall man with a hawk nose and wire-rimmed glasses.

"Where exactly do you think you are going?"

I straighten and look the man in the eye. "I am with His Highness, part of his personal guard and serving as his valet."

The man hums. "Indeed. Well, your services are useless here. We will make sure that His Highness is properly cared for. We have secured additional guards, many sent by the palace, and have procured His Highness the most highly trained valet available. Lord Maxinburg will provide His Highness the best of the best while avoiding any and all impropriety and scandal."

I grit my teeth, biting back my retort. Sometimes I forget how much disdain people have for me. They overlook my years of training and experience in service, choosing only to remember the gossip and my most recent employment.

"Perhaps I can come inside and at least set my bags down where I'll be staying?"

"Regrettably, the manor is currently overloaded by very important guests and their servants, and we haven't room inside to spare," he says in a tone that doesn't sound regrettable at all. "I do believe there may be a spare bed in the stables, however. Feel free to check there."

The slight is more than obvious. He means to offend. Part of me wants to fight it, remind him that I work directly for the crown prince and therefore I technically outrank him, but I don't. Even as I glare at him the fight leeches away, disbelief and anger fading into acceptance. I'm tired and this man doesn't deserve my energy. I straighten, shifting my bag on my shoulder, and storm away. When I get to the stables, it takes me a minute to find the stable boy. He can't be more than twelve, thirteen at the oldest.

"I was told I was bunking here," I say, startling the boy as he tosses hay to the horses.

He spins around to face me and his eyes widen in obvious fear. He stumbles back a step and manages a nod. I sigh.

"Have you ever plotted against the king or any member of the royal family?"

I didn't think it was possible for his eyes to get any wider, but somehow they do as he shakes his head so violently he almost tips over.

"Have you ever supported any cause that promised harm against the king or any member of the royal family?"

He shakes his head again.

"Do you ever intend to do either of those things?"

This time he manages a weak, "No, sir."

"Good. Then you have absolutely no reason to fear harm from me, unless of course, you're foolish enough to attempt any harm to me directly."

The boy relaxes a little but doesn't seem entirely reassured by my words. At least he no longer looks like he might shit his pants.

"Now, I've had a long journey and would like to set my things down and maybe sit a bit myself. Could you please direct me to where I'll be staying the night?"

The boy mumbles something incoherently but when he shuffles away, I follow him. He leads me to a sparse backroom that has a tiny bed in one corner next to a table and a small cot shoved along the opposite wall. I sigh and turn to the boy.

"I take it that's mine for the night?" I ask, nodding to the cot.

The boy starts to nod, but pauses, swallowing audibly. "Unless you'd rather have the bed."

"The cot is fine."

The boy watches me as I cross the room and toss my things down onto the cot. When I turn back to him he flinches. Is this truly my future? Disrespect from heads of households and fear from stable boys?

"If you have work to do, don't let me keep you from it."

The boy needs no further encouragement to scurry off. I sink down on the cot and attempt to rest, but it's pointless. Even as tired as I may be from constant travel, I can't just lie here and do nothing. It was made clear I'm not welcome inside the house, but that doesn't mean I can't at least make sure things outside are safe. I spend the remaining hours until nighttime exploring the grounds, satisfied enough that Ty and Freya are indeed safe. Once darkness falls, I stick closer to the house. At one point I pause outside what I assume is the dining hall, taking in the shadows crossing in front of the glowing windows. I wonder which silhouettes belong to Ty and Freya. I feel like I should be able to tell, but even though I have a decent guess, I can't be completely sure.

I sink down onto a lone bench. Tonight is a stark reminder that their lives are separate from mine. Now that we're closer to the palace, the real world is sinking back in. My purpose has been almost entirely served. I've protected my prince and his fiancée. Soon they'll be safely back inside the walls of the palace, surrounded by guards and soldiers sworn to protect them. I am superfluous. I only need to finish the journey and get them home. What happens to me next?

Before I had purpose. I was Ty's right hand and then his someone. He now has all the king's guard and Freya. Then I was his protector from afar, hunting down the members of a cult that were out to end him. Maybe I should go back to that. If this trip was any indication, they are still far too strong. Even though I managed to take out many significant players and disassemble their system to some extent, there is much left to be done.

Resolve sinks into me like a stone. I cannot be with either of them in the way I long to, but I can protect them. People fear me because I am a killer, so I will kill. Once we get back to the palace and Ty and Freya are bonded and wed, I'll leave. That will be my place. That will be my purpose.

CHAPTER THIRTY-SEVEN

BASH

Dark clouds roll through the morning sky as I make my way to the main house. We'll need to be on the road soon if we're to outride the storm. I weave my way through the crowded hall and find the dining area where a take-and-go breakfast has been prepared for the serving staff. Several people eye me with wary disdain as I help myself to some toast and eggs, washing them down with some lukewarm tea. Once I'm done, I hunt down the head of house, who I've come to learn is called Mr. Fredricks, cornering him in one of the bustling servant hallways.

"Since I'm not allowed to tend to my charges," I say to the frowning man, "I'm sure you'll make sure they're ready to go within the hour."

"I most certainly will not since they are staying another day."

I go very still and even this fool of a man can sense he's on dangerous ground. He looks nervous for a moment before he straightens to his full height, staring me down defiantly.

"A storm is coming, severe by the looks of it, and I will not be responsible for sending His Highness out in it."

I'm on the verge of informing him I was planning on getting ahead of the storm instead of delayed by it when a familiar voice carries down the hall over the cacophony of servants.

"You *will* find Bastion Shamblefoot immediately."

I dodge around Mr. Fredricks and head toward Freya's voice but stop short at the corner. Freya is standing at the bottom of the stairs leading down from the main house, her face set in a scowl.

"I'm sorry, my lady," a servant says, wringing their hands, "but you aren't permitted—"

"I'm not permitted to what? Ask after my own servant? To step foot in the servant halls? Please, do tell me, your future queen, what I am and am not permitted to do in this house. I would *love* for you to tell me."

I bite back a smile as the servant stammers a reply I can't make out from this far away. Whatever they say, however, doesn't seem to calm Freya in the slightest, her eyes flashing her frustration. Before she can unleash any more fury on the poor help, I step forward. Her eyes fall on me and her shoulders sag with relief.

"There you are," she says when we're close enough to talk without yelling. "We were worried."

"I'm fine," I say, coming to a stop in front of her, the servant she was talking to bustling off. "Are you and Ty okay?"

Her smile is tight as she nods. "We're fine, but we were told we wouldn't be leaving today?"

"Yes, Your Highness," Mr. Fredricks says, stepping to my side and inclining his head to Freya. "We thought it would be best—"

"I don't remember addressing you," Freya snaps, leveling him with a glare. "In fact, I've grown quite tired of your meddling."

"Your Highness—"

"I am not done speaking, and you will not interrupt me. In fact, is there a place where I could speak to Bastion without your constant hovering?"

Pride swells through me at her commanding tone and the way she has this dull man sweating before her. She may not think she's cut out for palace life, to rule, but she's fierce and protective and everything Ty needs in a queen.

"You may use my office, if you'd like, but—"

"I would, yes."

The man's shoulders tense for a moment before he surrenders, motioning for us to follow him down the hall. He leads us to a small, cluttered room off to the side, holding the door open for Freya and giving me a nasty look as I pass inside as well.

"I will be right down the hall," he says, his voice indicating it's as much a warning as anything.

Freya gives him a sharp nod, and he goes to leave, shooting me one last look of disdain before he closes the door, leaving it open a crack. As soon as he's gone, Freya spins to me, her entire body relaxing.

"Are you really okay?" she says, her voice just above a whisper as her eyes frantically scan me over. "We haven't seen you or heard from you since arriving. He won't admit it, but Ty is worried. He almost stormed the servant quarters himself when you didn't show up last night."

The corner of my mouth twitches up into a small smile. "Mr. Fredricks is just an ass. I was instructed that you and Ty had been given 'proper servants' for your stay and then I was relegated to the stables."

Freya scoffs. "As if his staff is—Wait, did you say you've been relegated to the stables? What does that mean?"

"It means I've been given a cot in the corner of the room with the stable boy," I say, trying to keep the bitterness from my tone.

Freya's eyes flash. "Bash! That's entirely unacceptable! I'm going to—"

I catch her elbow as she turns to storm out, a laugh escaping me before I can stop it. She twirls back around to face me and I release my hold.

"Why are you laughing? The way they're treating you isn't acceptable."

I shrug. "I can't say I'm not used to it."

There's something in her expression I can't quite read, but it's some mix of concern and indignance with what is more than likely pity.

"Bash, you are worth more than ten of them, and don't you forget it."

I open my mouth to protest, but she plows forward, shaking her head.

"No, you told me before the ball that everyone wanted to be me, that they were jealous, but I think these people want to be you. No, no listen! You are right hand to the prince who will one day be king. He cares for you and often treats you as his equal. They want to bring you down a notch and crush you below their boots because they want what you have. You are amazing and skilled and you deserve better than how they treat you."

She's so fervent and I can tell by the fire in her eyes she means every word. My breath catches in my chest and my heart beats so fast I'm almost afraid it will break free. The urge to kiss her is almost overwhelming, and I find myself moving a step closer to her without ever having made the conscious decision to do so. I stop myself, closing my hands into fists at my sides to keep from reaching for her.

"Thank you," I say softly, not trusting myself to say more.

"It's all true," she insists. "And what is this with them undermining you, saying we aren't leaving today?"

"Ah," I clear my throat. "They feel it best for us to wait the storm out."

"Is that what you feel is best?"

"My plan was to ride out ahead of it, but I won't deny waiting it out is an option."

"Do we have time for that?"

I sigh. "Technically? Yes. There are six nights until the Fae moon, so we have a couple buffer days and only one necessary stop between here and the palace. I would be more comfortable heading out in case something like, oh, I don't know, an attack along the road occurs, but . . ."

I trail off with a shrug that I hope seems indifferent. I don't want Freya to make any more of a fuss than she already has and get her into trouble. She seems satisfied enough by my answer and glances over her shoulder with a sigh of her own.

"Well, now that we know you're alive, I should probably head back upstairs and suffer with Ty." She turns back to me with a groan. "I swear every noble within less than a week's riding distance is here and most of them are extremely tedious."

"I'm sorry," I say, managing to keep my smile under control, but I'm sure my eyes give it away.

Freya scoffs, hitting my arm playfully as her own eyes twinkle. "No, you're not." She sobers little, cocking her head to look up at me. "But you are *sure* you're okay?"

"Yes." I give her a reassuring nod. "Especially now that I've seen you."

Freya's lips part slightly at my boldness before they tip into a soft smile. "Good." She walks toward the door, pausing once it's open to look back at me. "I'll make sure you're taken care of and treated with the respect you deserve. We miss you, Bash."

"I miss you, too, Princess."

She gives me one last smile before she disappears into the hallway, and it's all I can do not to follow her.

CHAPTER THIRTY-EIGHT

TY

Thanks to the weather, I'm forced to endure another full day with the most pretentious and tedious people alive. Lord Huckleberry has a full twelve-point plan to "revitalize" the kingdom's tax program, and, thanks to our delayed departure, I'm stuck listening to the entire thing laid out in excruciating detail. At least I feel slightly better off than Freya, who gets stuck in multiple conversations detailing ball gowns and teatime etiquette. Don't these women care about anything else? When thunder rolls over so hard it rattles the windows, however, I'm grateful to be indoors and not potentially caught in the storm.

I should be talking things over with Freya, but somehow every time we have a moment alone, I can't bring the conversation forward. She doesn't seem overly eager to broach the subject either. I suppose it might have something to do with all the people hovering around us, picking apart our every action. I know we need to talk, but now just doesn't feel like the right time. So instead of discussing things like two

"

proper adults, we spend the day and evening in awkward, stilted conversations, avoiding prolonged eye contact.

When morning comes, we rise early, which has the advantage of giving us a head start to our day before most of the nobles have even thought about rising. We ride under heavy cloud cover across thick, muddy streets. I wonder if we waited long enough for the storm to pass, but we don't reach the drizzling, windy weather until mid-afternoon. With our combined magic, even as weak as it is, we're able to combat the annoying drizzle for a while, but when lightning starts flashing in the sky followed by crashes of thunder, I'm more than eager to be off the road.

"Keep your eyes open for shelter," Bash instructs, like I haven't been doing that for the past half hour. "A farmhouse would be ideal, but even good tree cover could work. We have our tents, but some shelter from the worst of the storm and wind would be ideal."

However it's neither of those things we end up spotting, or rather, that Freya ends up spotting. It's a meager little building in the center of a field that looks one good wind away from being a heap of rubble. Without a variety of other options, we ride toward it. Bash seems pleased to discover there's also an overhang that's been built on to protect the horses.

"Looks like a shepherd's shed," Freya says as we step inside the drafty building.

"A what?" I ask, looking around, though there's not much to take in. It's one open room with nothing but a few blankets piled in one corner, a locked chest in the other with a cracked lantern on top, and a pile of wood next to a dusty fireplace.

"A shepherd's shed," Freya repeats. "It's not uncommon

for farmers and shepherds to set these up in case they get stuck away from the main house and barns overnight or in storms like this one."

I kneel next to Bash who is already stacking wood in the fireplace.

"Think you can light it?" he asks, looking over at me.

I swallow. Can I? I take a deep breath and extend my hands, palms out. I pull on my magic and after a few tries, flames roar to life. I sink back on my heels with relief, but when I grin up at Bash, he's not looking at me. His attention is focused out the rattling window.

"Bash?" I say, pushing up from the ground. "Everything okay?"

He offers me a tight smile and a nod. "I think I'm going to go make sure the horses are secured and get them properly situated. Then I'm going to survey the area for any threats. I want to be sure potential attackers don't take advantage of our circumstances."

"But the storm," Freya starts, her brow furrowed with worry.

Bash's smile is a little more sincere when he turns to Freya. "It isn't here in full force yet. Better to check it all now than to wait until it's too strong and regret it." He looks back to me. "I plan on being thorough, so I might be a little while."

His meaning sinks in. *Talk to Freya.* How he knows I've been avoiding the whole thing in the hope it magically goes away, I'm not sure. Then again, he really does know me better than anybody. He gives me one last heavy look before slipping out into the howling wind. I turn to Freya, nerves twisting in my stomach.

"We should . . ." I trail off, motioning vaguely to the area in front of the fireplace.

Freya nods and we sink down together in front of the flames. For a couple minutes, neither of us speak, the silence heavy.

"Freya, I—" I say at the same time she says, "Ty, about the —"

We both laugh and she waves for me to go first. I clear my throat, looking into the flickering fire to avoid her eyes.

"Bash told me I mentioned the letters the other night and that it upset you."

"I—Yes. Did he say why?"

I shake my head. "Only that we need to talk." I force my attention to her. "I'm sorry if you felt like I invaded your privacy through the letters. It was never meant to be that."

"No, that's not why I was upset. Not really. It's more complex than that. I just . . . What exactly did you instruct Cora to do?"

I frown as I study her. She's worried about something, but I can't quite figure out what.

"I honestly don't remember the details, but in essence Cora was asked to stick close to you in a casual way and to get to know you, to build a friendship."

Freya nods, chewing nervously on her lip. "And she was your idea?"

"Not exactly. It was Klarissa's idea, so if you really hate the whole thing, feel free to blame her." Freya gives me a look and I sigh. "Rissa meant well. She thought you might need a friend of sorts in the chaos of your life suddenly changing and it wouldn't hurt for her to share the details of that friendship so I could get to know you little by little as she did. The soldiers were there for your protection, but Rissa said they were unlikely to be reliable when it came to knowing anything about you. She was very against us leaving you in your village and believed that us keeping our complete distance wouldn't do anyone any good. She insisted I should do something to get to know you so we wouldn't be complete strangers when we finally married."

I scoot a little closer to Freya, my knee bumping hers. She stays silent, her eyes fixed on the fire.

"I was against the idea, but not because I felt it would have been unfair to you. I thought it was unfair to me. I didn't want to get to know you or to like you. I was still mad at the world, but Rissa dug in her heels, going as far as to find Cora herself and sending her to you. When the letters first started arriving I was furious. I even burned the first one. I only opened the second because Bash insisted. I barely scanned it over, but it was enough for you to become more than a girl I briefly met once. You became a person, a living, breathing person who I was going to marry."

I reach over and take one of Freya's hands in mine. She startles slightly, finally looking at me, but she doesn't pull her hand away. Feeling encouraged, I continue.

"Sometimes I read the letters in anger. I looked for your flaws in their lines, but there were very few to find. More often than not, reading the letters calmed me down. As much as I hated to admit it, they did connect me to you." I trace my thumb across her knuckles as a small smile pulls on my lips. "They broke down my walls and, even though I was still fighting it, created a path to where I am today. I am sincerely sorry if they upset you."

"It's not the letters themselves that upset me," she says, her voice small.

"Then what is it, Freya?" I ask, gently taking her other hand. "Let me know what I need to do to make this right. I will do anything."

She takes a slow breath, her chin trembling as she holds back tears.

"Freya, please."

I'm aware I'm begging. I don't care.

"I need to know that Cora was never instructed to be more than my friend."

I frown. "What do you—" Her meaning becomes clear and I straighten, my eyes widening as I furiously shake my head. "No, Freya. No. I would never. Rissa wouldn't either. I swear it. If there was anything more than friendship between the two of you, I had nothing to do with it."

She relaxes a little, drawing a shaky breath. "Okay. Thank you."

"If you want to talk about it, about her, I'll listen," I say, pushing aside the jealousy that threatens to rise.

She's quiet a moment before she speaks again, her voice barely louder than the wind outside and the crackling fire. "After our marriage was arranged and you left, I felt lonely, rejected. Then Cora arrived and I thought maybe I could have a chance at happiness, even if it could only be temporary. It all started like you intended as friendship, but then we grew closer. We became so much more."

Despite my best efforts, jealously spikes in me, but I stay silent. It's not like I was celibate during that time.

She shifts but leaves her hands in mine as she looks back into the fire. "I felt guilty at first, knowing she and I could never stay together, knowing I would never marry her because I had to marry you. I told myself probably much the same as you did when it came to Bash—that another solution would be found." She sighs, raising her gaze to meet mine. "I guess we were both a little foolish."

My mouth cocks up into a smile. "Perfectly matched." My

smile falls as I tighten my grip on her hands. "As envious as I am that someone else got to be with you, I'm glad you had that little bit of happiness. If it helps at all, there was never any indication in her letters you were more than friends. She protected that part of your relationship very well. I'm sorry if I inadvertently hurt you."

"It hurts to know she was only there because of you, but it helps to know that at least her affection toward me was genuine."

I swallow, the next question on my tongue. I have no right to the answer, but some part of me needs to know.

"Did you love her?"

Freya's eyes widen a moment before her whole face softens. "Maybe. I don't know. I don't think I was ever in love with her, if that makes sense, but I did love her in a way. People don't really fall into bed together over and over if there's not some sort of feelings there."

I choke on a laugh. "That's never been a problem for me." Freya frowns and I barrel on. "I've slept with dozens of people, and I can truly say I only ever felt anything for one—well, two now—of them. You and Bash, if that wasn't obvious. Despite longing for a soulmate-level relationship, I didn't need any sort of emotional connection to someone to find sex satisfying."

"You didn't feel anything for any of them?"

"I felt physical attraction," I say with a shrug. "Most of them I actually hated beyond what they could offer in bed. Think for a moment about the ones you know about. Do you really see me falling in love with a single one of them?"

She pauses for a moment, her head tilted in thought. "No, I suppose not. I mean, when I first arrived, they fit with the version of you I had in my head."

"Ouch."

She laughs. "But now that I know you, no, I don't see you caring for them."

"Good. I did feel a little guilty stringing some of them along, but I never pretended to be in love with any of them. I made it very clear that it was sex and nothing more. I fucked them and then left immediately following. I didn't even stay to clean up."

Freya opens her mouth, like she wants to speak, but closes it, shaking her head.

"What?"

"No, never mind."

My stomach swoops unpleasantly. I've screwed up, I'm sure. Maybe I've said too much, and I shouldn't have brought up my flings and affairs.

"You can say whatever is on your mind. I want you to know you can always be open with me. You can call me a whore or whatever you want."

Her brows scrunch together as she frowns. "I would never call you that, Ty. You're not a whore simply because you find pleasure in sex with people."

"Even though we were engaged?"

"It was a technicality, an arrangement we had little to no part in. I won't begrudge you for what you did then. No, I was only wondering if . . ."

She trails off mumbling so low I can't make out what she says.

"What was that?"

Her cheeks color and she looks down at her lap. "I was wondering if after we marry whether you'll eventually miss the casualness of sex, the no-strings part of it. If you'll one day regret being tied to me, and it will all become little more than routine and obligation."

"Never," I insist, not even waiting a beat. "I love you, Freya. The sex I had before with all those people was empty and meaningless. It temporarily satisfied an itch and nothing more. You fill me and complete me. Being with you is a joyful experience I crave. I can never be satisfied enough by what you offer. Those people before you? They were crumbs jumbled together that didn't even equal a full bite of a meal. But you, Freya? You are a seven-course feast.

"My day doesn't truly begin until you're in my sight and my day ends the moment you disappear behind your own bedroom door. Having you by my side every night, waking up to you beside me, will be the culmination of everything I have ever wanted. You, Freya, have become my happily ever after."

A tear escapes and I cup her cheek, brushing it away with my thumb. She smiles, leaning into my touch.

"You're mine, too, Ty."

I inhale sharply, leaning in to kiss her before I can talk myself out of it. Her lips crash into mine as she meets me halfway. This isn't the first time we've kissed, but there's something different about this kiss that hasn't been present before. It's more than need and lust and want. This kiss is a promise, wiping way everything else. It's me and Freya and the rest of our lives.

CHAPTER THIRTY-NINE

BASH

When I return to the shed, Freya and Ty are snuggled together under a blanket in front of the fire. I smile to myself. They look peaceful and happy, and even though that hurts a little, it still somehow makes me feel lighter knowing they'll be okay. I don't have long to relish in that comfort however, before our peace is disturbed by men in black masks crashing through the windows. I instantly have a dagger in each hand, but before I can cut them down, two of them have crossed the room to my charges. One immediately has Freya beneath his blade and the other has Ty.

"Move another step and they're dead," a voice snarls behind me.

I spin and come face to face with a man that should be dead, a man I killed. His sharp blue eyes cut into me as his mouth, or what's left of his mouth beneath a jagged scar, tips up into a cruel smirk.

"You can't be here," I manage, my voice coming out too unsure. "You're dead."

The man's laugh is cruel. "Clearly, I'm not, but they might be soon."

He nods to Freya and Ty behind me. I cheat my body enough that I can see them out of the corner of my eye but keep my focus on the man in front of me.

"Let them go. Let them go, and I'll do anything. This is between you and me."

"Begging is beneath you, Bastion," the man says, clicking his tongue as he walks further into the room. "They've made you weak." He looks past me to his men. "Kill them."

A scream rips from my throat as both men slice through the flesh on both Ty and Freya's necks. Their eyes go wide with terror as they drop to the floor, crimson spilling down across their clothes.

"You have minutes to save one. Who will you choose?"

Panic overwhelms me as I rush forward, but I freeze, hovering over their bodies. I can't choose one if it means losing the other.

"Will you choose the prince, the heir to the throne, the man you love? Or will you choose the pathetic peasant girl who somehow managed to worm her way into your heart?" he mocks. "Choose quickly, Bastion, or you'll lose both."

No. NO. I can't lose them. I can't. I can't . . .

"Bastion! Bash!"

The world around me is shaking. No, I'm shaking, or rather something is shaking me.

"Bash, wake up!"

I gasp, sucking in air as I open my eyes to find Freya's face inches from mine. I bolt upright, my heart pounding so hard each beat chokes me. My hands are shaking as I reach for Freya, placing one palm on each of her cheeks as my eyes flick frantically over her. One hand slides to her neck where there should be a long slice, but there's nothing there but clear skin.

"Bash?" Ty's voice comes from behind me, filled with uncertainty.

I twist to face him. He's as close as Freya, sitting next to me on my other side, his bleary, sleep-filled eyes blinking at me in confusion. I shift so I'm facing him and I proceed to check him over as well. My rough fingers trace along his neck and across the sharpness of his collarbones back up over his throat. I can feel his heart fluttering beneath my fingertips. He's alive. *He's alive.* They both are. It must have been a dream. A nightmare. They're fine. They're *fine.*

All the fight and panic leeches from me and I fall back on my heels as my breathing steadies. A cool hand touches my cheek and I look up into Freya's concerned eyes.

"Are you okay?"

I swallow. Am I okay? No. I am definitely far from okay. I shake my head, unable to form words.

"Hey," Ty says, scooting closer to me and draping a blanket over my shoulders, his hand lingering on my shoulder as he tugs me against him. "We've got you. It's okay."

Freya shifts beside me and suddenly she's pressing a skein of water into my hand. Almost entirely on instinct, I lift it to my lips and gulp the water. By the time I've drained it, I'm coming back to myself. Ty's steady hand on my shoulder helps ground me as I close my eyes and draw a deep breath, releasing it slowly. After a few more breaths, I feel calmer, opening my eyes.

"I'm sorry," I manage, my voice hoarse and weak.

Freya offers me a small smile that doesn't reach her eyes. "There's no need to apologize."

I clench my teeth, the muscles in my jaw twitching as I hold back another apology.

"What time is it? Did I wake you?"

Ty glances over his shoulder toward the window. "My guess is that it's a little past midnight."

I nod, processing the information. "I did wake you."

"It's fine. Really," Freya says, her voice gentle but firm. "Do you want to talk about it?"

I take one more deep breath, running a hand through my hair.

"It's nothing. Just a nightmare."

"That was more than a nightmare," Ty counters, his hand tracing soothing circles on my arm. "I've never heard you scream like that Bash." His hand stills. "It . . . I can't . . ."

He sounds so broken. So scared. Shame burns my cheeks. I can't look at him or Freya.

"We're okay, Bash," Freya says softly, leaning forward to brush a quick kiss on my cheek. I raise my eyes to meet hers and nearly melt under the compassion and understanding shining there. "Whatever you saw in your nightmare wasn't true."

"Freya's right," Ty says, giving my shoulder a squeeze. I turn and meet his eyes. He forces a weak smile, but I can still sense his worry. "We're okay."

I relax and release another long breath. They are fine. They're not dead or hurt. They aren't bleeding out while a maniac demands I choose between them. He's not here. He's dead. He has to be. I killed him. I remember the metallic smell of his blood, the sticky feel of it on my hands. His blood. Not theirs. Not theirs. *Not theirs.*

"I . . ." I shoot to my feet, startling Freya and nearly knocking Ty over. "I need air."

I barely make it outside before I retch up the contents of my stomach. I wipe my mouth with a shaking hand before I dry heave, stomach muscles clenching in protest. I brace one hand against the wall of the shed as I breathe slowly in and out, heavy rain pouring down on me. I should get back inside, but instead I lift my face to the rain, letting it careen down my face. It's cold and wet and it brings me to the present. I stand there another moment, letting it thoroughly soak my clothes. When I finally stumble back inside, I find Freya heating water over the fire while Ty is playing with a deck of cards.

"Feel better?" Freya asks, offering me a smile as she digs through her travel bag.

"What are you doing?" I hedge, avoiding the question.

"Making tea," she says like it's the simplest thing in the world.

I stand just inside the doorway, blinking at her in something close to awe as she puts tea leaves in three travel mugs.

"Do you need sugar?" she asks, removing the kettle from the fire and pouring steaming water into each cup. "It was nice of Klarissa to make sure we had proper tea supplies before we left."

Ty snorts, shuffling the cards with a flourish I taught him. "That would be her concern. Tea."

"Fine," Freya says. "Then you don't get any."

Ty sticks his lip out in a petulant pout. "I didn't say I didn't want any."

"Sure sounded to me like you didn't."

"Come on, Freya. I was kidding."

Freya attempts to hide her smile as she looks back up at me. "So, sugar?"

"I, uh . . ."

"He takes it black and plain, like his coffee," Ty answers for me, dealing the cards into three piles. He hesitates, looking up at me with half-cocked grin. "Still true, right?"

"Yes." I shake my head. "I'm sorry, what is happening right now?"

"I'm dealing cards for Backhanded Jack and Freya is making tea. Oh, did Rissa send any of those little tea biscuits?"

"I see that, but why?"

"Yes, she did, but you don't get any because of your bad attitude," Freya says, deliberately ignoring me as she stirs sugar into what I assume must be Ty's tea given the excessive amount.

"I was joking."

"Mm-hm."

Freya walks over and hands me a mug. I cup my hands around it, absorbing the warmth. She hands a second mug to Ty before fetching the third mug for herself along with a tin of biscuits, which Ty practically snatches from her hand as she takes a seat on the floor across from him.

"You should probably join us now," Ty says, shoving a biscuit in his mouth, "or I can't guarantee any biscuits."

Ty looks up at me expectantly. I stare down at him in awe before I start laughing uncontrollably.

"Bash?" Freya says, a hint of her previous concern creeping into her voice.

I keep laughing as I sink down between her and Ty next to a stack of cards. Despite my laughter, tears flood my eyes. When Freya goes to reach out to me, I wave her off. When I finally catch my breath, I wipe the tears from my cheeks.

"Feel better?" Ty asks.

I manage a nod. "Yes."

"Good," Ty says, rolling his shoulders. "Now prepare to lose, because I am going to wipe the floor with you."

"Wrong," Freya counters, her forehead pinched as she studies and adjusts the cards in her hands. "I'm going to win."

I chuckle, looking over my own cards. "You're both wrong." They look over at me and I grin. "Because I never lose."

Ty's laugh almost startles me, but I'm held steady by Freya's bright eyes. Without another moment of hesitation, the game begins and soon we're all caught up in laughter and frivolous fun. Outside the rain continues pounding against the shed while the wind rattles the windows, but inside we are warm and safe. In the morning we'll be exhausted, but right now I'm happier and more at ease than I've been in a long time. I sincerely hope I can snag more nights like this before I disappear again.

CHAPTER FORTY

FREYA

We get on the road a little late, but given we didn't get back to sleep until nearly dawn, we needed the rest. Even now, riding under a bright, clear sky, no hint of last night's storm remaining beyond the muddy roads, I can't get Bash's screams out of my head. I can't imagine ever forgetting the wild look in his eyes when he first woke up or the way his panicked, trembling fingers trailed over my skin as he made sure I was okay. Even Ty was clearly surprised by Bash's nightmare, and his panic was palatable when we were first trying to wake Bash. It terrified us both, and I will do whatever I can to protect Bash from that kind of pain ever again.

We pause around midday to eat some lunch, Bash going as far as to spread a blanket out across the soggy ground for a picnic. He insists it's so we don't arrive muddier or more disheveled than we already are, but I think he's trying to capture some of that same casualness and camaraderie we shared last night. I'll admit, it feels nice not to rush for a change. Once we get back on the road it doesn't take long before the towering estate of some duke comes into view in the distance, whatever casualness there was dissolving into stiff formalities and general chagrin. Maybe once Ty and I are officially wed and bound, he, Bash, and I can travel a bit and see the kingdom without all this added stress.

When we come to a stop in front of the house, we're greeted by the normal line of well-manicured staff and our hosts. The man who steps forward is striking with bright blue eyes and graying blond hair. Despite his bright smile, however, there's something about him that seems uncomfortably familiar. Something that has me wanting to get away from him as soon as possible.

"Your Highness," the duke says, inclining his head. "I'm glad to see you finally made it."

The slight is obvious, but Ty doesn't take the bait, snapping on one of his most charming smiles.

"I am quite sorry for our late arrival, but the storm delayed us a bit."

"No matter. No matter," the man says in a tone that says it is indeed a matter. "I'm glad you're here now. Shall we get you inside so you and her ladyship can refresh a bit from your journey? It looks like it was quite taxing."

Another slight, I'm sure, but Ty takes it in stride as well, falling into step beside the duke as we're guided inside.

"I'm afraid my dear Cressida isn't able to be here, but I do have another guest who is eager to see you."

Cressida. The realization crashes down on me in full force. That's why this man seems so familiar. He looks just like an older, male version of Cressida, the girl who literally pushed me off a cliff. He must be her father or an uncle.

"Such a pity," Ty replies, his tone dry. "I'm sure I'll see enough of her when I return home."

"Indeed." The man's eyes take on an almost evil glint. "I suspect you'll see both of us a good bit as I intend to join her soon. Given all the changes happening, the queen believes my presence may be helpful."

Ty's eyes flash but before he can get in a word, the duke waves it off.

"We can discuss everything later. For now, please, recover from your journey and join me for drinks in the drawing room when you are ready. It will be a delight to entertain both of you."

Glad to be rid of the duke, Ty and I ascend the large staircase, following a servant meant to direct us to our rooms. We walk in silence, but questions and concerns flood my head. Ty is dropped off at his room first and then I'm directed to a room a good way down the hall. A maid arrives a moment later to point out some of the features of room, including a handful of formal dresses sent from the palace. She helps me change into fresh clothes before leaving with a bow. With her gone, I feel like I can breathe again, looking around the room. I've barely had time to take in everything before the door is flung open and Ty strolls inside wearing fresh clothes of his own.

"Something is up," he says, slamming the door and dropping sideways into a chair with his legs slung over the armrest.

I cross my arms and glare at him. "I could have been changing."

He looks over at me with fresh interest, a smirk curling on his lips. "Pity you aren't. Please, if that's what you intended, don't let me interrupt."

I roll my eyes, biting back a smile. "I've already changed."

His eyes flick over my new dress and he shrugs. "I

wouldn't mind if you feel the need to change again." He sits up in the chair, swinging his legs around so his feet thump on the ground. "I'm more than happy to help."

My cheeks warm and I turn away to examine books on the nearby shelf.

"What were you saying when you barged in?" I ask, pretending to study the book titles. "You think something is going on?"

"Ah, yeah. That. You heard the things he was saying, right? About joining me at the palace and things changing?"

"Is that surprising information?" I ask, turning to face him.

He sighs and shrugs, sinking down in the chair. "Not really. He's always been the kind of man to stick his nose where it's not wanted and things are changing, but lately he avoids the palace, sending Cress there in his place. I guess it's hard for him to manipulate my father when he's too ill to chat."

"Is Cressida his daughter?" I ask hesitantly.

"Oh, yeah. I guess you wouldn't have necessarily known that. Cressida Vanderhof is daughter of Lionel Vanderhof, the Duke of Brookeshire, where we are now. It's one reason she acts so entitled. Her father is one of the highest-ranking men in the kingdom, and his land is within spitting distance of the palace. She can have breakfast here, pop in a fancy carriage, and be in Rosana by dinner, bugging the hell out of me. Of course, she has rooms at the palace, so she often stays there anyway."

"Will I have to worry about her father pushing me off cliffs?"

Ty chuckles. "I doubt it." His smile falls away as his brow furrows. "The duke is far craftier than that, which is why I'm concerned. He's planning something or he's in on something. I just know it."

Before Ty can elaborate on his conspiracy theories, a servant comes to the door, fetching us for drinks. Ty doesn't seem overly thrilled, but he mutters something about snakes being easier to handle when they're close and offers me his arm. When we step into the lush drawing room, my eyes go immediately past the duke to the other man in the room, my blood running cold. Ty doesn't seem to notice and steers me toward the two men, a false smile plastered on his face.

"I'm glad to see you looking refreshed after your journey," the duke says, stepping closer. "What would you like to drink? I have some excellent brandy that is truly delightful."

"That would be fine for me. Freya, would you . . ." Ty trails off as he turns to me, finally sensing my mood. He follows my gaze to the other man who's watching me with a shadowed expression, his mouth twisted into something that's not quite a smile.

"Ah, how rude of me not to introduce you," the duke says, his glee barely concealed. "Though, I'm sure you've met at least once or twice, Your Highness, given your current circumstances, but perhaps you've merely forgotten. This is my good friend Lord Grayson Mayberry, Earl of East Hingling."

The earl inclines his head, stepping forward. "It's an honor to meet you again, Your Highness."

Someone else says something, but I barely pay attention over the beating of my heart and the ringing in my ears. When the earl turns his full attention to me, I unconsciously take a step back. The warmth of Ty's hand as it presses gently but firmly against the small of my back steadies me slightly, and I lean a little closer to him.

"Remind me where we met before? I'm afraid I don't recall." Ty chuckles depiste the stiffness of his posture. "I meet a lot of people."

The earl dips his head, his smile tight and his eyes gleaming. "Perhaps it would help if I reminded you of what land I hold? East Hingling rests in the far northeast of your kingdom and is flush with farmland. It produces some of the best wares that even the palace finds . . . enticing."

His eyes settle on me and I fight the urge to squirm. Ty still doesn't quite grasp what's happening.

"It does sound familiar, now that—"

He freezes, his hand pressing harder into my back as realization hits. His previously cheerful disposition, fake or not, vanishes in its entirety.

"We met briefly when we passed through the first time I met Freya. East Hingling is where she's from."

The earl's grin widens, showing off sharp teeth. "Yes, indeed, Your Highness! As I said, my land has produced the best of the best, even so much it was deemed fit for the palace."

"I'm sorry, I'm sure I'm misunderstanding your meaning, but it does seem you are implying that the woman I love is little more than imported property."

Ty's voice drips with venom as his hand slips around my waist, drawing me closer. The earl has the audacity to laugh.

"If you don't wish to see it that way—"

"I don't see it that way because it isn't that way. By implying it is that way is to make my fiancée and your future queen a thing rather than a person, and such insubordination will not be tolerated. It is treason."

"Now, now," the duke cuts in with a chuckle, thrusting a

glass of brandy into Ty's free hand. "I'm sure Lord Mayberry meant nothing by his statement."

The earl's smile sharpens. "Naturally." He turns to the duke. "Before we were joined by their Royal Highnesses, you were telling me about your latest trip to the south. Perhaps you could regale us all with your tale?"

"Of course! I would be happy to continue." He pauses, turning to Ty. "If that's all right with you, Your Highness."

Ty nods once, his hand gripping his glass so tightly I'm afraid he may shatter it. "Please do."

As the duke launches into his story, Ty leans in, dropping his hand from around my waist.

"Are you okay?" he whispers, his lips barely moving as his eyes stay trained on the rambling duke.

I swallow and manage a nod. The earl narrows his eyes in our direction, and I force a tight smile, pushing down the nerves twisting my stomach.

"We'll talk later," Ty whispers, his hand finding mine. "I promise."

I squeeze his hand and hold on for dear life.

CHAPTER FORTY-ONE

TY

I tell myself all through dinner that slitting the Earl of East Hingling's throat is too kind of a way to end his life, which is the only reason he's alive by the end of it. Well, that and the fact Cressida's father is obviously waiting for me to fuck up. Maybe I shouldn't have threatened his daughter. Oops.

The duchess also joins us for dinner, but she looks bored out of her mind. Freya still attempts some conversation with her, and I can't hold in my smile when the duchess relents a little and even seems to enjoy talking to her. It's only a bonus their conversation ruffles the duke's feathers.

Once dinner has ended, the duchess sashays away, and Freya mentions turning in for the night. I'm about to suggest the same, hoping maybe I can sneak into her room for a bit, when the duke claps a hand to my shoulder and suggests we take after-dinner drinks to discuss things between us men. Freya assures me she'll be fine, but I escort her into the hall and make eye contact with Bash hidden in the shadows. One look is all it takes for him to follow her upstairs.

"It seems your tour has been rather interesting," the duke says, settling into his chair with a glass of whisky on the rocks.

"I suppose. It did start out with my carriage being ambushed after all," I say, taking a seat across from him with a glass of my own.

The duke arches an eyebrow. "I heard it started with your bride-to-be disappearing with your guard and a disastrous dinner with Lord Longfellow."

I take a swig of my drink to keep myself from immediately snapping his head off.

"It seems you have your facts a little confused."

"Oh? I have it from a very reliable source."

"Not so reliable it seems."

"So Lady Freya and your guard didn't vanish together while visiting Netherfield?"

I shake my head. "No. They stepped away from the main crowd for a bit to chat with the baron's son, but they were well within my eye line the entire time. My guard, Bastion, did grow up on the baron's land, you know."

Even though it's the truth, it's bitter on my tongue, but I can't let the duke know.

"I do remember something to that effect now you mention it."

"The dinner, then," the earl jumps in, leaning forward in his chair. "What about that? Even as far away as I was I heard about the disaster that took place."

"Some mistakes were made on the part of everyone in attendance," I say, struggling to keep my voice steady.

"Everyone?" the duke says, his eyebrows practically touching his hairline. "Even Lord Longfellow himself?"

"And his wife and son and, yes, everyone." I throw back

my glass, draining the contents. It burns but I manage to hold back my wince as I set the glass on the table next to me. "It seems I've finished my drink, so if you'll excuse me—"

"Wait, wait," the duke says quickly as I go to push up from my chair. "We don't have to discuss the tour and its disasters. We can discuss your plans for when you get home to the palace."

There's a glint in his eyes that tells me he has an agenda. He's leading this somewhere, and I feel like it's important to follow. I settle back in the chair but refuse another glass when offered. I need to keep my head clear.

"Do you still plan to go through with the bonding and marriage ceremony when the Fae moon arrives?" he asks, twirling the glass in his hand so the ice clinks.

I frown. "Of course."

"Even with your father as he is?"

Fear clenches my heart, stilling it. "My father?"

"Yes, given your father's updated condition, I would think you would rush to marriage with a farmer's daughter with a little less haste."

His eyes are too bright and his smile too strong. He knows something, and it irritates me he's holding it back as some sort of sick leverage. He wants me worried and flustered and guessing, but I am the crown prince, damn it. I will not be strung about like one of his puppets.

"Speak plainly," I say, my voice level and cold.

The duke's cheer flickers for a second before returning as he says, "Your father's recovery is astounding."

The air in the room thins and I struggle to catch a breath. "His recovery?"

"Had you not yet heard?"

He knows damn well I haven't heard, and I almost want

to lie in an attempt to wipe the smug smile from his face.

"News has been few and far between from the palace since my tour started," I say, opting for honesty.

"Ah, then I am pleased to share the good news. You father is up and about again. Not consistently and not every day, but he's leaving his bed, even if he stays mostly to his rooms should a spell overtake him."

I swallow. Hard. "You heard this from who? Cressida?"

He laughs. "No, dear boy. I *saw* it for myself. I visited myself very recently, returning home only two days ago in anticipation of your arrival."

My heart pounds in my ears as I try to make sense of his words. Not only is my father recovering, he's entertaining at least the occasional visitor. This means I don't have to be king yet. Relief washes over me. I have time. I don't have to rush things. It's not so dire. Magic is . . .

Magic is failing.

I reach for my own magic, not to bring forth a flame, but to test it. It's barely a whisper. I reach deeper and manage to grasp hold of it, but it's weak, a flickering heartbeat.

I stare down the duke, but there's no tell he's lying. He's far too gleeful. There's more to this. I straighten in my seat.

"There's no point in waiting, though, even if my father is recovering. Freya's blood is pure enough and we have the priest, the crystal, and all the arrangements are made. The ceremony will commence as planned in three days. I love Freya and I still choose to marry her."

I expect his smile to fade, but it only grows, something wicked gleaming in his eyes.

"I would not be so sure. This changes things and we both know it."

"It changes nothing for me."

The earl snorts and I turn my ire to him. "Do you have something to add?"

His grin is cruel as he meets my eyes. "Only that if you decide you do not want your little bride, I can be sure she has a safe home to go to."

I'm out of my chair looming over the man in an instant. He has the decency to look afraid for a moment before he leans back in his chair, taking a sip from his glass. I have a dagger in my boot that would look lovely lodged in his throat. But no. I have to control myself. These two are playing a game and if I make the wrong move, I lose. I swallow my pride and turn to the duke.

"It has been a lovely evening, but I am afraid my travels have made me quite weary. I bid you both goodnight."

I turn on my heel and storm toward the exit, but the duke calls out to me before I can leave the room.

"Things are shifting, young prince. They're turning, and you better prepare yourself for the change that is to come."

I refuse to look back at him, marching through the door. Once it closes behind me, I race up the stairs, not even pausing for a moment to catch my breath until I throw open Freya's door, gasping for air. Bash and Freya are sitting at a table laughing over a card game, but they both freeze and turn worried eyes to me. Bash is up and across the room before I have the door fully closed.

"Who do I need to kill?" he asks, a dagger already in his hand.

"I don't know," I confess. "I don't know."

"What happened?" Freya asks, her voice unnervingly calm.

I straighten and meet her eyes. "Tell me why you're scared of the Earl of East Hingling."

She swallows and Bash's attention darts between the two of us a moment before he reaches for the door handle.

"I'll have his body disposed of before we leave in the morning."

"Wait!" Freya calls out, rising from her chair.

Bash stops, his jaw clenched, but he doesn't pull his hand back as he looks at her over his shoulder.

"Wait," Freya repeats a little less urgently. "He's never done anything to me directly. He's never hurt me or anyone I know personally."

"Then why are you scared of him?" I press as Bash turns to face her, folding his arms across his chest, dagger still in his hand.

"What do you know about him?" she hedges.

I shrug. "Not much."

"He's had several wives, all much younger than him," Bash supplies, his voice hard.

Freya nods, gnawing at her lip. "He's on his fifth wife. She's only a year older than me. None of his wives have lived past the age of twenty-three."

My eyes widen. "He's murdering his wives?"

"There's no proof of that," Freya says a little too quickly. "From what we always heard, they died of natural causes, one of them in childbirth."

"It's not hard to fake natural causes," Bash says.

"No, and that's why it startled me to see him so close. He's not well thought of in our village, and while he's never been cruel to us, he's never been benevolent. You heard how he spoke tonight."

Bash turns, reaching for the door again. He's got it half opened before I can ask where he's going.

"To ensure he dies of natural causes."

I catch his arm and if looks could kill I would be a pile of dust.

"Just wait. There's something else going on." I nod to the door. "Shut that and come sit down."

For a moment I think Bash is going to ignore my request and leave to at least rough up the earl a bit, but he sighs and closes the door. I head over to the table they occupied before and sink into Bash's vacated seat while Freya resumes hers across from me. Bash remains hovering nearby, his dagger away and arms crossed.

"What's wrong, Ty?" Freya asks gently.

I swallow, trying to find the words, the place to start. I fold my hands on the table and stare down at them, grounding myself. Finally I look up at Bash.

"Your magic is still weak, right?"

He frowns. "Very weak."

"Mine too. Which is why I thought it was odd when the duke told me my father is recovering."

"What?" Freya gasps.

"No," Bash says quickly. "If your father's health was improving, magic would be getting stronger, not weaker." His voice softens. "I know you want your father better, Ty, but the evidence isn't there. Whatever the duke heard, he was mistaken."

"That's it, though. He didn't just hear it. He claims he saw my father and even spoke to him."

Bash scowls so hard his eyebrows might as well be one. "But that . . . It doesn't . . ."

"Exactly."

"But it's good your father is doing better," Freya says, reaching across the table and placing a hand over mine.

A small smile finds its way onto my lips. "Yeah. It is." The smile falls away. "But as much as I want my father better, I can't dispel the feeling that something is wildly wrong."

"Did the duke say anything else that made you suspicious?" Bash asks.

I nod, licking my lips. "Yeah, he kept talking about change all evening, even at dinner." I glance to Freya for confirmation, and she nods. "And he seems to think our marriage won't happen, at least not yet, even though I assured him I'd still choose Freya, even if the wedding is delayed."

Freya smiles, squeezing my hand. "I'd choose you, too."

"Where does the earl with a death wish come into play?" Bash asks.

I shake my head. "I don't know that he does, except he made an unsettling comment about making sure Freya had a home to go to should our wedding not happen."

All color leeches from Freya's face as her eyes widen. "He what?"

"You will never have to worry about that man laying a finger on you," Bash says, his voice low and lethal. "I swear on my life because he won't live until morning."

"As much as I wish you could, you can't kill him here, Bash," I counter with a sigh.

He turns his venom-filled gaze to me and I almost shrink away from him, even though I know I'm not the one his wrath is aimed at.

"Why not?"

"They'll know it was you."

"I'm very good at covering my tracks."

"I have no doubt, but people like the Duke of Brookeshire already don't like you and are looking for a reason to have you removed. Don't give any fuel to their fire. I need you, Bash. I literally wouldn't be here without you."

"About that," Freya cuts in, drawing our attention to her. "Don't you think this half of the journey was a little too easy?"

I frown. "What do you mean?"

"I mean, we were attacked three times before we got to the temple. We haven't been attacked once on our way back."

Bash shrugs. "Our plan with the decoys and varying the route home worked."

Freya shakes her head. "I'm not so sure. I can see it working at first, but this cult is clever. They would have regrouped and tried again. Our stops with Klarissa and here had to have been expected given their connections and importance to the palace."

I look at Bash, waiting for him to insist again the plan merely worked, but his closed-off expression only heightens my fears. He agrees with her.

"So what do we do now?" I ask.

"We wait," Bash replies. "We don't know exactly what we're up against. We're less than a day from the palace, so things should unfold soon. We stay alert. We look for patterns or breaks in patterns. We stick together. That starts with tonight. We're all sleeping in the same room."

Despite the seriousness of the situation, I can't hold back a slight laugh. "Oh, the duke will love that."

"At this point, I don't even care what he thinks," Bash says, his voice almost a growl. "And if I leave this room tonight, I can guarantee the earl will never leave his alive."

I turn to Freya and offer her a lopsided grin. "Ready for a sleepover?"

She rolls her eyes, but a smile plays on her lips. "Fine, but I'm not sharing my blanket."

CHAPTER FORTY-TWO

TY

I wake in a warm nest of blankets, snuggled between two of my favorite people. Freya is curled into my chest, her head tucked comfortably under my chin, and Bash is curled around me, his arm draped across my waist, holding me tight. I can honestly say I don't think I've ever felt this safe or comfortable, and I let myself dream for a moment that this could be an everyday reality. True reality, however, is a bitch, and she pops my happy bubble in the form of a servant entering the room. I close my eyes, pretending to still be asleep as I tuck in closer to Freya, but Bash immediately wakes. His arm jerks from around me, taking his warmth and comfort.

"I-I'm sorry," the servant stammers. "I didn't mean to interrupt your morning."

The mattress shifts as Bash quickly slides from the bed.

"You didn't interrupt anything," he says hurriedly.

With half my happy nest gone, there's no point in pretending to sleep. I sigh and roll over, glaring at the servant, even though it's not their fault my perfect morning is already in decline. They're only doing their job, but I don't have to be happy about it. Freya shifts beside me but doesn't wake.

"If you could have breakfast brought up for all three of us, it would be most appreciated," I say, irritation obvious in my voice.

The servant glances nervously at Bash. "All three?"

Bash opens his mouth, likely to tell the servant breakfast for him isn't necessary, but I answer before he has a chance.

"Yes, all three, and given that you did disturb my morning, your discretion is appreciated and advised."

The servant looks borderline panicked as they nod and back out of the room. Bash shoots me an admonishing look, but I can't make myself care. The duke already hates me, so there's no point trying to win his favor now. After a few failed attempts to get Bash back into bed, I finally give up and rise myself. By the time breakfast arrives, Freya is also awake and my nest of happiness is officially gone.

We take our time getting ready, but a couple hours later we're officially on the road, headed home. I feel equal parts light and heavy, the realizations from last night still hanging over my head. What will I find when I get back to the castle? Is my father actually better, or was the duke trying to manipulate me in some way as a petty revenge for something beyond my control?

We arrive at the palace gates midafternoon, and I don't like the way people are looking at us. It makes me think the duke may have been telling the truth. It does nothing to sway my worries when a messenger greets me the moment we step through the main door.

"The queen has requested your immediate presence in the throne room."

I force a smile despite the fact I feel like I could hurl on the messenger's shoes.

"My companions and I have only just arrived and would appreciate a few minutes at the very least to recover from our journey."

"The queen was insistent you come immediately," he says, refusing to meet my eyes.

I turn and look at Bash, whose face is set in a deep scowl. This isn't good. My mother hates doing any sort of business publicly. She prefers to control things in private. Something is definitely going on and Bash knows it, too. I turn back to the messenger.

"Please inform my mother we will be there shortly."

The messenger nods and scurries ahead while I try to remain regal and not panicked. I am not succeeding. I stop outside the throne room in an attempt to gather my thoughts and settle my racing heart. My world steadies when I feel Freya's hand slip into mine.

My hopes the confrontation with my mother would be a mostly private affair despite the public location are dashed the second I walk through the door. Far too many nobles stand along the walls and lean against the tall marble columns. The entire mood shifts as all attention turns to me. I keep my head held high as Freya and I walk side-by-side, hand-in-hand down the red carpeted aisle to the throne, Bash a few steps behind.

"Good afternoon, Mother," I say, trying my best to keep any disrespect from my voice. "I believe I was summoned."

"Yes, you were, Tybalt. I wanted to make sure you heard from me the changes in store for you before any gossip could dilute the facts." She turns her sharp gaze to Freya and I tighten my grip on her hand. "As for you, my dear, I wanted to thank you in person for your willingness to take on the task we unreasonably set before you."

"It is an honor, Your Majesty," Freya says, bowing her head.

"Indeed. However, I know it upset your life, and I am sorry all the suffering you were caused due to the circumstances ended up being needless. I have already ensured additional compensation for your troubles."

I frown, trying to make sense of my mother's words. Freya seems to catch her meaning faster, inhaling sharply, her hand squeezing mine almost painfully. Surely I'm misunderstanding my mother's words and the idea forming in my head isn't what is really going on.

"What are you playing at, Mother?"

"I play at nothing, Tybalt," she replies, her voice sharp and her eyes sharper. "We rushed into things a bit too soon when other options were waiting to be discovered."

I shake my head. "Freya is the option. The only option."

"That is no longer true."

My world tilts as my mother motions to someone off to the side. A slight girl with long, dark hair steps forward dressed in a stunning purple gown. No, not any purple. She's wearing the shade specific to the highest nobility. To royalty. Yet she's entirely unfamiliar. She comes to a stop directly next to my mother's throne and my mother smiles at her. *Smiles.* No. Surely not. No.

"Tybalt, meet Princess Amarelia Poshswallow of the Panbrio Isles."

No.

"It seems when we first visited the isles in search of a queen for you those years ago, we only checked the compatibility of her two older sisters."

No.

"Upon further research it was discovered she fit the requirements."

No.

"Tybalt, please say hello to your future bride and Elodia's future queen."

"No!"

My voice reverberates around the room, deathly silence falling in its wake. I step closer to throne, my hand clutching Freya's tightly.

"I have my bride. I have my queen."

My mother meets my gaze without a flinch, her eyes flashing. "Yes, you do, and she stands beside me."

"How old is she, even?" I ask, eyeing the girl with her wide, blinking eyes. "How old are you?"

The girl stumbles back a step, shooting my mother a worried glance. Great. My mother already has the girl under her full control.

"She turns eighteen on the 15th of Samaneer."

"So she's only seventeen which means her magic, if she even possesses it, won't be strong enough by this Fae moon or the next. Samaneer is months away." I laugh on the verge of mania. "It won't work. It can't work. I can't marry her."

"Which brings me to some good news." She actually smiles, her shoulders relaxing. "Your father's health has vastly improved. There is no need to rush into an unwanted marriage out of necessity."

"My marriage to Freya is not unwanted. I want it. I want her. I love her."

My mother purses her lips, looking at Freya like she's trash on the bottom of her shoe. "She is unsuitable in every matter beyond her blood. The tour has proven this."

"I don't know what you heard, but Freya did well. Many of the nobles loved her."

"And many reported quite the opposite."

I open my mouth to speak but my mother waves me off, standing in one smooth motion, much like a beast pouncing on its prey.

"Enough, Tybalt," she says, her voice fierce. "This is not the place for further conversation. The decision has been made. Princess Amarelia is a far more suitable bride than a farmer's daughter." Freya flinches beside me. "She has been trained as royalty since birth, and her blood has enough Fae magic for our purposes."

"She's from the Rebel Isles. She's an outcast."

My mother's mouth tightens into a firm line and the look she gives me would have smarter men backing down.

"We are reorganizing our alliance with the *Panbrio* Isles," she bites out, emphasizing the official name over the one they were dubbed after the civil war several generations back when they gained their freedom from Elodia. "This discussion is over. Please retire to your rooms. Separately, as there is no need to further your relationship."

My mother turns and begins to walk toward the exit behind the thrones.

"You can't make me marry that girl!" I shout, my voice echoing around us.

My mother stills and I doubt anyone else in the room is breathing. Slowly, she turns around, leveling me with a look that tells me I pushed her too far.

"Don't test me, Tybalt. The decision has been made." She looks to guards standing nearby. "Escort the girl to her room and make sure the prince has no contact."

Before I can fully understand what is happening, Freya's

hand is ripped from mine. I spin around to pull her back to me, but two men already stand between us with two more on either side of her. Her eyes are wide and terrified, tears already wetting her cheeks.

"Ty!" she calls out, her frantic eyes meeting mine.

I lunge toward her, elbowing the guard closest to me in the face with a sickening crack. Blood pours from his nose as he staggers back. The other guard wraps his arms around me, effectively pinning my arms to my sides. I struggle against him, kicking wildly in an effort to break free.

"Stay your hand, Bastion Shamblefoot, or I will have you exiled from my kingdom at best, executed at worst," my mother says, her voice cold.

I catch a glimpse of Bash out of the corner of my eye. He already has daggers in each hand and his jaw is set with displeasure. He meets my eyes and I know without a doubt if I say the word he will unleash his full fury and bathe the floor in blood.

"Stop struggling, Tybalt. You are making a scene," my mother says with a sigh in the same tone she used when scolding me as a boy. "If it continues, I will have both Freya and Bastion exiled together."

The fight seeps from me and I still. I can't risk losing them. I can't. The guard holds me a moment longer until he seems sure I won't attack him, but eventually he releases me. I take a step back.

"Touch her and you will regret your actions!" I yell at the men flanking Freya. "I swear on the life of my father, if she is harmed, you will not live long enough to regret it."

They begin to usher her away, more of my mother's men circling her as she's removed from the room. I turn back to Mother but she's slipped away, the girl with her. I release a shuddering breath and look back at the only other person that matters.

"Bash," I say, my voice breaking.

He's standing feet away, but his eyes aren't on me. They're fixed on the door. Everything about him is tense and lethal.

"Bash," I say again, and this time he turns to me. His gray eyes are wild as they meet mine. I stumble toward him and he catches me.

"Let's get you to your chambers," he says, already steering me toward the door.

I remember nothing of the trek to my room. Nothing matters anymore. When the door closes behind us, I sink into the nearest chair.

"I can't go through this again," I mutter, staring off at nothing. "She can't do this to me." I look up at Bash who's staring down at me, anguish shining in his own eyes. "How can she rip away another person I love?"

My voice breaks and Bash sinks down to his knees in front of me, reaching a hand to cup my cheek and brush away my tears.

"I'm sorry, Ty," he says, his voice so soft I think it might shatter me.

I swallow. "You have to help her, Bash. My mother doesn't care about her anymore. She never did, but she needed her. Freya's useless to her now. You have to stay by Freya's side. Protect her. Swear to me you'll protect her."

He meets my eyes, an intensity in his gaze I've only seen once or twice. "I swear."

CHAPTER FORTY-THREE

BASH

The oath I make to Ty is both the easiest thing I've ever promised and the most difficult. Freya is leaving the palace. I'm surprised the queen didn't have her escorted straight to a carriage to leave tonight. But no matter if she leaves tonight, tomorrow, or in a week, she's leaving, and I have a duty here. Or a duty to Ty at the very least. If I leave his side, I should only leave it to take out the remaining members of the *draíochta*. The cult that is also a risk to Freya. Even if she's removed from the palace, they'll still know she exists. They know about her blood. She's still a risk to them, a risk they'll likely still want eliminated. I need to find a way to protect her and keep my promise while also protecting Ty.

It's my nightmare all over again. If I choose wrong I could lose one of them forever, if not both of them. It's an impossible choice.

Right now, however, I need to focus on settling Ty down so I can check on Freya. I ring down for tea and convince Ty to write Freya a note. Even if his mother can keep him from seeing Freya, she can't stop all communication. When he rises from the desk, he seals the letter with his official seal and passes it to me. I tuck the letter into my pocket and turn to leave.

"Bash," Ty calls after me. When I turn back to him he tries for a smile that doesn't reach his eyes. "Help her get over me, yeah? Like you had to?"

"What do you mean?"

He shrugs, likely opting for casualness but it comes across more defeated than anything. "You're the only person I know who's been in love with me, in a relationship with me, who had to get over me quickly under very similar circumstances. Knowing she's okay and has a chance to find happiness may be the only thing that can get me through this. If I can't be happy, maybe at least she can be, and I can make myself be okay with that. So, maybe you can share some tips to help her move on faster?"

I stare at him, trying to make sense of his words. "I . . ." I shake my head. "I don't think I can do that."

Ty frowns, genuine hurt flashing across his face. "You can't? Why not?"

"Because I never got over you, Ty."

His eyes widen in surprise. "You . . . didn't?"

"No."

He takes a step closer to me. "You still love me? You're still *in love* with me?"

I swallow, wanting to look away but I'm too lost in his eyes to do so. "Just as much as I was when I kissed you on your seventeenth birthday. Even more so."

He takes another step closer, putting him well within arm's reach. "Bash, I . . ."

"It's okay that you no longer feel the same about me," I say quickly.

"But I do," he whispers. "The kind of love I feel for you isn't the kind that can be so easily smothered." He moves a fraction closer. "I assumed when you left you did so to get me over me, and coming back meant you succeeded."

I swallow hard. "I rather spectacularly failed."

Ty moves in to kiss me, and I almost let him. I jerk away at the last moment, my heart pounding painfully. He pulls back, confused.

"I can't," I grit out, looking away. "Please, Ty. If I can't keep you, I can't do this. It hurts too much."

Ty nods, licking his lips as he steps back. "I understand." He takes a deep breath, exhaling slowly as he looks past me to the door. "Then protect Freya." He meets my eyes and forces a smile. "For me."

I nod, not telling him I don't need the incentive. I was always going to find a way to protect Freya. I leave, heading toward her room, only to find guards posted outside.

"We're under direct orders not to let anyone in," one guard says, smirking.

The second guard is one I know who I've gotten along with well enough. When I turn to him, he adds, "It's true. Unless you are bringing food or have been directed here by the queen."

He gives me a meaningful look and I straighten.

"Ah," I say, taking a step back. "Good to know."

Several minutes later I return, holding a tray of sandwiches and tea. While the one guard who I don't know gives me a shifty look, the other smiles, stepping to the side and opening the door.

Freya is curled up on top of her still-made bed wearing

the clothes she traveled in right down to her boots. She barely stirs when I enter the room.

"I brought some food," I say, holding up the tray. "And a letter from Ty."

She sniffs, curling in on herself tighter. I set the tray down on the nearest flat surface and tuck the letter underneath. I hesitate only a moment before I crawl up on the bed behind her. I wrap my arms around her and she sinks back against me. Her body trembles as she cries, and I soon find tears wetting my own cheeks. I feel sorrow for her and her heartbreak. Sorrow for my own. Sorrow for Ty. For several minutes we stay that way, not really finding comfort but managing to steady ourselves despite the turmoil assaulting us.

Eventually she runs out of tears and turns to face me. I loosen my hold on her but don't release her, the desire to keep her close too strong to ignore. In this position we're inches apart, our noses nearly brushing. For a brief moment I consider kissing her, comforting her with something physical, but in my gut I know this isn't the time. She is mourning. *We* are mourning.

"It shouldn't hurt so much," she whispers, as much to herself as to me. "I didn't want this. Less than a month ago I wanted out. And now I have my out. I suppose this is what they mean when they warn you against wishing."

She laughs but it's without humor and it makes my heart ache. I tighten my hold on her and she presses her forehead to mine, closing her eyes.

"How do I do it, Bash? How do I go back to being a farmer's daughter and nothing more? I never fit in here, but I don't think I can fit in back home now. Not when a piece of my heart remains in the palace." She opens her eyes, going nearly crosseyed as she meets my eyes. "How do I move on?"

"Well," I mumble, my voice rough, "when it happened to me, I went out and slaughtered a bunch of people in the name of the Crown, so I'm not sure I'm the person to ask."

She huffs a laugh and closes her eyes again, tucking herself against me. "I don't know. I wouldn't mind bringing down a cult right now as distraction."

She says it as a joke, but something clicks for me. Maybe I don't have to choose between protecting Freya and protecting Ty. Maybe I can have both. Maybe I can stay with Freya, watching over her, loving her, while still finding what remains of the *cultas draíochta.*

"Run away with me," I say, the words tumbling out before I can stop them.

Freya sits up, blinking down at me. "What?"

She sounds confused, maybe a little surprised, but not put off or disgusted. It gives me hope. I sit up, crossing my legs.

"You said you don't know if you'll fit in back on your farm, so don't go there. There's a good chance the cult will go after you anyways. It won't be safe. So don't go home. Run away with me, and help me track down the cult and destroy them."

She studies me for a moment. "How? I'm no good with a sword or any sort of weapon. I'm not fast. I would only hold you back."

I shake my head, determination swelling through me. "Maybe not, but you're clever. Damn clever. And while you may not be particularly proficient with any weapon, I've seen how far you can come with a little instruction, especially when you're determined. I can teach you more."

I pause, but she doesn't say anything. I think she's actually considering it. I can have this. The gods owe me. *The gods fucking owe me.*

"Neither of us can have Ty," I continue. "He's been snatched from us, but through this we can help him and be with him from afar. It will keep us connected to him."

She shakes her head, looking away. "I don't know. I wish it could work, but . . ."

Feeling her slip through my fingers, I reach out and take her hand in mine. She jerks her attention back to me, her lips parting.

"If you say no, I will take you home myself or at least find somewhere safe for you to go, but I really believe you could help me. Before when I was hunting down the *draiochta,* I killed so many of their members, but it wasn't enough. There is so much more at play, so many threads twisted together and I can't untangle it on my own. I need someone to help me gather intel and get into places where I can't and figure out the puzzles that elude me. I think you could very well be that person, Freya. I think we could make an amazing team." I trace my calloused fingers over her knuckles, my heart hammering in my chest. "So I ask again: run away with me?"

Her eyes hold mine and I barely dare to breathe as she considers my offer. I'm afraid she's on the verge of declining when a small, defiant smile curves on her lips.

"Yes, Bastion Shamblefoot, I would love to run away with you."

ACKNOWLEDGMENTS

For some reason, I can sit down and write a book without too much trouble, but my brain shuts off when it's time to do the acknowledgments. Well, here goes my attempt.

First of all I have to thank Lana, who once again had to put up with reading the absolute worst version of this story. You helped turn the trash of a first draft into something the rest of you might actually enjoy reading. I like that you're mean. It makes me better.

Also, huge shoutout to R who had to read this story while it was on draft two. Your input was invaluable and some of it totally made my day. (I hope you like the additions where I did indeed make Ty grovel a bit more. You were right—he needed to grovel.) I cannot thank you enough for always being there to hash out ideas with me or talk about our books and stories or simply to talk about life. I love having you as a friend and a reading/writing buddy. (Was that too sappy for an acknowledgments page? Oh well.)

Of course, I also had a wonderful team of Beta readers to thank. You all gave lots of feedback that helped take this book from good to great. So thank you Kara, Mandy, Karin, Jessica, Rebecca, Chrissa, Konstantina, Reanna, Shannon, Rosalind, Autumn, Megan, and Melissa. (Did I get everyone? I hope so. There were a lot of you.) Y'all seriously rock and I cannot thank you enough! Whether you gave me a play-by-play where you yelled at me the whole time (Megan) or you waited to yell at me until you were done or something in-between, I am sincerely grateful.

Andi, my editor and the keeper of the commas, thank you as well. I think at this point in our working relationship you know my writing voice better than I do at times. Thanks for putting up with the fact that even after seven—now eight!—books together, I still don't know how commas work half of the time and still can't spell "focus" correctly 99% of the time.

I also cannot leave this section without mentioning my amazing partner who not only did the incredible cover art, map, and character art for my book but also had to put up with my incessant ramblings. They had to listen to me gush about my characters and kept a straight face when I went on rants when my characters wouldn't behave. Honestly, I'm lucky to have such a supportive partner.

I'm sure I could go on and on mentioning everyone who helped make this book possible, but alas, the ink in this mortal world is limited. Just know that if you were one of the people cheering me on whether it was in a Facebook group, TikTok, some other social media platform, my Patreon, or in person, I appreciate you. I do this for my readers and you all prove to me every day that I chose the right career.

If you've made it to this point, thank you. I love you and wish you all the best.

ABOUT THE AUTHOR

AMBER D. LEWIS is a highly combustible combination of caffeine, mismatched coffee mugs, and shiny things. In her spare time (and, quite frankly, when she's supposed to be doing other things) she writes fantasy and other stories.

facebook.com/amberdlewisofficialauthorpage

instagram.com/mugshots_n_bookthoughts

bookbub.com/profile/amber-d-lewis

goodreads.com/crymeariversong11

tiktok.com/@thewriteamber

patreon.com/amberdlewis